# The White Darkness

Other books by Geraldine McCaughrean

*Forever X*
*Gold Dust*
*The Kite Rider*
*A Little Lower than the Angels*
*A Pack of Lies*
*Plundering Paradise*
*Smile!*
*The Stones Are Hatching*
*Stop the Train*
*Not the End of the World*

# GERALDINE MCCAUGHREAN

# The White Darkness

OXFORD
UNIVERSITY PRESS

# OXFORD
## UNIVERSITY PRESS

Great Clarendon Street, Oxford OX2 6DP

Oxford University Press is a department of the University of Oxford.
It furthers the University's objective of excellence in research, scholarship,
and education by publishing worldwide in

Oxford New York

Auckland  Cape Town  Dar es Salaam  Hong Kong  Karachi
Kuala Lumpur  Madrid  Melbourne  Mexico City  Nairobi
New Delhi  Shanghai  Taipei  Toronto

With offices in

Argentina  Austria  Brazil  Chile  Czech Republic  France  Greece
Guatemala  Hungary  Italy  Japan  Poland  Portugal  Singapore
South Korea  Switzerland  Thailand  Turkey  Ukraine  Vietnam

Oxford is a registered trade mark of Oxford University Press
in the UK and in certain other countries

British Library Cataloguing in Publication Data

Data available

ISBN-13: 978-0-19-271983-6 (hardback)
ISBN-10: 0-19-271983-1 (hardback)
ISBN-13: 978-0-19-271991-1 (restricted edition)
ISBN-10: 0-19-271991-2 (restricted edition)

1 3 5 7 9 10 8 6 4 2

Typeset by Palimpsest Book Production Limited,
Polmont, Stirlingshire
Printed in Great Britain by Mackays of Chatham plc, Chatham, Kent

For Richard Oates or Titus Morant

The mind is its own place, and in itself
Can make a Heaven of Hell, a Hell of Heaven.

John Milton, *Paradise Lost*

# Chapter One
## 'Titus'

I have been in love with Titus Oates for quite a while now—which is ridiculous, since he's been dead for ninety years. But look at it this way. In ninety years I'll be dead, too, and then the age difference won't matter.

Besides, he isn't dead inside my head. We talk about all kinds of things. From whether hair colour can change spontaneously to whether friends are better than family, and the best age for marrying: 14 or 125. Generally speaking, he knows more than I do, but on that particular subject we are even. He wasn't married—at least, he wasn't when he died, which must have substantially cut down his chances.

Uncle Victor says I shouldn't marry at all. Uncle Victor knows about these things and he says that 'marriage is a bourgeois relic of Victorian sentimentality'. That suits me. No one would match up to Titus. And we have a kind of understanding, Titus and I.

Uncle Victor is marvellous: he's done so much for us— for Mum and me, I mean. And anyway, he's just so clever. Uncle Victor knows a fantastic amount. He knows at what temperature glass turns to liquid, and where Communism went wrong and how the Clifton Suspension Bridge was built and just what the Government ought to be doing: you can't fault him. He's read books about everything: history, geography, politics, astrology, animals . . . The Fount of All Knowledge, Dad used to call him.

I would get stuck doing my homework, and Dad would say, 'Ask the Fount of All Knowledge.' And I'd telephone Victor and he would tell me. Quite often he knew more than the teachers, so they'd think I'd got my homework wrong, but as Victor says, 'What teachers don't understand is that the body of learning is still growing. They reckon it stopped the day they came out of college. That, or they're bog ignorant. Lot of ignorance in yon schools.'

It's true that none of my teachers knows much about Antarctica. When Dad and Victor and I went to Iceland, one of the teachers had been, too, and knew all about Dettifoss and the hot springs and people having stinking saunas in their back gardens. But none of the teachers at school has been to Antarctica. Some of them know about Scott of the Antarctic going to the South Pole and not coming back. But they mostly mean John Mills in the movie. I don't.

In the general way of things, I don't know much about anything. Uncle Victor says I'm 'the victim of a shoddy education system'. But I do know about the Polar Regions. The bookshelves over my bed are full of books about the North and South Poles. Ice-bound almost. A glacial cliff-face teetering over my bed. I remember: the night after Dad had been rushed into hospital, one of the shelves sheared off and crashed down on me. I woke up thinking the house was collapsing—books gouging at my head, bouncing off the bed-frame, slapping flat on the floor. I looked at the hole in the wall and the rawlplugs on the pillow and I didn't know what to do.

About the shelf. About anything.

So I went back to sleep, and dreamt I was sailing towards the Ross Ice Barrier, and that crags were splitting off its face, plunging down, massive as sea-going liners foundering.

Come to think of it, Uncle Victor gave me most of my ice books. Every birthday and Christmas. Books about

The Ice and the North Pole; about Shackleton and Scott, Laurence Gould and Vivian Fuchs, Nansen and Barents, Franklin and Peary; about penguins and polar bears, whales and seals and boreales . . . About Captain Lawrence Oates—the one they called 'Titus'. Uncle Victor understands how the whole idea creeps up on you like pack ice—pressing in and pressing against your head, then crushing the hull and tumbling inside . . . If we ever did a project at school on Antarctica, I could shine. Like Mount Erebus in midsummer, I could, I could shine!

Except that I don't think I would choose to. It's all bound up with Titus, and I know better than to mention Titus at school. I do now, anyway. I made that mistake once. I won't do it again.

'Symone has a pretend friend! Symone has a pretend friend!'

It was the conversation about snogging. Like the ant nest in the larder: you think you've done everything to be rid of it—that it can't possibly come back again—but there it is: 'How many boys have you snogged?' There is no right answer. You say 'None' and you're sad and frigid or they know someone whose brother would be willing to snog you for a quid. You refuse to answer and you are sadder still—or hiding something, or prefer girls, or . . . It's not that they care; they only want to tell you how many they've snogged—chiefly because they like saying the word. It makes them feel as if they are wearing red underwear. But on and on they go: 'How many boys, Sym? How many boys have you snogged?'

Why is it that all the words to do with sex are ugly? Words to do with love aren't. No wonder Titus thought women were a nuisance. No wonder he died without ever . . . getting mixed up with all that.

Anyway, I said that I could do without it. (At least that's

3

what I tried to say. I don't explain things very well out loud.) I tried to say that I was happy to stick with imagining for the time being, thanks all the same. Later, maybe. If I ever met anyone who could compare with Titus . . .

And after that I was the mad girl—sad, frigid, and mad; all three—the retard who had an imaginary friend: 'Like little kids do, oo-hoo. Like little kids do!'

The day I came into school and said my dad had died, I heard Maxine say to Nats, 'Don't worry. I expect she just *imagined* it.'

So that's when I sealed myself inside. Laced up the tent, so to speak. Filled the locks with water so that they would freeze. That's when Titus and I looked at one another and decided we could do without them, so long as we had each other. *'You and me now, Sym.'*

'You and me now, Titus.'

*'Warm, isn't it.'*


'Who fancies a trip to Paris, then?' said Uncle Victor.

Mum was surprised, because money's been so short lately.

'It's one of those newspaper promotions,' said Victor. 'Free tickets on Eurostar and two nights in a two-star hotel.'

I wanted Mum to smile and widen her eyes and say 'How lovely!' because it was such a kind thought. It seemed wrong of her to pucker her forehead and look harassed and confused. It's not the last place on earth a person might want to go, is it: Paris? But Mum just looked uneasy. 'Sym has exams coming up.'

'Say again?'

'Sym has exams.'

'The child worrits her life away on exams! Exams in what? What are they trying to measure? Her potential? Her usefulness? Her knack at taking exams, is all! You'd

4

like to go to Paris, wouldn't you, girl? Cradle of Art and Town-Planning?'

'I'd like to go up the Eiffel Tower,' I said.

Mum's face accused me of treachery; in mentioning the exams she had thrown me an invisible hint and I had muffed the catch. Why can't she say things out loud? Why does no one in this house say anything out loud? Anyway, why wouldn't she want to go to Paris? Uncle Victor is only trying to cheer her up! 'Can't we go after the exams?' I said, trying to satisfy them both.

'Lillian will write you a note, won't you, Lillian: *Regret any inconvenience* manner of thing. The only real school is the School of Life!'

It's one of Victor's favourite sayings, that.

It suited me. Every way I look at it, it suited me. No Chemistry exam meant no revision either. I loved the thought of telling Nikki I wouldn't be around for the Chemistry papers because I was going to Paris. I'd send her a postcard, in case she thought I was making it up. The weather outside was horrible, but even Paris in the pouring rain had to be better than school and exams.

So I got the weekend case out of the loft, and Mum packed it and cancelled the dentist and wrote a note to school and got some euros from the Post Office and found some guide books at the library and looked out the passports and hoovered the house (in case we all drowned in mid-Channel, I suppose, and neighbours had to break in and were scandalized by the state of our carpets). Meanwhile, Victor found a 360 degree virtual view from the top of the Eiffel Tower, on the computer. He had his passport in his jacket pocket—said he carries it with him at all times. It made him sound like a spy waiting for his next mission.

\*　　　\*　　　\*

5

'Can't do Chemistry next week,' I told Nikki, casual as anything. 'Be in Paris.'

'Lucky cow,' said Nikki without looking up from her magazine. She was filling in a questionnaire to find out what kind of boy she should date.

'Two nights and three days,' I said.

'*Oh là là*,' said Nikki flatly.

The article was called *Foto-Fit!!!* Exclamation marks infest all Nikki's magazines. Like head lice. Given the amount of time she spends with her head in a magazine, you'd think Nikki might have caught some, but oddly, whenever she speaks, there's no sign of an exclamation mark anywhere.

'Uncle Victor is taking Mum and me.'

'Can't he afford a week?'

Beside each question in the questionnaire was a row of photographs: boys' faces, boys' legs, boys differently dressed . . . '*PICK THE BUFFest BOY!!*' said the caption.

'The Eiffel Tower. Everything,' I said.

'Snails' legs,' said Nikki with a grimace.

Even Titus was mildly intrigued by the magazine article. '*Buff? Buff as in polished? Well bred?*' he said inside my head.

'No, Titus.'

'*Buff as in Blind Man's?*'

'No, Titus.'

'*Buff as in "Steady the Buffs"?*'

'I don't think so . . .'

'*Buff as in envelopes?*'

'No, Titus.'

'*Buff as in stark naked?*'

'Captain!'

'*Sorry.*'

'Buff as in "fit",' I explained.

'*Ah,*' said Titus, but looked doubtful.

So I assured him, 'You're fit. You're really fit!'

And he agreed: *'Up to a point I was very fit . . . Until death set in. Death is inclined to undermine one's fitness.'*

'No, no. Not that kind of fit. "Fit" as in "handsome", I meant.'

But now he looked plain mutinous. Words ought to retain at least some of their meaning from one century to the next, or conversations can't keep their footing.

Actually, I've never looked at a boy and thought 'fit!!' or 'Be still my beating heart'. Those obscene jerks they offer us with their forearms; trying to outdo each other in dirty words at the back of the bus: none of that stirs me to curiosity—doesn't stir me to anything, except perhaps a slight desire to see them fall off the bus into the path of oncoming traffic.

'We're going Eurostar,' I told Nikki, but she was engrossed. Of course I should have been telling my teacher really, not Nikki. The letter from Mum was still in my skirt pocket; I wanted to leave asking until it was too late for Mrs Floyd to say no.

The teachers at school don't like me. Uncle Victor says so, and he ought to know; he always insists on going to Parents' Evening now Dad's gone. Uncle Victor says teachers are a 'barrier to enlightenment', so he spends a lot of time up at the school trying to enlighten them. The geography teacher in particular seems to vex him: 'You learn your subject [he told her once] then regurgitate it year after year! Round and round, staler and staler. Like astronauts drinking their own piss.' I don't think Miss Cox took in his argument: didn't take in anything except the p-word.

The next string of photos in Nikki's magazine was not of boys but of their interests—a computer, a car, a Walkman, a football, a book. As if boys can only have one interest.

*'Where are the horses?'* said Titus. *'I'm a horse man.'*

'That would count as cars, I suppose. Or sport. How about sport?'

'Well, polo, of course. I played tennis a lot in Egypt. Raced camels. Boxed in India. At Hut Point we played football to keep . . . er . . . oh dear . . . fit. And ice hockey. Are you including motorized sledges among cars? Motorized sledges are a waste of time and money. For a thousand quid I could buy myself a team of polo ponies.'

'Not any more, you couldn't. How about music?'

'So long as I don't have to dance to it.'

'Books?'

'Aha, well. Perhaps the books for my major's exam.'

Cold hands, Titus. Cold hands. It's what he wrote asking his mother to send him, the day he set out for the Pole: the books for his exams. He would need them, he said, when he got back.

Sometimes, quite unbidden, Titus says something and it's as if he has laid icy hands on the back of my neck. But why, in that instant, did other words congeal against my brain: *Sooner Chemistry than Paris.*

Maxine drifted past.

'Sym's uncle's taking her to Paris,' said Nikki, and a surge of happiness went through me, because Nikki had been listening after all.

'What, for a dirty weekend?' said Maxine. With any thought behind it, it would have been a vile thing to say. But Maxine doesn't do thinking. Maxine is just so full of sewage she only has to move sharply to slop over at the mouth.

'Holiday,' I mumbled.

'Me, I'd go down the Moulin Rouge—get off with all the rich men,' and wrapping her arms behind her head, she shut her eyes and flicked her hips at us. 'But don't you bother, Sym,'—looking me over, contempt weighing down her eyelids—'you can't give it away for free, can you?'

I could feel my cheeks burning, my guts churning. What's wrong with me? Is there something wrong with me? What's

8

wrong with me? We're fourteen. It's illegal. 'Adults-only', it says on the box. And yet everyone I know at school seems to be pushing and jostling to play. Or talking about it. Lots of talking about it. And what with not doing talking, really, and not wanting to talk about it anyway . . .

Nikki began doodling glasses and moustaches on the boys' faces in the magazine. 'Bet your uncle drags you round loads of dreary art museums, Sym,' she said, filling up the awful silence, dredging me out of Maxine's sewage. And I thanked her by nodding and wincing and smiling ruefully.

''Spect so.'

'In the rain.'

''Spect so.'

'*I'm game. I'll come,*' said Titus brightly. '*We were always going on holiday when I was young. My adoring mother fled the English winters,*' and he gave his low, ironic laugh. '*Thought the cold might be the death of me.*' That's right, Titus. Put things into proportion.

And I cheered up instantly, knowing that he would be there in Paris, and Maxine wouldn't.


The trains at Waterloo Station were all as shiny and sleek as intercontinental missiles. A mere excursion to the other side of the Channel seemed beneath their dignity—film stars finding themselves on a bucket-and-spade weekend when they had been expecting to go to the Cannes Film Festival.

'Have you *been*, Lillian? Sym?' said Uncle Victor loudly, from some distance away. Mum tried to ignore him, but Victor only repeated it more loudly still: 'Have you *been*? Think on. You should both go before we set off!'—offering to mind our shoulder bags while we found the station toilet.

'Sometimes!' hissed Mum under her breath, investing

9

the word with a wealth of pent-up embarrassment and resentment.

We were no sooner back than the train doors opened with a mechanical gasp that seemed to come from inside my chest. I didn't lift my foot high enough to clear the sill, stumbling into the train. Elegant as a swan, me.

But Mum was still on the platform, rummaging through her handbag, crouching down to set it on the ground and look with two hands. Uncle Victor was unzipping our single suitcase, sighing patiently, lifting out clothes. 'Your mother has left her passport behind,' he said and managed a martyred smile.

'No! No, I had it! I know I did!'

'Calmly, Lillian, calmly. Think on. Calm oils the cogwheels.'

But though she searched through every pocket, every compartment of her shoulder bag, between every page of her library book and under the cardboard stiffener in the cheap suitcase, there was no sign of either her passport or her calm. 'Are you sure I didn't give it to you to mind, Victor?'

Victor's hands padded slowly, methodically over the luggage. Mum's darted and flickered in growing panic. 'So stupid!'

'*You* aren't stupid, Lillian,' said Uncle Victor smiling and shaking his head, 'but sometimes the things you do are . . .' Mum didn't appreciate the distinction: she almost zipped Victor's hand into the suitcase.

The clock over the station clicked round. The guard appeared holding a green paddle the shape of a ping-pong bat. Mum had begun to cry with frustration and annoyance. My stomach swung like a cat flap. 'We'll just have to catch a later train!' I said.

But apparently the tickets were valid only on the eight o'clock. When the doors finally closed, Victor and I were

10

on the inside with the suitcase, Mum was on the outside, her arms full of her own freshly ironed holiday clothing. It dangled from her grasp and she stooped awkwardly to stop the silky blouses slithering to the ground. She looked like a marble Madonna holding someone dead on her lap, head cocked sideways in grief.

'*Back on Saturday,*' I mouthed through the window and kissed the glass.

'It's a common mistake,' said uncle, cracking open the newspaper. 'Lack of organization. Success comes down to getting organized. Keeping your eye on the ball. Think on, Sym.'

'Maybe someone pickpocketed her,' I suggested.

'Say again?'

'Stole Mum's passport. Someone. Maybe.'

'And happen she'll find it just where she put it, more like. The ladies, eh? God bless 'em.' It was said with a conspiratorial wink—which must mean I'm not really female but an honorary man. A good thing, I think. A compliment.

'*So! We're off,*' said Titus settling into the seat beside me, stretching out his long legs, opening *The Life of Napoleon* as Waterloo slipped slowly behind us in a flicker of brick and scaffolding.

And it didn't matter: Mum hadn't wanted to go in the first place. And at least I'd have Titus. Now, if he were to rest his head against my shoulder, I would feel the black crispness of his curly hair under my cheekbone, smell the pipe tobacco inside his leather jacket. If I were to shut my eyes and imagine his arm around my shoulders, we could be going anywhere in the whole round world and not just on a three-day, educationally informative trip to Paris.

'Just you and me, eh, Titus?'

'*Just you and me, ma chère.*'

And Uncle Victor, of course.

11

# Chapter Two
## Freeze Frame

I remember the day Titus arrived in my head—not when I first heard of him, I don't mean, but the day he arrived, like some distant cousin you've heard tell of but who suddenly comes to visit. I remember. Uncle Victor had given me the box-set DVDs for my birthday: *The Last Place on Earth*—an old TV series made before I was born.

I had the house to myself, because Dad was bad in hospital and Mum had gone to see him. So I plugged the DVD player into the TV, turned the sound right up and I sat down and I watched all the episodes straight off, one after another—six hours—the cellophane wrapping still scrunched up in my hand, my breakfast bowl on the table.

I knew this story—thought it held no surprises for me. But I was seeing people that I'd read about, so already I felt I knew them. I was like one of those relatives on the dockside waving the men goodbye, minding about whether or not they came home again.

And then it came real.

I watched so intently—concentrated so hard that there was no sofa, and no screen, no chime from the clock, no traffic outside, no whine from the fridge or thump from the central heating. And it came real. So real. So real. So real. So real. So real.

When one disc came to an end, I suppose I must have

put in another, but I don't remember doing it. I knew this story: it shouldn't have held any surprises for me. Five men trekked to the South Pole. A Norwegian expedition made it ahead of them, so they didn't even have the joy of being first. And then they didn't quite get home.

If he had been there, Dad would have said, 'What do we want to watch this for? We know how it turns out.'

Mum would have said, 'I wonder where they filmed it? Wasn't he in something else?'

Even Uncle Victor would have spotted an inaccuracy in somebody's cap badge or the rigging on the *Terra Nova*.

But me, I didn't think anything. I let it soak into me like water into salt, until I was invisible, absorbed. It blew me away. That's what people say, isn't it? It blew me away—like wind ripping a tent loose of its guy-ropes, or the blizzard submerging a man in powdery, edgeless Death.

And there, at the heart of it, was Captain Oates: so sublimely beautiful that his image passed clean through my retina and scorched itself on my brain. And his voice flowed into me, so sensuous that I was wading across the River Jordan, up to my ears and deeper in milk and honey, towards Paradise on the other side. He was perfect—as I've always known he would be if ever the blurred photographs, the expedition portraits, were to come to life. Like everything perfect, he set up a ferocious pain inside me—a flickering, griping sort of pain, because nothing so marvellous is ever within reach, is it? Nothing so beautiful can ever last. I was powerless to rewrite the past—to change the outcome of the story; to save Oates from dying—in the film—in real life . . . The DVD-player grew hotter and hotter in my lap, so that after Oates got up, and went outside into the blizzard, and crawled away into the snow to die, his body warmth was still there in my lap, slow to cool. He lingered in my lap.

13

And then the phone rang.

And it was Mum to say that Dad had died.

I thought there was really bad static on the line, but it was only the cellophane clenched in my hand, crackling by the receiver. And all I could say was 'Oh', because it had been on the cards for weeks. I had been half-expecting the call all day. The news held no surprise for me.

And besides, Dad never liked me.

# Chapter Three
## Swallowing SIM

Uncle Victor likes me. Uncle Victor is very fond of me. He calls me his 'right-hand girl', his 'apprentice', his 'journeyman'. I was a disappointment to Dad, apparently, but Victor could see my potential. The two of them were business partners, in the shot-peening line of work. He isn't a blood relation but he has always been around, so some time when I was small, Victor Briggs became my 'Uncle Victor'. And he's been as kind as any real uncle—paid for the funeral, did Parents' Evenings. Suggested Paris.

The hotel in Paris was . . . odd. It wasn't quite the sort of place you would expect to book through the *Daily Telegraph*, with or without tokens. It was in the Algerian quarter—*L'Hotel Gide*—over the top of a Greek restaurant serving Moroccan food. In the adjoining two-star bedrooms, the sheets had two star-shaped tears in them.

'Look. Only two singles anyway!' I said.

'Say again?'

'Where would Mum have slept?'

'Ah. Quite. Typical French,' said Victor.

I looked out of the window hoping to see Montmartre—or the Eiffel Tower—or the Moulin Rouge. But there were only some derelict tower blocks, a flyover, and below, in the yard, a public toilet.

'Shall we phone Mum?' I asked. 'Say we've arrived?'

'Let's eat first,' said Victor.

We had a Couscous Royale for dinner. It sounded better than it tasted. There was a Greek mythical fresco on the restaurant wall that one of the waiters must have painted. I worked out it must be Phaeton, careering around the sky in his father's sun chariot, charring the green places into deserts, dooming both Poles to everlasting cold because he couldn't control the horses. There was also a TV on the wall over my head, showing a football match between France and Morocco, so that each time I looked round everybody in the restaurant was peering my way. The sound was turned full up—I had to switch off my hearing aid—but Uncle Victor didn't seem to notice. He didn't seem to notice that it was Wednesday, either, because he was eating protein.

Normally Victor eats protein on a Monday, carbohydrates on a Tuesday, dairy on a Wednesday, fish on a Thursday, and fruit on a Friday. On Saturdays he only eats food supplements like cod liver oil and selenium, and on Sundays he only drinks things liquidized, with herbs out of the garden. A few years ago, I helped him with this experiment to find out if you could get by living only on very high doses of vitamins; but I think Mum must have objected, so we stopped. He worked out a seven-day diet for me last year, but it made me throw up, which was annoying for him, because he couldn't keep an accurate record of my calorie intake.

'Do you think we could go up the Eiffel Tower tomorrow?' I asked.

'Say again?'

'Eiffel Tower. Tomorrow. Can we?'

'Complete sentences, Sym. Think on. If you can't speak out plain, at least be thorough.'

'May I borrow the phone, please? I said I'd phone Mum as soon as we were settled.'

Overhead, the French scored and someone threw a chunk of French bread at the television set. It landed in my couscous, spraying me with orange food dye. Victor picked up the round bread roll from his side plate. I thought, in horror, that he was going to retaliate, but he just began hollowing it out with the tines of his fork.

'Mobile. Can I borrow?'

'Phones,' said Victor with a detached, fretful look. 'B****r phones.'

It was more startling than the baguette splashing down in my dinner. He does hate mobiles, I know—says they interfere with signals in the brain. But he isn't usually given to swearing. Grudgingly he passed me the phone and the attachment he invented to protect his brain from it—a plastic funnel with the spout cut out. I took them outside into the street to get a signal. The pavement was full of puddles the same colour as the splashes on my clothes; also Algerians, watching the football through the restaurant window. They eyed me up and down and one of them said something in French that I wished I did not understand. I thought Home would be last-number-dialled, but it wasn't. Victor had made several calls to someone called BROOK

The Algerians stared openly while I pinned the plastic funnel against my head with the phone. Victor's safety device might save your brain cells, but it also stops you hearing anything. Even after I turned my hearing aid back on, it was all I could do to make out a voice at the other end. I thought it was Mum's, until I heard the bleep of the answerphone. Mum was out. So I told her the hotel was lovely and that we were having a great time. I tried to sound like Nats does on a mobile—competent and grown-up—but my voice came out flat and slightly tearful, a jumble of sentences half-begun and tailing away. 'Give

17

my love to . . .' I began to say, but could think of no one in England who wanted it.

I'm so clumsy. I'm so awkward. The plastic funnel slipped, fell to the ground and bounced away down the alleyway. An Algerian boy ran after it and brought it back, pressing it into my hand, his other hand holding mine from underneath, his face leaning close to mine. *'Merci. Merci. Merci. Merci beaucoup,'* I said, in the hope that he would let go. My cheeks were blazing. My hands were sweating. Falling over the step, graceful as a swan, I fled back into *L'Hotel Gide*.

Uncle Victor had finished scooping out the bread roll and was holding it over the flame of the electric candle on the table, so that the light glowed golden through its crust. 'Look at that,' he said. 'Hollow!' and, 'Has Lillian found her passport yet?'

'I don't know. She's out.'

'People should have to pass an examination to own a passport. Same as a driving licence. Government should ration travel. Some of these people take three holidays a year, you know? Worse than joyriders.'

'I'd really like to go up the Eiffel Tower,' I said, hoping that didn't constitute a frivolous and unnecessary journey.

'I thought somewhere a bit further afield. A jaunt. Now we're here. What say?' The corners of his mouth twitched with comedy.

'Jaunt?' Remembering Mum's ungrateful frown at the mention of Paris, I smiled eagerly, though for some reason the cat flap banged again inside me. 'Where?'

'Well, seeing as you've broken free of your mother's apron strings for once . . . I reckoned we should head down south. Two, three weeks.'

How had I known—straight off—that he did not mean a tour of the Tuileries or a coach trip to Fontainbleu? How had I known, just from the tilt of his head, that

18

Victor was talking long distances? The boy driving the badly painted chariot was losing control. His horses had pulled the reins out of his hands. From the end wall of the restaurant a fat, pink Zeus hurled a thunderbolt at him, trying to stop his reckless joyrider before it was too late.

'*Immortals ought to have a licence before they drive flaming chariots,*' said Titus in my ear. '*Especially if they do it in the buff.*'

France scored another goal, and a fight started up. Victor and I escaped upstairs.

'Whereabouts, uncle? What about school? We don't have the right clothes for sun. There wouldn't be swimming, would there? I've got homework. I'll have to ask Mum. Mum wouldn't like . . .' My objections and misgivings soon lay piled on every flat surface in my tiny room.

But Victor just smiled and packed them neatly away again. 'Only real school is the School of Life, lass. Think on.' Hands on his thighs, knees tucked tightly together, bouncing slightly with excitement, he sat on the broken bedroom stool grinning at me in the dressing table mirror. 'What say we don't tell Lillian, eh? Let's keep it our little secret.'


'What does your mum say?' we asked when Maxine told us about her latest boyfriend.

'Yeah, right, like I'm gonna tell my mum, durr,' she said, eyes rolling like metal balls around the rim of a dusty bagatelle board.

'Well, how did you meet him?'

'Internet.'

'*NO!*'

Maxine's revelation—that she was going out with a thirty-year-old man she had met over the Internet—triggered a clamour of horrified screams and shrieks. Object

19

achieved, I'd say: Maxine loves to cause uproar. Nats—
who is sensible and motherly and can say these things—
started to mention Stranger-Danger, but Maxine only
writhed like a slug sprinkled with salt.

'Join the real world, will you? 'Swhat people *do*.
Leastways anyone with half a brain.'

'But you ought to tell your mother if you do go out
with him,' said Nats. 'Tell someone.'

'Waldron says it's *our little secret*,' said Maxine smoothing
one eyebrow with a little finger.


'Mum would go frantic. If she lost track of us,' I told
Victor, with an apologetic snicker. 'I wouldn't like her to
worry. Can we *not* keep it a secret, please?'

For a second, Uncle Victor's features altered as if a cold
wind had blown in his face. His lips thinned, his eyes
narrowed. 'Your father always said you were wanting in
the courage department. "Spineless shrimp", his precise
words.' Then his whole expression brightened and he
beamed at me, bald head gleaming with irrepressible good
will. 'Righty-ho! Whatever you say. I'll go right now!'
And he sprang to his feet. 'I'll find one of yon cyber-café
places. Email her. Put her in the picture, right? You wait
here.' He was laughing hugely at the thought of someone
his age frequenting a cyber-café. Anyway, I thought that
was what he was laughing about.

It was quite a relief. Mum might worry, but not to the
point of calling out the police when we didn't come
home. And she would be pleased to get an email, even
if she didn't like what was in it. She and I sit down at
the computer every evening, like spiritualists at a seance,
and check for messages from friends we don't have, family
we don't possess. I think she is half hoping Dad will one
day email her from beyond the grave. (Wouldn't email

me, that's for sure.) But tonight there would be an email about how Victor and I were staying away a few days more. Two weeks, maybe. Or three. Telling her just where we were going. Wherever that was.


Nine o'clock. It was very cold in my bedroom. Children were playing on the stairs—also a draught that made the door thump every so often, as if someone was trying to come in. I climbed into bed fully dressed thinking I shouldn't go to sleep until I heard Victor come back safe. 'Paris, eh, Titus! How poetical is that?'

But the only poetry he seemed to want to recite was the Periodic Table that I'd learned for the Chemistry exam before I knew I was going to miss it. '*Hydrogen, helium, lithium* . . .'

His voice has a velvety, musical quality that I can always, always, always hear. Me, I mumble. I must do: Victor never hears what I say. But when Titus speaks I can hear every word. For me, that's like when the optician slides home the right lens and all the e's and g's and o's and c's come perfectly round again and it isn't a struggle, even to read the bottom-most line.

'. . . *beryllium, boron, carbon, nitrogen* . . .'

Titus's voice plaits together strands of tenor and bass into a silk rope that could save you from the highest tower or the deepest dungeon.

'. . . *oxygen, fluorine, neon, sodium* . . .'

Every serif, every cross-stroke, every flourish; every accent, every aspirate. His voice touches places inside me like someone moving through a house, flicking light switches . . . No peering into the corners for what's been said. No struggle to hear. Because he's on the inside of my eardrums, isn't he? And even if he were on the far side of glass, his diction is so perfect that I could read his lips! And even if it was dark and there was shellfire or an arctic gale blowing, I'd still be able to understand him, because our thoughts nestle against each other, like pigeons on a wire.

Ten o'clock. The light went out in the yard. The children disappeared off the stairs. The TV set downstairs was switched off.

*'And then there are the Noble Metals,'* said Titus, *'though I rather tend to confuse them with the Golden Numbers in the Prayer Book.'*

'He's been gone a long time,' I said aloud into the darkness.

*'Left his raincoat, too.'*

In the dark, I could feel Victor's mac resting across the foot of my bed. I thought I might phone Mum again— even risk nuking my brain by holding the phone right hard up against my ear. Just to say: Paris wasn't *so* wonderful. She wasn't missing *so* much. A bed, for instance.

But Uncle Victor had taken the phone with him, of course. There was nothing in the mac pocket but a passport. Even in the dark my fingers recognized the stiff card cover, the brittle pages inside. I sat cross-legged on the bed, wondering what it gave as Victor's occupation. 'Shotpeener?' Even I don't know what one of those is quite.

'What would you put in yours, Titus? Polar explorer?'

*'Plorer. I never made it to be an ex-plorer,'* said Titus tersely. *'Look in the passport.'*

So I turned on the light, though we both already knew whose name, whose occupation, whose photograph would really be on the back page.

Full Name: *Lillian Jennifer Wates.* Occupation: *Secretary.*

Well, Victor always keeps his own passport in the breast

pocket of his jacket, doesn't he? Like a special agent waiting for his next assignment.

Eleven o'clock. I kept trying to think what I'd say when Victor got back. About finding Mum's passport. Not that he would have taken it on purpose, of course. Of course not. But there are worse things you can say than, 'Did you steal Mum's passport?' You can suggest someone made a mistake—slipped up—forgot. Everyone makes mistakes. But some people you can tell and some you can't. Victor you can't.

The smell from the toilet in the yard below was pretty unendurable. Tomorrow, Nikki and Maxine and Nats and everyone would sit down to do the Chemistry exam, and I felt an absurd, wrenching desire to be there. Nobody might ever again ask me questions about the Periodic Table, and there it was, in my head, learned, and as useless as a pair of binoculars to a blind man.

'Tell me the Noble Metals, Titus,' I said. 'Or the Golden Numbers, I don't mind which.'

*'Would you settle for the Four Horsemen of the Apocalypse?'*

Then Victor came back, and he was grinning from ear to ear. 'All set!' he said, jolly as Santa Claus. 'We're all set!' and his eyes gleamed with impish delight, fists dancing in front of him like a man driving a fiery chariot. Putting down the mobile phone on my dressing table, he set it spinning with his forefinger, fast and faster, until it spun off the glass surface and fell to the floor.

'So where are we going, uncle?'

'Can't you guess, lass?' he said, perching on the end of my bed.

Not south to the Loire, then, or the sea. Not south in

23

search of educational museums or improving cathedrals or swimming. How could I ever have thought Uncle Victor would be so unkind? I'm his 'right-hand girl'. He taught me chess and bought me all my ice books and videos. Uncle Victor's a genius and a true original! And he's about to grant me my dearest wish.

'In all the world, where's the one place you'd like best to go?' he said, grinning so broadly that the pink of his dentures showed. 'Money no object.'

When Victor said south, he meant the southest you can go. He meant catching a plane for Buenos Aires. And from Buenos Aires another plane south to Punta Arenas. And from Punta Arenas . . .

We hugged and danced about wildly till the dirty carpet came adrift from its gripper rods, and the room bared its carpet-tack teeth at us on all sides. 'You got through to Mum? What did she say? Does she say it's all right? She says we can go?'

'Chance of a lifetime,' said Uncle Victor. 'Her very words. "Chance of a lifetime. Too good to miss." Now, if she'll just leave us in peace to enjoy ourselves . . .' The two halves of the mobile phone had come apart, spilling the SIM card out of its slot. Victor picked it up and, with the air of an undergraduate in Rag Week, tipped back his head, opened his mouth and dropped the SIM card into his gullet, choking and laughing and crunching down on the delicate contacts. I laughed until the tears oozed from my eyes.

*Oh, Titus! Titus! We're going to Antarctica! Think of it, Titus! The Antarctic!*

The man inside my head did make some response, but I didn't catch it. The excitement was so huge, and Uncle Victor and I were both laughing so loudly that I could not properly focus my mind.

\*　　\*　　\*

24

It is a knack. When I was little and it was cold, I used to put my hands in my pockets and instantly my fingers became tribesmen sheltering in a cave from a blizzard. They cuddled together for warmth and ate bear's meat and drank hot mead. I could *think myself* into that cave. The transporter room aboard the *Starship Enterprise* is rubbish in comparison with a little child's imagination.

Nowadays I can call Titus to mind whenever I like— at least I can usually. But what with the smell from the toilet, the mice in the ceiling, the drunks fighting in the yard, and my heartbeat thumping the mattress under me, it took a while that night. In the end, I managed to focus the shafts of moonlight falling through the window, like sunbeams through a burning glass and—presto!—my Captain's head was on the pillow next to mine.

Except that his back was turned. And to judge by the sheet rippling over my skin, someone in the bed was trembling violently. Another lorry thundered past on the flyover, shaking the hotel. That must have been it. Not Titus trembling at the prospect of Antarctica. And surely not *me*? Just heavy traffic shaking the hotel.

That must have been it.

# Chapter Four
## Dreams

I was a disappointment to Dad, Victor says, because of my hearing and my clumsiness (and he ought to know: he and Dad used to see each other every day). But Uncle Victor likes me. He tells me I am *'Sym-patica!'* And he's been so good to Mum since Dad died.

First it was just a matter of coming round, mowing the lawn, knowing the Qualcast is too heavy for her. (Besides, he says Mum does it wrong, and that the grass needs to be cut north-south and east-west but never diagonally, or the blades of grass twist as they grow.) He's been generous, too, considering he must have lost just as much when the company went bankrupt. But apparently he managed to put a little money aside during the good days—being more prudent than Dad. That's how he was able to pay for the funeral.

Mum tried to take out a bank loan to pay for it: that was when she found out that our overdraft was already on the limit. She tried to extend the mortgage, but that was when she found out Dad had already done it— borrowing more cash against the value of the house, trying to keep the company afloat. I was there.

'Where did it go?' she kept saying. 'Where did it all go?'

And the bank manager went and changed the sand tray in the bottom of his budgerigar's cage, because he was so embarrassed at the way she was crying. He didn't want to show us out of his office until she had stopped. But he didn't lend us the money, all the same. Uncle Victor had to do that.

And now Antarctica! And his generosity didn't stop there. He took me into the middle of Paris and bought me clothes! Apparently our fellow travellers in Antarctica would be well heeled, and Victor did not want me to feel 'at a disadvantage' socially. I wanted to say that *being me* was all it took to be at a disadvantage socially. But that might have sounded ungrateful. And I did so *want* the red devoré camisole, the swirling red silk skirt with its deckle-edged price ticket. (How could Victor afford this?) The gilded mirrors in the changing room multiplied my reflection into an army of Syms and all of them looked . . . fantastic. Sales ladies in soft jersey suits stood about and discussed me. I wanted to squirm away out of their sight.

But I wanted the stuff.

*'What do you think, Titus?'* I said, spinning round to make a red silk skirt swirl out.

But he only shrugged, having no interest himself in fashion or nice clothes. *'I like you whatever you wear,'* he said without looking up from his book.

Me, I recognized all those scarlet-clad girls reflected in the mirror. They were the kind Maxine and Nikki and Nats would have been desperate to hang out with: the Chic Chicks; the Chic Clique. To tell you the truth, *I* wanted to hang out with them—those sleek Sym-look-alikes in the gold-glass tunnels of light.

I studied myself, trying to see what it was that still irked me. 'I wish I could have been blonde,' I said, flicking my mousy hair to and fro.

*'I wish I could have been grey,'* said Titus.

27

He has a certain way of putting things in perspective, does Titus.

*Click* went Victor's credit card on the counter of the salon. *Click*, like a gambling chip on a roulette table. At the door of the shop, one of the assistants put an arm around me and nodded in Victor's direction as he strode off down the street. '*Ton papa?*' she asked, searching my face, worry in her eyes.

'*Mon oncle*,' I said and smiled broadly to reassure her. I hardly needed rescuing from Uncle Victor!


Then we went to some left-luggage depot where Uncle Victor produced a docket and was given, in exchange, a huge suitcase. I mean huge!

'The cold weather kit,' he said. 'I sent it on ahead.'

The ancient family suitcase was dwarfed by this great crate of a bag. It put me in mind of King Osiris floating down the Nile in a sealed coffin, slowly suffocating while Queen Isis sent all the birds and crocodiles frantically searching for him. Then and there, in the middle of the cracked concrete floor, watched by surly faces behind the grilles, Victor crouched down and redistributed our luggage.

The huge suitcase seemed to be already full—of brightly coloured clothing with glossy tags in unpronounceable languages: Ullfrotte, Brynje, Barrabes, Hvitserk, Brenig . . . But he laid on top of them my red silk finery, and bundled our Paris clothes any-old-how into the family suitcase. I supposed we were going to pick it up again on our return. But instead Victor took it outside on to the rainy Quai de la Tournelle. He set off across the Pont de Sully while I followed behind, towing King Osiris. I was busy negotiating the dimpled pavement by the traffic lights so I didn't see him rest the old case on the bridge parapet.

But I saw it hit the water.

It was a long drop. The impact made the cheap zip gape its teeth in surprise, and the contents spilled out. Victor's tracksuit, my best sweatshirt stayed afloat as the case sank from under them—floundered on the surface for a while, gathering river litter into the crooks of their sleeves. Then they were swept away, balling up and rolling over in the current, floating downstream beyond sight.

I hate water. I have a horror of drowning. At the sight of my school shoes capsizing and sinking I could not quite remember how to breathe. But Victor's face was a scrawl of eager happiness.

'You've still got Mum's passport, though?' I said, before realizing my mistake. Victor neither noticed nor answered.

'Think on, lass. New beginnings. Let's start the way we mean to go on!'

Out with the old, on with the new. Uncle Victor has no idea, bless him. He has no idea how good it would be—to take a second run at things. In high jump they give you three chances to clear the bar; in school they only give you one. After junior school, Victor thought I ought to be home-educated, instead of going to secondary. Dad said no: he saw quite enough of me already. The Local Education Authority said no, too. I was glad. I was clinging desperately to good memories of school: friends, skipping in the playground, gold stars, dusters wiping the chalk off blackboards. Friends. Sleepovers. Friends.

But secondary school isn't junior school. It isn't Mallory Towers. It isn't Hogwarts. It's notes on the blackboard saying '*Sym Wates is a sad loser.*' '*Sym Wates runs on nerd-power.*' '*Sym Wates washes in the bog.*'

It was my own fault. I should never have invited Hilary over to our house to play *Spirit of Speed* on the computer. But Uncle Victor was there for some reason, tidying out the filing cabinet, and he began telling Hilary about the plans to home-educate me. Except that somehow, suddenly, it sounded like my idea.

'Doesn't want to turn out mediocre, our Sym. Doesn't want to be run-of-the-mill ignorant. Got her eyes set on higher things than most. Doesn't want to get held back by the dead-weights.'

Also, after she had gone, I found there was a new notice in the toilet: uncle had been practising his beautiful calligraphy again. It said:

> *Visitors may use this toilet but please remember: a single bacterium can multiply 700,000 times in a day. You are requested to maintain high levels of hygiene.*
> *Thank you.*

The words spread through school like a germ and multiplied quicker than bacteria: that Sym Wates thought she was too good for ordinary school—too good to consort with anyone at ordinary school—also that visitors weren't welcome at her house. Sym Wates was a misfit weirdo.

Whereas in fact I'd give anything to fit in.

If only I was fit to.


An elbow jabbed me awake.

'If you ever dream that you are hanging from a cliff by your fingertips—jump.'

'Where are we?'

'Jump,' said Uncle Victor again. In his flat Yorkshire accent—*joomp*—it had a kind of military authority. It cut through the roar of the aircraft engines, the drone of voices. The sense of what he was saying, though, could not quite cut through that fog of sleepiness that fills up aeroplanes like smell fills up a dustbin or cold fills up a fridge. After eight hours in the air, being awake seemed less real than the dreams that dozing brought on.

'Got that? Ever dream that you're hanging from a cliff—or a tall building—or a bridge—jump.'

'Why?'

'Wake up straight off. Never fails.'

'Do you dream it often, then?' I asked.

'Say again?'

'Do you often dream you're . . .'

'Everyone dreams. Proven fact. Every ten minutes. Eyes go jigger-jagger behind the lids: that's dreaming. You watch.' And he directed my attention to the lady sitting alongside.

Me, I dream I'm in the school play and I don't know my lines. I rush from person to person asking to see their script, but they won't let me, so I search and search until I find a script, but all the pages are blank—white as snow. Not a word, and the curtain's going up and I don't know what to say . . .

'Mine drizzle away . . .' I said. 'I don't think I ever . . .'

'Me, I write mine down,' said Uncle Victor. 'Always keep a book by the bed. Columns. Black-and-white or colour. Pleasant or not. And the setting. That's all you need. The detail's not important.'

'Need? Need for what?'

'Say again?'

I like to do my dreaming when I'm awake; but I didn't say so, because that would sound loony. Some nights I don't sleep at all—not from midnight till morning, because I'm with Titus and I've got such a good imagining going, and, next day, flashes of delight go through my stomach like electricity—as if something real and marvellous has happened and I've just remembered. But if I admitted to that, Uncle Victor would say that's why I'm so slow-witted—because I waste my time and energy daydreaming.

31

I would have liked to get an imagination going on the plane, but my head was full of headache and recycled air—pressurized like the aircraft cabin. *If for any reason the pressure drops inside your head, masks will fall from your skull* . . . The pressure in my head had been mounting steadily since take-off. Uncle gave me one of his herbal medicaments, but it just filled my mouth up with the taste of unravelled sock wool.

Uncle Victor has an allotment and he makes all his own medicines, stitching them into little muslin pouches the size of tea bags 'because doctors are all in the pay of the big drug companies'. Also doctors refuse to accept a man's diagnosis of what's wrong with him. 'My body. My symptoms, and yet they persist in thinking they know better,' says Victor.

Uncle Victor took lessons from a Chinese herbalist in Whipps Cross and got a postal degree in allopathy from Phnom Penh University; knows what everything does for you. Apparently, it was Uncle Victor's tea bags that kept Dad alive six months longer than the doctors could have. Without them, also, the dying would have been worse, says Victor. The dying would have been worse? How much worse could it have been?


The cabin lights dimmed, and everyone around about woke up enough to drape blankets over themselves and settle down to sleep. My legs were twitchy with sitting still for so long. I tried to curl myself into my seat and put the blanket over my head. Like a tent. But the seat was full of plastic cutlery and cake crumbs, empty plastic bags and free newspapers. Information flashed up regularly on the cinema screen: we were travelling at 786 kilometres per hour over the ground, and at a height of 12,000 metres.

When I was little, I used to have a herd of imaginary horses. They all had names, and I kept a record of their fodder on the Vernon Football Pools coupons that came through the front door once a week. When we went on holiday down to the caravan park, my horses would run beside the train, keeping up, stretching their necks, leaping hedges and drains and signal boxes, clattering through stations. Tireless.

'What do you dream of, Titus? Do you dream of hanging from the lip of a crevasse by your fingertips?'

*I dream of huskies appearing out of a blizzard: first their breath, then the black dots of their noses, then their masks, with the noise of a sledge's runners behind. Arriving in the nick of time. I dream of One Ton Base coming into view and the smell of hoosh. I dream that Death and the pain were both a dream and I've woken up fit and well and the blizzard has blown itself out . . . And naturally I dream of you, Sym. At least . . . whenever you dream of me.'*

Out of one side of the blanket I could see the woman whose eyes shivered beneath her lids as she dreamt. I couldn't tell from outside whether she was dreaming in black-and-white or colour. Out of the other side of my itchy plaid tent, I could see Uncle Victor, wide awake, his overhead light encasing him in a cone of yellow. His eyes were stretched wide as he made calculations on a paper napkin—noting down the facts on the screen: the ground speed, the temperature outside, the remaining flight time . . .

*Keep up, Titus. Planes go so much faster than trains.*

# Chapter Five
## Sigurd

As far as I could tell, Uncle Victor didn't sleep the whole way to Buenos Aires. I dozed now and then, without sloughing any weariness, but whenever I woke up, Victor was still sitting bolt upright in his seat, checking on the progress of the plane.

He has what people call a 'military bearing'. His spine is very straight. At home he doesn't sleep in a bed. He has a vibrating chair that he bought at the Ideal Home Exhibition back in 1980. I put it down to that. That chair was always the first place I went when I was little and we visited his house. It looked like a dentist's chair standing in the middle of his living room, and at the turn of a knob on the left arm, it would start to throb. It can throb in two directions—upwards from the feet or downwards from the neck, or just quiver all over like a rabbit on a motorway. Apparently, that improves circulation.

It looks bigger standing in our living room, now that Uncle Victor has moved in with Mum. Oh, I don't mean it like that: 'moved in with Mum'! Just 'moved in'—in case we need tight jars unscrewing or gutters painting or the benefit of his advice. It helps with paying the huge mortgage too, of course. His Therapeutic Vibro-Chair® doesn't face the fireplace, but turns its back slightly on the other furniture: a home-educated chair. We have to walk round it to get to the kitchen—but it has to face due north apparently, because of the atoms in the body.

'Hammer a slab of pig iron when it's lying in a north-south magnetic field, and the atoms all swing about to face north. There now. I'll leave that with you. Think on.' Twenty-five years of sleeping north-south in the Therapeutic Vibro-Chair® must have aligned the atoms in Uncle Victor's body and brain into a little fleet of ships all sailing the same way. That's the object, anyway. Over the years, he has measured an increase of 10 points in his IQ.

And maybe the Vibro-Chair® is why uncle was content to sit upright all the way to Buenos Aires. Me, I craved to lie down long. My legs were twitching as though I was wearing the red shoes in that story: the shoes that skip and jump of their own accord and dance you to an early death.

Uncle Victor's teabags caused a stir at customs in Buenos Aires. The guard dogs patrolling the Nothing-to-Declare area took a keen interest, pushing past me to sniff at the big suitcase. I felt their stiff fur, hot and greasy and terrifying, pressing against my arm. We were summoned to a table by a man with epaulettes and a gun, and instructed, with huge arm gestures, to open the bag. But the customs officers, when they unearthed Victor's teabags, were merely amused. They said something to the effect of 'The English and their tea!' and grinned at me. After all, why would anyone smuggle drugs *into* South America? The cold-weather gear did hold their interest for several minutes. The blazing sun boring its way through the roof of the concourse made ski suits look outlandish: like aliens living in our suitcase.

'From here you go . . . ?' asked the man with the

epaulettes, although he had already looked at the label on the case.

'Tell them, Sym,' said Victor.

'Antarctica!' I said proudly, and the customs officers bared their teeth at me again in nicotine-stained smiles.

Beyond the barrier, Jon, the representative of Pengwings was waiting to greet us. Jon was young and rugged, with huge circles of sweat around the shoulder-seams of his shirt. Within two minutes we knew that he had travelled to China, Peru, and the Lebanon. Within half an hour, he had gathered up four more Pengwings passengers arriving by plane and loaded us into a coach to take us to the hotel. The four wanted a tour of the city, and so did I too, although I was daunted by the sight of the coach wavering and sweltering in its own heat haze.

As it turned out, the air conditioning was so powerful that we shivered in our seats. The sun's heat could no more board the bus than the skinny dogs and cats jumping out of its path. As we cruised up and down I could feel Victor shuddering and I turned to say that I was cold too. But when I looked, he had his lips bunched up between his teeth and he was trembling, not with cold, but with pent-up rage.

'Waste of time! Airport hotel. Would have saved all this traipsing back and fro. Save three hours easy.' And I realized that he was still travelling—would still be travelling until the moment he set foot on Antarctic ice. I nestled close to him, partly for warmth, partly because I understood how he felt. Also, I had just realized what lay in store. The four in the coach were only the tip of the iceberg. There were going to be *other people* on this expedition—the ones my new clothes were intended to impress. And I don't do strangers.

*     *     *

36

None of the other people on our trip looked as if they would ever stay at *L'Hotel Gide*. No strangers to hardship, mind. Some had been trekking in the Andes or safariing in the Okovango or had walked the Great Wall of China. They were, for the most part, bronzed and polished; their watches showed Pacific Time and the phases of the moon. Most seemed to own palm computers, cameras with lenses as long as my forearm, and tiny mobile phones. (The richer you are, I've worked out, the smaller your telephone and the bigger your telephoto lens.) Not that their mobiles would work once we reached Antarctica, but the fact was, our fellow passengers, with the exception of Tillie and Brenda, all possessed lots of everything and had brought most of it with them. They were rich in years, too: the majority were over sixty.

Everyone said, when they saw me, how glad they were to see a young face. But I'm not sure I believed them. When I'm struggling with arthritis and gout, I think the last thing I'll want to see is someone fourteen. Anyway, whatever they said they said it very loud and slowly, seeing my hearing aid and assuming I was a halfwit. I said nothing to disabuse them. Halfwit is what I do best.

Mr Pogsbaum (already asking if the hotel had a snooker table) had a body like the net under a corner-pocket bulging full of balls. Mrs Pogsbaum was as thin and stiff as a snooker cue, unable to bend at waist or knees because of arthritis. Extraordinary, to go south with joint pain. But perhaps Mr Pogsbaum did not give her any choice, or perhaps she did not stiffen up until after they left Florida.

Colonel Oliver (retired) and Hue Fah were on their honeymoon; a garland of dead flowers still hung round the bride's neck as they stood waiting in the lobby. They had been living together for twenty years, but apparently Hue Fah had suddenly 'taken it into her head that she wanted a piece of paper, odd woman'. Bewilderment still lingered in Colonel Oliver's milky blue eyes.

Tillie and Brenda were friends and had been holidaying together for years, escaping their husbands to visit Petra by coach or St Petersburg by train; every year somewhere more ambitious. Antarctica was to be their best—Brenda had inherited some money—but their last, because next year they were both retiring, and money would be eaten up by duller things.

There was a black American journalist—a travel writer—preparing an article on the trip, but who had either written it already or was convinced it would be tedious past bearing, because he had brought eight paperback thrillers to read, a laptop, and sixteen movies on DVD.

Clough—I don't know if that was his first or second name—was a Lancastrian, so he instantly took against Uncle Victor for being 'Yorkshire'. He was a bird-watcher so naturally assumed the trip would be chiefly given over to bird-watching. At first he parked his luggage trolley alongside Ms Adolphus, who had penguin transfers all over her suitcases. But he moved further off when he discovered she was a one-bird enthusiast. Ms Adolphus knew everything there is to know about penguins—'the most wonderful creatures alive!'—and made yearly visits to commune with them on a spiritual level.

A blond man and boy were standing on the stairs of the hotel, surveying us all as we milled about in the lobby. While Victor was checking in, the man caught my eye and smiled as if he had known me all his life, and yet I had never laid eyes on him or his son before. If I had I wouldn't have forgotten.

'Who's that?' I asked Uncle Victor tugging on his sleeve, but he said how was he to know and not to stare. The man looked like Beowulf, Viking-slayer-of-monsters. His son, too, had shoulder-length, curling, blond hair and Viking-blue eyes. He came down the stairs without needing to look down at his feet. I was still thinking, *'I wish I could do stairs without looking'*, when they introduced themselves: Manfred and Sigurd Bruch from Norway.

Victor spun round and grasped the man's outstretched hand between both his. 'Grand!' he said—which Manfred certainly was, in his white jeans and whiter collarless shirt. Sigurd was all in black.

'So you too are heading south,' said Mr Bruch to me. 'How agreeable for my son.' His voice was rich to the point of opera; he rather put me in mind of our school Head, who's Welsh and given to singing.

And then they had gone, out into the sunshine and the garish racket of the street, to see something of the city. I thought for an odd moment that Victor was going to run after them. But the receptionist was thrusting registration forms at him, and there was a queue forming behind us.

Madame Mimi Dormiere-St-Pierre arrived late, magnificent in a big pink snowsuit that made her look like a baby in rompers, what with her sparse tufts of hair and the big rattle of a microphone into which she dictated her thoughts. She was writing a novel, and quickly promised to include us all in it. The stopover in Buenos Aires had come as a surprise to her, she not having read the itinerary very closely—'All those boring papers!' Hence the snowsuit. She was about as French as apple pie, and discovered to her joy that she owned a beach house very near the couple from Florida. Mimi was so rich she even had a satellite radio phone that could be used anywhere in the world, including Antarctica.

All this I found out by watching and listening, of course, not asking. (God forbid!) And I tell you, it's no mean feat to eavesdrop when you're wearing a hearing aid. A lot

39

of voices all talking at once in an echoing hotel lobby blur together into a blizzard of sound.

I couldn't wait to get to my room with its seven Sky TV channels and mini-fridge, sofa, writing desk, double bed just for me, and a view so sunny that the light ricocheted sharp as curare-tipped arrows off the cars far, far below.

'Can I phone Mum?' I called through the connecting door.

'Best not,' came the reply.

Stretching out full-length on the satiny bed, I was faced with an envelope on the pillow. It was for a Pengwings party in the penthouse restaurant at seven o'clock, and called itself—predictably—The Icebreaker. My heart sank.

For some crime committed by my ancestors in the dark and forgotten days, I came into the world already tarred and feathered. With shyness. It hurts terribly—every bit as much as hot tar choking every pore—and I wish I could be rid of it. But it hurts a lot less than having someone try and *peel the shyness off*. That's like being flayed alive.

Also, Titus and I went to a deal of trouble to surround ourselves with pack ice. We don't appreciate icebreakers, do we, Titus? 'How about you and I have Room Service and watch *I Love Lucy* in Spanish? I'll tell Uncle Victor I'm ill.'

*'You're going to have to harness up with these people sometime, you know. Have to decide who you're going to pull with. Who's going to be on your team?'*

'I thought I'd use dogs.'

*'Not quite the thing. Not quite in the spirit of British endeavour,'* said Titus rather bitterly.

'Ponies, then.'

*'I shot them all, remember? Or brained them with an ice axe.'*

'Cold hands, Titus. Ease up. I'll be in *your* team, then—

with Teddy Evans and Birdie Bowers and Cherry and Atch—'

*'Currently unavailable.'*

'Manfred the Viking, then, and that nice Brenda woman and Jon the tour-guide . . . and you.'

*'What about Sigurd?'* said Titus.

'Who?'

Uncle Victor came in and unfastened the suitcase, looking for the washbag and his shaving kit. My red silk skirt spilled out on to the carpet like blood.

*'Sooner or later, you have to meet them, you know, Sym,'* said Titus putting his arms round me from behind and resting his chin on my head. *'I need an opportunity to size them up.'*

'And I suppose it is a chance to wear the red silk,' I conceded.

*'I shall come as I am.'*

'And you won't wander off, will you?'

*'Not for a minute.'*


The whole noisy hubbub of the penthouse restaurant engulfed me the moment I was through the door. Rods of sound pierced my head like a conjuror's swords rammed into a box full of conjuror's assistant:

—pans banging in the kitchen;

—the sharp twang of Mr Pogsbaum's Texan accent, 'When we were in Afghanistan before the war . . .';

—the head waiter swearing at a waitress in Spanish;

—Ms Adolphus saying, 'So they monitored the heartbeat of these poor little preggie Adélie penguins and they got all stressed out soon as anyone came closer'n thirty metres.'

Oh yes, little penguins, I know how you feel.

Me, I stood beside the coat-stand, rubbing sleeves with someone's linen coat on one side, holding hands

41

with Titus on the other, and baring my teeth at anyone who came within thirty metres. Smiling. I like people. I like watching them. It's just that I'd prefer to do it from a mile away using very powerful binoculars.

I scanned Colonel Oliver and Hue Fah from head to foot, looking for concealed Romance. But there wasn't any—unless it was in the way she slipped the medication between her husband's lips between fetching him glasses of water.

Madame Doolier-St-Pierre had exchanged her snow-suit for a gypsy blouse with mirror-sequins, but her fuschia-pink crinkle skirt still overlapped big, fleecy, après-ski clogs. She was intent on cornering the American journalist to discuss creativity and publishers, but he left after ten minutes to telephone his children in Maine. She should have caught him at home: she proved to have another weekend villa in just his neck of the woods.

On a round table, Clough had spread out his map of Antarctica, which was smothered with small, neat hand-writing. The round, white, frilled shape of Antarctica was dwarfed by the larger, white, frilled circle of the table-cloth underneath. People glided up, pored over the tiny writing, and read out the euphonious names of birds: black-browed albatross, great shearwaters, prions, sheath-bills, black-bellied storm petrels . . . while Clough frowned and nodded and rocked up and down on the balls of his feet, swallowing huge gulps of champagne to hide his delirious happiness.

Jon was handing out sheets of paper about the trip, and I wanted one so badly that I almost ventured away from the wall. Almost but not quite. Still the swords of sound slammed through my head, sharp enough to shred everything sensible I had thought of to say, if anyone spoke to me.

42

*'This your first time on The Ice?'* Everyone was using the name as often as possible—'The Ice'—to prove they knew that professionals and experts always refer to Antarctica as 'The Ice'. They were like actors talking about 'Sir Larry' to imply they were once on hugging terms with Laurence Olivier.

Someone dropped a pile of plates beyond the green baize doors. I turned down my volume.

Beowolf the Viking moved effortlessly from group to group. It did not surprise me to learn that he was a film director (though I made a mental note to write and tell Nikki). Like a camera, Manfred fetched full-face smiles from everyone he spoke to. Like a photographer, he placed his beautiful son strategically alongside him—an arc-lamp that quickly lit up every face. Clearly Sigurd was as charming as his father. 'Sigurd'. What an amazing name. What an amazing phenomenon: a teenage boy who could charm! Long hair is a rarity round our way: boys wear theirs plush (like those bus-seats that leave marks on the back of your thighs) or spiky, as if they've been electro-cuted. I never saw the point of hair if it wasn't to grow, keep your head warm, and feel nice to the touch. Sigurd's hair invited touching. At least, it would have done, if I weren't me.

I began a kind of mental diary, editing events, selecting the highlights, ruthlessly slicing away any unsatisfactory fact.

*Pengwings holiday-makers are all millionaires: film producers, honeymooners, and novelists, beautiful young men with long golden hair, lovely young women in red silk skirts, one moment sipping champagne, the next thrown together by danger on a frozen Continent, forming fleeting friendships only possible far from home and dull routine . . .*

Except, of course, who would believe one word, knowing Sym Wates? Not me.


Uncle Victor was explaining to Tillie: 'Think on. T'bubbles in yon champagne, they cleave to t'oxygen in't blood-stream and remove it in't urine. Sap t'body of oxygen.' He always gets more Yorkshire when he's talking to strangers.

'It does make me weepy,' Tillie admitted, furiously sipping at the sparkling flute-glass in her hand.

'Say again?'

'We prefer sherry really,' said jolly Brenda. 'But we'll drink anything if it's free.'


'I bring you a drink.'

I cracked my head against the wall because I had not heard him coming. It was Sigurd holding two glasses of orange juice. The Adélie penguins' heartbeats raced with terror. 'I don't drink,' I said.

'Nor I. This is why I bring you juice. It is you or it is your father who chooses to visit Antarctica?'

'Both he's not my father he's my uncle Dad's dead thank you.' I took a sip from the glass and declared it to be very noisy. Inside me, Adélie penguins were reeling to and fro, banging into each other in their panic, knocking each other over domino-style.

'Your uncle, at home, his profession is . . . ?' ventured Sigurd.

'Yes!' I said. 'I know.'

Sigurd was fazed only for a moment. 'You like maybe the animals; the birds and the seals and big whales, yes?'

'Evans Bay. The Ross Ice Shelf. Scott. All that. Not saying anything against Amundsen, I don't mean just because he killed his dogs and didn't die and I know Scott was a snob and drew lines across the tent floor with his socks and everything but I can't explain it—or shot-peening my uncle he's a shot-peener but I can't explain that either.' I realized I was shouting but there was nothing I could do to adjust my volume. Even the silence that fell between us was deafening. 'I heard penguins stink,' I said, to fill it.

'I heard that also,' said Sigurd. 'That is a very attractive skirt.'

'Is that the itinerary? Can I see it?' I demanded.

He gave me his sheet of paper, bowing slightly from the waist, and insisted I keep it; he would get another for himself. I studied it so intently and for so long that I did not see either what it said or when Sigurd moved off. When I looked up he was moving around the room once more, continuing to light up groups of partygoers like Guy Fawkes lighting fuses. The Adélie penguins stampeding round the penthouse restaurant gradually returned to their roost inside me, moulting and shivering with post-traumatic stress.

'I feel sick,' I told the coat-stand, and went and sat on the stairs with my orange juice. The sheet of paper Sigurd had given me wavered in and out of focus. It was headed *Welcome to 'The Ice'*, and listed the lectures that would be on offer. It even suggested each of us might like to prepare a talk about our own particular interests, to deliver to our fellow travellers. Perhaps Hell might like to freeze over first.

My mind for some reason strayed to Maxine's first date with her internet-lover Waldron. She gave us a talk on that, too; a public lecture—not quite illustrated, but near enough. She recounted it so languorously and with such relish, sitting on the teacher's desk at break-time, head thrown back, legs crossed, shoes dangling from the tips of her toes. She told us of the roses he brought her, the BMW, the wild party they had gone to, given by Waldron's famous friends . . . When she got on to the kissing part, I left the room, her laugh pursuing me down the corridor.

Now I sat on the stairs and wished I was Maxine—*almost* wished I was Maxine—wished I was anyone, really, who could go to a party and come away the happier for it. For a while I was so filled with self-disgust that it did not leave space on the stair for Titus to sit down beside me. Then I moved over and hugged the banister. 'Why can't I do parties, Titus? What's wrong with me? Parties are supposed to be fun.'

'*I purposely never learned to reverse on a dance floor. That way the ladies would never want to waltz with me,*' said Titus sitting down beside me. '*Not twice, anyway.*' The colour was high in his cheeks from the heat of the restaurant.

'"*I heard penguins stink.*" Did I really say that? It's like saying, "I smelled a duck quack."'

Titus smiled down at his orange juice. (He doesn't drink, either.) '*I got the gist.*'

But I needed reassurance on a much larger scale. The tears were painful behind my eyes. '*You* never fitted in either, did you, Titus?'

He shrugged. '*I was Army. The others were Navy men.*'

But I persisted. 'Everyone says. You were quiet and you kept yourself to yourself. Like me. And Scott had trouble getting you to come out of your shell.'

'*Bagatelle!*' said Titus unexpectedly. '*While we were kicking our heels at Hut Point, waiting for the off, we played a lot of it, bagatelle. Like pinball, yes? You know how the ball bounces down the slope?*'

'Unless the board's dusty.'

'*A badger-hair shaving brush, that's the thing. Only proper use for a shaving brush in my opinion—dusting a bagatelle board. Anyway—where was I? The thing is not to push too hard,*

46

*you'll agree, or the ball rebounds straight back where it started. Take it gently and it bounces its way down the board—ping-ping—until finally it sinks home into a hole. 15. 250.'* His long fingers cut leisurely arcs through the air, following the descent of the bagatelle ball. *'Eventually they all fit in somewhere. Every last one. Everyone.'*

'Except for the dead balls at the bottom. Like me.'

Titus glanced furtively over his shoulder then lifted his eyebrows at me.

*'The thing is, girl, to keep going. Take them again and again and again till they all finally score.'*

'That's called cheating, Titus.'

*'So? I thought you were intent on fitting in. Sometimes cheating is necessary. You'll find your slot one day . . . And I'll have you know I did fit in. You have to rub along when you're living on top of one another in a hut at the bottom of the world. Even more so in a tent. Doesn't mean to say you can't keep something back. Reticence. Reserve. Uniquely British traits, but requisites of a gentleman, in my opinion. When I had nothing to say, or it was better not to say it, I kept quiet, yes. Biscuits keep best in a communal tin. But opinions? I don't think so.'*

And he looked at me with that level, penetrating gaze of his—self-contained and certain, and needing no one's good opinion. And I needed no one's good opinion but his. And the sound of Maxine's laughter, the words on the blackboard—*'Sym Wates is a sad loser'*—swirled away like loose snow in a blizzard. The Adélie penguins grew calm and rested their beaks on their chests. Their heartbeats slowed to normal.

# Chapter Six
## The Ice

By travelling west on the way here, we gained the best part of a day. Does that mean that by the time noon gets to England it will be second-hand really, covered in our footmarks and fingerprints?

There are days I would like to lose:

—the day the dog got run over;

—the day I wore my hearing-aid to school for the first time;

—the day the garage people came and repossessed the car, because Dad had not made the repayments;

—the day Dad looked across the breakfast table at me and asked Mum, 'Who's that?'


At first the doctors thought Dad had been doing drugs. It took Victor to write down all the signs and symptoms and history of the illness to prove it was a virus attacking the central nervous system. It began soon after Iceland, I think. Dad began to injure himself on the equipment at work. Then he started to forget things—birthdays, appointments, post codes—then to crash the car. Even when he thought he was holding a mug of tea upright, it would spill out into his lap and scald him. He forgot names: first friends and customers, then family. He got so frustrated and afraid that he went wild sometimes, ripping the cloth off a set dinner table, shouting, and smashing things. He couldn't tell the difference between people on the TV and people in the room. Even photographs had the power to taunt him. He couldn't tell the difference between doors and cupboards, searching for his clothes in the toilet, trying to get out-of-doors by way of the fridge. It was like living with a punch-drunk fighter—speech slurred, hands bruised, temper lost without trace.

'Who's that?' he asked, looking at me across the breakfast table.

'That's Symone, dear,' said Mum, high-pitched with horror and tenderness. 'That's our lovely Sym.' And for a moment a flash of recognition made Dad's eyes stagger in their sockets.

'Over my dead body!' he screamed. 'I won't have it in the house. Don't mention that name in my house!' And he threw the golden syrup so that it hit the mantelpiece and we all sat and watched the syrup drip, drip, dripping into the grate like big amber tears.


As early as Punta Arenas the lectures began. Clough could not wait any longer than that to tell us about the diet of the kelp gull, all the different cormorant species, whether a sheath-bill was a true wader or not, how to tell the difference between a dark-mantled and light-mantled sooty albatross. We members of the Pengwings Expeditionary Force sat on the hard, tubular-metal chairs in the Fuego Hotel bar and watched him talk.

Quite quickly I began to sink, like an oil-less duck. To keep myself awake I compared his performance-style with Uncle Victor's during his regular Tuesday-night lectures in the conservatory. Clough only scored 5- for diction, 4- for animation, but 8- for hand-gestures. Victor usually scores straight 10s for everything, of course . . . except hand gestures, which never progress much beyond that screwy jab of his forefinger.

'What would you give a talk on, Titus? If you were a talking kind of man.'

'*Beagle breeding*,' said the man in my head. '*I had some lovely pups coming along when I left India. Or how to keep a pet deer in your coalhole. Less success on that front, mind. It got loose and ate the memsahibs' roses.*'

'Not Polar conquest?'

'*Why dwell on my weaknesses?*'

'And so now we come to the most southerly of the fulmars . . .' said Clough.

I tried to tell myself that I was in the most southerly town in South America—already brushing the Antarctic circle—that tomorrow I would set foot on The Ice . . . Pengwings was the only outfit in the world that actually *flew* tourists there instead of subjecting them to weeks of being sick over the rail of some Russian ice-breaker. Given my fear of drowning, that was kindness past all my deserving. What is more, when we got there, Pengwings would fly us to lots of places the ships couldn't get to. Including Hut Point! What could possibly be any better?

But the flight south from Buenos Aires, the dull exhaustion of endlessly travelling had sapped all the excitement out of me. However much was it *costing* Uncle Victor for us to be travelling with Pengwings? However much was it *costing* to sit here, listening to Clough describing skua eggs? And was I turning into my mother that all I could think about was the cost?

'But which is the biggest of the mollymawks? And which the smallest?' enquired Clough. (I think they were rhetorical questions.)

Victor was starting to breathe out through closed lips—

a sure sign he was falling asleep. If I woke him up, he was bound to put Clough wise on the markings of the black-browed albatross. Better, though, than for him to start snoring. I whispered in his ear. 'What will it be? Your lecture. On. When it's our turn?'

When he turned his face towards me, there were deep, dark circles round his eyes. 'Say again?'

'What will you tell them about?'

Joy swarmed upwards from his mouth, till his whole shiny face was alight. 'Won't tell 'em!' he said, thrusting his head so close to mine that our noses banged. 'Won't tell 'em, girl! We'll SHOW 'em!'

Fossils, then. He must have brought along his photo collection of fossils. He can fit a two-hour slide-show on to a couple of CDs. I know: I've seen it. I smiled and smiled, but the news trickled down through me like iron filings.

'Now, the krill population is crucial—it goes without saying—to penguin reproduction,' said Clough, proving that it did not go without saying at all.

Titus groaned, turned up the collar of his leather jacket and slid slowly down in his chair, arms crossed, a look of martyrdom pinned in place by his eyebrows. *'Oh well, as Napoleon once said, Come what may, there's always Death.'*

'Cold hands, Titus. Cold hands.'


Next moment (or so it seemed) Victor was jabbing me with his elbow, insisting I look. We were aboard the DC-6, swallowed up inside the huge roar of its engines, and flying out over the Southern Ocean. I had chosen not to sit by the window—not wanting to see so much sea. Now Victor insisted I look.

Down below—an iceberg.

Like something lost overboard from a container ship,

51

angular and square. The pilot flew lower so that we could see through the water to the vaster bulk of ice below. A kilometre of ice. Acres and acres of ice. As natural a phenomenon as the white cliffs of Dover—except that the cliffs at Dover aren't carved out of elephant ivory. Cameras buzzed and whirred. But there was really no way of judging bigness—nothing to place against it for scale. Through the TV-shaped windows, it looked like TV footage of an iceberg. The extraordinary colour of the sea I put down to a sun-filter in the window glass. Nothing could be so inky blue. It was none of it real.

An hour later, the plane collided with some invisible barrier and dropped through the air. Cold engulfed the cabin. We had crossed the Antarctic Circle and it was as solid a thing as an electric fence. We had rammed the pillar of cold that stands perpetually over the Antarctic's frozen sea and land. Below us was a curding of sea ice—here, there, and everywhere—a mosaic of white puzzle pieces saying, 'Solve me! Solve me!'—the makings of a self-assembly world waiting to be glued together.

And then there it was: the perfect whole! The dazzling white shield of Antarctica, clinging to the curve of the planet! And I had to close my eyes.

I don't mean that I dared not look. I mean that the brightness forced my lids shut, like thumbs pressing on my eyeballs. The sheer blistering, agonizing dazzle of sunlit ice clawed, until tears welled over my lids and the irises screwed tight shut.

Jon handed out sunglasses to those of us who left home thinking to go to Paris and who hadn't thought to unearth ski goggles from the suitcase. Huge, moulded things they were, like the dentist uses, too broad for my head, so that I had to hold them in place. But now, at least, features emerged—the filigree lace of blown snow on volcanic rock; the fancy knotwork of a seal colony; the towering ruck of an ice barrier, snow pluming off its rim; dark hummocks of stone that were really the tips of mountains buried up to their necks; the black axe-heads of far-off mountain ranges.

Once, the pilot pointed out specks of blood. Not blood, no: a man-made settlement where everything was painted red. But I didn't choose to believe in weather stations and trucks and prefabricated igloos painted pillar-box red. I preferred to believe in meteorites nicking the planet's skin, needle-sharp starlight pricking it, the blood of dogs and ponies . . .

Hours more passed—hours rendered tiny by the immensity of the land beneath. And then: a blank.

God sketched Antarctica then rubbed most of it out again, in the hope a better idea would strike Him. In the centre is a blank whiteness where the planet isn't finished. It's the address for Nowhere.

The emerald ice-floes, the mosaic of growlers on a navy ocean, the tortured contortions of glaciers meeting the sea—these things had been beautiful as we passed over them—but the interior? That empty featureless plateau, rising up and up to high-altitude nothingness with no feature fixing its centre—it mesmerized me. The idea of it took me in thrall. It was so empty, so blank, so clean, so dead. Surely, if I was ever to set foot down there, even I might finally exist. Surely, in this Continent of Nothingness, anything—anyone—had to be hugely alive by comparison!

I was leaning right across Uncle Victor's lap, trying to get a better view, trying to make it real, so I could not help seeing his hands gripping the armrests. His fingers were clenched so hard round the upholstery that the padding had peeled clear off the metal framework.

'Are you all right, uncle?'

His clenched teeth raised ridges of muscle across both cheeks in the shape of handlebars. And I realized that he was concentrating too hard to hear me. I realized that, ever since England, he had been driving all the trains, steering all the coaches, holding all the aeroplanes in mid-air by sheer force of will.

And why? Just to get me here. Knowing how much I wanted it. How kind is that?

'Thank you, Uncle Victor,' I said. 'Thank you for bringing me. Thank you *so much.*'

'Say again?'

We landed on a runway of blue ice pitted by the sun's heat into a potholed ice-rink, raising a blizzard with our own propellers, bounding and bouncing on and on and on, unable to brake, slewing from side to side until flatness and melt-holes brought us to a halt. Madame Bolognese-sans-Pierre prayed loudly. Brenda and Tillie held hands and shut their eyes. The Colonel asked his bride for one of his heart pills.

But I wasn't scared! Such things don't scare me. I don't know why. Maybe it's because I have Titus to look after me. Or maybe I'm too scared of Life to be scared of getting killed.

Even when we climbed down from the plane on to the blue-ice, and tottered and slithered and clung to each other, helpless, out of our element, I could only laugh: usually it's just me falling over my own feet. Even when, within the hour, the DC-6 took off again, marooning us, alone, at the bottom of the world, I was glad to see the back of it. It left behind a legacy of silence—immense and solid. The clamour of silence was so loud that it herded the other visitors into a nervous huddle, cowed.

Didn't worry me! I know silence. I knew all along it would be here, waiting for me. And I do silence, me.


Camp Aurora is on the eastern, Siple Coast of the Ross Sea—well, on an island just off the Siple Coast—though there is no sea to be seen. No seagulls or candyfloss or guesthouses with *No Vacancy* signs in the window. (The holiday trade is never going to be big round here: the whole of the Siple Coast is Vacant.) No water in front of me, no crash of breaking waves, no killer whales or dolphins or seals or penguins, nothing wet for hundreds of miles, in fact. I liked that. I'm not fond of deep water.

Oh, the sea was down there somewhere, all right, but sealed under a lid of everlasting ice, then sugar-frosted with snow. I stood on the edge of Camp Aurora where icefalls tumbled away from me like frozen river rapids and formed a buckled chute downwards on to the Ice Shelf that exists in place of the sea. And I looked westwards across it—a thousand kilometres of flat, frozen nothingness.

I tried to convince myself I was standing on land—on the shore of a sea. But it was impossible. The Ice doesn't differentiate between land and water; it just smothers the whole continent, from the middle outwards, then keeps on spreading outwards over the sea, roofing over huge sea inlets for a thousand kilometres. This was the ice tray in God's fridge, a thousand metres thick.

Somewhere out there—far, far away across that shining silver plain—Titus hauled and marched and staggered and fell and crawled to his . . .

*'Paris. I remember saying I was game for Paris. Did you mishear me perhaps?'*

Behind us, beyond the clutter of oil drums and flapping tents, parked-up skidoos, fluttering flags, tanks,

55

aerials, and red, blood-blister igloos, a handful of little mountains sheltered Aurora from the worst of the southerly winds. But even they looked lost amid the immensity of wrinkled whiteness stretching east to the edge of forever; hefty wrinkles, as you'd get on an albino rhinoceros the size of Essex. I've read about you. You are sastrugi, I thought, moulded by the wind out of ice and snow. I know you. Sastrugi. It sounds like a villain in a fairy tale.

'Titus. Do you know the story of the princess held prisoner in the tower?'

*'Her body encircled by three bands of iron.'*

'Can't move, can't blink her eyes, can't speak a word. However hard she tries?'

*'Unless some friend can foil the evil magic, three nights in a row . . .'*

'. . . keep her by his side until morning.'

*'With a noise like the crack of ice, one of the iron bands broke, and she was free to blink her eyes,'* said Titus.

'You heard it too, then. The crack.'

*'Sym, I hear everything you hear.'*

The silent crack was so loud that it travelled outwards and outwards and outwards to the edge of Space. I blinked my eyes to dislodge the snowflakes resting there; also in sheer wonder. And for the first time in years I could see the possibility of Happiness.

# Chapter Seven
## Talk

I don't know if I'm stupid. I might as well be. When I open my mouth nothing intelligent comes out. Inside my head I'm as articulate as anything, look. But try and get a thought out and it's like pushing raw potatoes through a sieve. There are things roaming around inside my head as clever as Theseus in the Labyrinth. It's just that nobody ever gave them the necessary piece of string, so they'll never find their way out.

*'Look at goldfish in a bowl,'* says Titus. *'Are they gormless—nothing to say for themselves? Or are they addressing the world in Classical Greek on parthenogenesis among the lower pelagic life forms, and we are just too dense to lipread?'*

'Quite, Titus. Thank you.'

*'You're welcome, Sym. My speling was awfull, you know? Couldent spel or puntuate atal, not to save my life . . .'*

'So much for an Eton education.'

*'Not that it would have done, of course.'*

'Done what?'

*'Saved my life.'*

'No. I suppose not.'

*'Oddly enough, no one remembers me for that: Captain Oates the duffer at English.'*

'Astounding. I wonder why. Anyway, I won't be doing a talk about you. You can rest easy.'

'*Excellent. Least said the better. I deplore the whole Polar hero thing, myself. And getting up in public.*'

'I'd sooner die.'

Titus considered this for a moment. '*Well, no. Taken all in all, I'd rather not have.*'


Being always part of the group got a bit wearing. For all the vastness of Antarctica, we were forever on top of one another: we tourists, plus Vicenzo the Otter pilot, Hugh the camp doctor and Popsie the cook, Jon the tour-guide, Mike and Bob the technicians. We were either sheltering in the tents and plastic igloos or clambering into the ski plane for another excursion. The various voices jangled inside my head like a gamelan band; no getting away from them. And the muscles behind my ears hurt from so much smiling. Aurora Camp was surrounded by safety flags, telling us where we might walk and where to avoid. After a while, even the safety flags felt like sentries deterring escape.

'*Going to the pictures again tonight, dearie?*' said Titus teasingly each day when they announced the evening's entertainment. (He was never a joiner-in when it came to lectures and slide-shows.) And encouraged by his cynicism, I would sometimes skip lectures and walk to the perimeter of the camp to look out at the distant Queen Maud Mountains, the nunataks, the wind-sculpted snowdrifts. The Ice Shelf itself. Mirages of things far beyond the horizon hung in the sky, as though by levitation, coloured gold by the sun.

It churned up such foaming, fuming feelings. Antarctica doesn't need anyone's admiration, so why should it go to the trouble of being so beautiful? Of riming ice caves with emerald green and turquoise? Or pumping vuggy ice full of rhinestones? Why moon dogs and corniches of snow like freeze-frame waves? Why, when we overflew the coast were there turquoise sculptures of ice rolling over and over in waves of indigo? It terrifies me, the sea. I know it would kill me if it could. I know this whole Continent would kill us if it could once sink its teeth into us . . . And yet I've never seen anywhere so beautiful, so marvellous.

Our excursions, during the first week, were by twin-engine ski-plane to sites fringing the ocean—a colony of elephant seals, minke whales nudging through tessellations of pancake ice, a rookery of penguins . . .

Ms Adolphus would marry an emperor penguin if she could. Me, I'm spoken for already, but I might be persuaded to vote for an emperor penguin in a General Election. We stood and watched them while they stood and ignored us, and Ms Adolphus told us their feats of endurance, trekking miles or standing hunched and hungry in the winter dark, for the sake of their chicks. 'The daddies do just as much as the mummies,' she said, hands bunched under her chin, face wreathed in smiles. There is something even pinker about Ms Adolphus than there is about Mimi Dormouse-St-Pierre in her fuschia rompers.

Is instinct not so strong among human fathers, then? Maybe not. Or are there actually some rogue emperor penguins who, in the depths of Polar winter, let the egg tucked under their belly fat roll away into the dark? Or take against it and lean down and smash it with their beaks? No? No. That would go against Nature. I think I could have enjoyed lying curled inside an egg, cradled on my father's feet while the half-year darkness raged with snow. But my father didn't like me. Uncle Victor is forever reminding me.

'You are correct about the stinking of the penguins.' Sigurd returned the binoculars, which we were sharing between us. There was a smell like an open cesspit. Their noise was every bit as thick. So maybe you can hear penguins stink, after all.

59

I asked Sigurd if he knew about the man in America who changed his name to Penguin because he was so obsessed with them. But I forgot to speak aloud, so Sigurd didn't answer. Obviously. A penguin carcass was being flayed by skuas nearby. It did nothing to settle my queasy stomach.

I told Sigurd how in 1910 Wilson, Bowers, and Cherry-Garard almost died on a scientific expedition to fetch back a single emperor penguin egg from Cape Crozier. To my astonishment, I found I had said it out loud, because he remarked, 'This is story for a film!'

'Your dad would have to pay the film crew extra,' I said.

'Danger money?'

'Smell money.'

He laughed, and a plume of steam came from his mouth that turned to a diamond dust of ice and caught the sun as it fell. For a few seconds there was a rainbow hanging in the air between our faces.

'The prehistoric penguins might be better,' I said. 'Two metres tall. And turtles the size of Volkswagens. *Return of the Killer Penguin*: now there's a film.'

Sigurd looked at me, to see if I was serious. 'They lived? I will tell my father.' The green sunscreen on his pale skin was like warrior warpaint. 'You will ride snowmobile with me sometime, yes?'

Behind us Colonel Oliver studied his itinerary anxiously, to see where we were and where we would go next. With a gouge of his thumbnail, he ticked off the 'Penguin Colony'. Hue Fah chivvied his hand back into its mitten— but it made him drop his itinerary. One or two people made a grab as the sheets of paper blew past their feet, but they got away and away and away, rising into the air, looping over and over, disappearing against the white brash-ice. I gave the Colonel mine: I had reached my destination. This whole continent was where I wanted to be: now, yesterday, and tomorrow.

'You are a kind person,' said Sigurd. 'And you, too, know much about The Ice, I think. You will give a talk to us about these dinosaur-penguins, yes?'

I shook my head violently. 'My uncle might. He knows everything.'

'To be sure? Everything?' and he laughed.

'No, really. Everything,' I hastened to assure him. I don't like it when people doubt Victor's genius.

'I have heard this. That he is very clever. I do know this,' said Sigurd, suddenly serious. I checked for sarcasm, but polite Sigurd would never have stooped so low. He and his gracious father were always civil. I mean, whenever Sigurd came up and talked to me, you'd almost have thought he *wanted* to. And he did it often. He made me feel as if he had come looking specially for me—but I dare say that's a knack; something you learn if you're brought up to be charming. Everyone liked the charming Sigurd. I liked him.

My clever uncle Victor, on the other hand, was not turning out to be the most popular man on the trip.

Unlike Titus, you see, Uncle Victor doesn't think reticence and reserve are the requirements of an English gentleman. He feels he has to give people the full benefit of his knowledge, whether they want it or not. So while Ms Adolphus sang the praises of emperors, he was busy putting the others right about the date of the first flight over the South Pole. He corrected Jon about the wording of the International Antarctic Treaty. He broke it to Tillie that pemmican was horse and not penguin-meat. He told Mr Pogsbaum how swigging whisky from a hipflask would not warm him but open the pores of his skin and make him die of cold . . . Theoretically they ought to have been happier for knowing these things, but people don't seem to work like that.

So when, that evening, Mike and Bob gave a lecture on fossils, I truly feared for them.

61

We all squeezed into the 'Leisuredome', a moulded-plastic, scarlet igloo where people went to read and play cards and write up their diaries. The talk was entitled *Seymour Island: Realm of Dinosaurs,* and Mike and Bob spoke of fossil-pavements, intrepid little marsupials crossing to Australia by way of Gondwanaland; a billion fish wiped out by a meteorite half a world away . . . Bob and Mike were good talkers—and quite as interesting as giant penguins, in their own way. They were palaeontology students who took any vacation job they could to get themselves back to The Ice. Like Kay in *The Snow Queen,* a sliver of Antarctic ice must have embedded itself in their hearts; I could almost see it when I looked in through their eyes. But now they were doing Uncle Victor's special subject, and I feared for them. I kept waiting for him to interrupt, to take issue with them, to put them straight. So did everyone else: I could tell from the way they flinched whenever Victor cleared his throat or shifted position.

But he didn't interrupt! When he smiled his patient smile, made popping noises with his lips, I would have sworn he was loading the ammunition to shoot them down. But he only went on smiling and nodding, beads of sweat gathering in the crease between his eyes.

'Are you all right, uncle?'

Bob asked if anyone had a question. The Expeditionary Force looked round—as one man—at Victor. He simply glanced across at Manfred Bruch and gave a deep, merry, Old-King-Cole sort of chuckle. Even the igloo itself breathed a sigh of relief, I swear.


Poetry.

In the end, that was how it began to unravel.

We were having a barbecue back at Aurora Camp next day, dining alfresco with the thermometer at thirty-three degrees below. As you do. It was the most lavish barbecue I ever went to (despite the biting wind and the smell of kerosene), with salmon fillets and champagne and kebabs of hot fresh fruit. Clients of Pengwings are used to the finer things of life, and besides, they were on their holidays. So they ate as they ate at home, though presumably at about a thousand times the price.

*'We dug up Christopher's head but it was rotten.'*

'Not now, Titus. I don't want to be sad.'

*'We dug up Christopher's head, but it was rotten.'*

'Shut up, Titus. That was then, this is now. What's wrong with eating potted shrimp?'

Unfortunately, I was feeling too queasy to enjoy the shrimp. Jon said that feeling lousy is part of getting acclimatized to Antarctica and that The Ice is really the healthiest place on Earth. But it still wasn't a good time for Mrs Pogsbaum to say: 'Guess it's time for our youngest member to entertain us!' (Maybe she was in such pain from her arthritis that she thought someone else ought to suffer too.)

'Yes, Sym, tell us something about yourself!' said Brenda, promptly taking my photograph.

*'Oui, bien sûr!'* said Madame Dormouse-sans-Pee. That's probably the full extent of her French. Her number one home is in Long Island.

Uncle Victor beamed with pride. 'There's not much Sym doesn't know about this place. I say, there's not much she hasn't read up on.'

'Right, lass!' said Clough with a malicious glare at Victor. 'Let's see what's in you.'

There's this sketch, done eighty years back: Captain Scott's photographer jumping from ice-floe to ice-floe while killer whales rear up out of the sea trying to kill him. That's how I felt. These people came at me like killer whales, agape with smiles, hungry for a taste of my stupidity.

'Perhaps Sym does not wish it,' said Sigurd.

'I—'

Ms Adolphus came and put an arm round me, half squatting so as to look me in the eye. Then she said very loudly and slowly, as to a little child, 'What's your loveliest thing, sweetie? Your absolutely favouritest hobby?'

It made me so mad that my neck arched convulsively and my head came up. 'The Ice,' I said. 'That's my thing.' I promptly dropped my potted shrimps and they spilled out onto the ice, whispering amongst themselves: 'gutless, spineless little shrimp . . .'

'Help me, Titus! I'm Sym the sad weirdo who runs on nerd-power.'

*That was there. This is here,'* said Titus. *'Tell them why the sea is cobalt blue. Tell them how Ponting was nearly eaten by whales. Tell them how Shackleton shot his carpenter's cat. Tell them there are trees here that only grow one-quarter of an inch high and lions even smaller. Tell them how ships find their way through pack-ice by reading ice-blinks off the clouds. Tell them how Bill Wilson once saw nine suns in the sky . . .'*

'She's a mite shy,' Uncle Victor was saying—quite superfluously really, since two minutes had passed and I had yet to utter a sound. Ms Adolphus patted me sadly on the head and withdrew, convinced I was simple. Mrs Pogsbaum rubbed her hip. The barbecue spat.

'On Scott's birthday,' I said, 'he and his men ate seal soup, roast mutton, redcurrant jelly, fruit salad, asparagus, and chocolate. Well, not chocolate with the asparagus, I don't suppose.'

The assembled company looked at me and laughed, but not unkindly.

'Ah yes, Captain Scott!' said Colonel Oliver and checked his itinerary, remembering that Scott featured somewhere on it.

'They put together a newspaper,' I said. 'During the

winter. In the billet at Hut Point. One of them wrote this poem . . .'

Madame Dogrose-sans-Phew promptly switched on her tape recorder and thrust the microphone at me.

'It's called "The Barrier Silence",' I said and shut my eyes. I was in my bedroom again, reaching up to my Ice shelf, tearing one page from among the thousands of pages compressed there between the wardrobe and the wall . . .

'And this was the thought the silence wrought
    as it scorched and froze us through:
Though secrets hidden are all forbidden
    till God means man to know,
We might be the men God meant *should* know
    the heart of the Barrier snow.'

Why that one, Titus? Of all the bits of snowy doggerel in the world, why did you have to hand me that one? If I live to be your age, I'll never understand why you fed me that one.

I opened my eyes and Sigurd rewarded me a very nice smile, for all the world as if he had understood it. Everyone else, though, was looking at Victor, who was rocking from foot to foot and wagging both fists in agitation like a man feeding rope through his hands. He had pushed back his hood to stand bare-headed in the wind. And there were tears streaming down his face.

Was it my fault? Had I moved him to some unbearable pride in me, by remembering a six-line verse? Or was he suddenly touched once more by the tragedy of Scott and Titus and the rest? I was still wondering, when he suddenly burst out, 'By God but we *are*! We *are* the men!'

I thought I saw Manfred Bruch, at the back of the

group, frown slightly and pass a hand in front of his mouth: a signal signifying silence. But I don't suppose Victor could see him through his tears. Anyway, the stopper was out now, and like a bottle on its side, some secret was about to flow out of him to the very last drop.

'I didn't come here on any footling jaunt, you know! I didn't come here on holiday! This trip here, it's the climax—the culmination of a lifetime's work! Happen you think you've read the books and you know all about this place, but I'm telling you, you don't know a thing—nary a thing!'

The aircraft that had taken us on the excursion to the penguin colony took off and flew away. Eyes trailed it towards the end of the sky. Despite the food and the grill, people were starting to feel chilled through. No one had any idea what Victor was talking about. Including me.

'Forget Newton. Forget Gallileo. Forget Stephen bloody Hawking. You people don't understand what's going on here!'

The black journalist gave a bark of laughter, picturing, maybe, an international conspiracy of terrorist penguins.

Uncle Victor jabbed his lecture-finger at him. 'Fifteen year I've bent the power of a good mind to proving it, one way or t'other. And it came to me! The proof! A revelation! Symmes was right!'

I heard Bob mutter under his breath, 'Twenty quid says he's been contacted by aliens.'

'Or found Jesus?' murmured Mike.

The others were looking not at Victor but at me, as if I might have the key to the mystery. But I could only gape back at them, thinking, *No, I'd know if Victor had found Jesus*. The sound of my own name—something like my own name—had thrown me completely.

'You'll see! You just wait and see! You see if I'm not right!'

Without realizing it, everyone took a step backwards,

away from the man shouting and weeping and exultant with happiness. Except for Manfred Bruch. He stepped smartly through an obstacle course of camera cases, fuel drums, stove, and tables to stand in front of Victor and pull his fur-trimmed hood forward again over his head. 'You are braver man than I, Mr Briggs, to show your ears to such wind.'

I noticed he did not let go of the hood, but kept a grip of the fur to either side of Victor's head, pulling their faces close together with a short, sharp tug. Victor fell silent. The party broke up very fast. The women cast uneasy looks at us, then went to the tents, the Leisuredome, the radio-tent, or the toilet. The men went in search of the dregs of champagne, the Japanese whisky, or something else to eat. For all the vast surrounding emptiness, it was hard to escape further than ten metres from one another.

Manfred Bruch led Uncle Victor to the Hagglund—a big articulated truck on caterpillar tracks—and they got into the rear van. Sigurd offered me his help to climb in after them. On the inside it was rather like a high-tech motor-home, festooned with electric cables, ear protectors, seat belts . . . and the sticky web of unspoken secrets.

'Are you all right, uncle? I'm sorry if I . . . Want a handkerchief?'

But Victor had done with tears. Those still lying in the hollows of his eyes had frozen into strange platelets of frost which quickly dropped away: scales falling from his eyes. His face was resolute. 'Sorry, Bruch. Apologies. Don't know what set me off.'

'We did agree, did we not? Absolute secrecy. We do not want the prize snatched from under our nose. Yes? We do not want to be like Captain Scott, yes, robbed of his triumph?' Bruch's voice was richly soothing. His big fur mittens were folded around Victor's. 'What kind of surprise party, my friend, without surprise?'

67

'It's just that we're so close! And then the lass spouting her rhyme . . . It brought it home to me. We're here. This is it. You don't know what it's cost me to get this far, Bruch.'

'Oh, but I do. I do! Believe me!' It was Manfred's turn to hold his head in his hands, to contain his emotions. 'After I study your work, and truth becomes plain . . . I am so filled with excitements—so bursting out with my joyful news, I think, I have to share my secret! With just one person, I *must share this secret*! And so I tell my wife. My Anka.'

'Yes, yes,' said Victor who had clearly heard this before (though I could not imagine how).

Manfred's face reproached him for his heartlessness. 'She is gone,' he said, blue eyes widening with shock at the memory of it. 'We lose her for ever, Sigurd and I. She says I am mad and she leaves us.'

Sigurd turned his head away and looked out of the window. Manfred reached over and gripped his son's shoulder, mutely apologizing for having caused a mother to walk out. Then recovering himself he said softly and bitterly, 'Find out for yourself, if you must, my dear Victor. Go out now and tell our secret! See how they laugh in your face.'

Victor shuddered visibly at the thought. ''nough said.'

'Have no fear, my friend. Soon enough they will cheer us, these doubters. Until this time, tell no one. This is crucial. Tell no one.'

We sat, all four, plump as Michelin men in our snow-suits and hoods and gloves, the wind rocking the van.

I did not like to intrude on their troubles, but I had to ask it:

'Does that include me?'

# Chapter Eight
## Worlds within Worlds

The world is hollow. It's a lot to take in.

Like cracking an egg and finding nothing inside. Or a full grown elephant.

Apparently John Cleeves Symmes had it all worked out in his head 140 years ago—that planet Earth isn't solid; it's a hollow sphere. And inside it hang a series of lesser spheres stacked one inside the next. And there are holes top and bottom that let in the daylight . . .

It's like cracking your skull and finding inside it a series of smaller and smaller skulls. It cramps your brain just trying to think it.

I had a Russian doll when I was little. It twisted apart at the waist, and inside it was another one. And inside that, another. And inside that . . . Dad used to spread them out on the carpet—all the tops and bottom halves, all mixed up, big and small, and I had to put them back together. In the end, the dog got hold of it and swallowed the smallest wee one, the baby: I liked that one best. And the others got so bent that they wouldn't screw back together again or stack. Not however hard you pushed. There was nothing for it but to put them on the fire. The paint blistered, I remember: five faces peeling off . . .

I'm sure Victor's right. You don't spend fifteen years studying something and then get it wrong. Not if you're Uncle Victor, you don't. He's a genius, with an IQ of 184.

And it wasn't as if he was denying the whole of Science and Geography: his methods for tracking down Symmes's Southern Hole had been very scientific.

'Two tectonic plates collided just yonder. East Antarctica, West Antarctica. That's how I narrowed it down, see. Symmes's Hole has to be somewhere along that seam! And the Earth's crust's thinner hereabouts than anywhere! Well known fact! So it's got to be here somewhere! Symmes's Hole. You can see that, surely? Don't let's give Mr Bruch here the idea you're thick!'

He said the name as often as possible: Symmes's Hole. After fifteen years of self-imposed silence, he savoured it like a holy wafer that enriched his soul even as it melted on his tongue. I tried to picture how it was spelt, this place with my name. Symmes's Hole.

'Any questions?' said Victor.

I had plenty: like why he had never thought to tell me, never told his 'apprentice', his 'right-hand girl', his 'journeyman' about John Cleeves Symmes or this quest to find the Southern Hole. But I said nothing. I suppose he'd wanted to be sure—to have all the facts at his command—to wait for the proof only his own eyes could give him—give us.

'Your uncle is a very shining man,' said Manfred Bruch leaning towards me across the van. 'Truly. A genius.'

'Oh, I know.'

'It will be an honour to film the summit of his life work!'

It was astonishing to think that this lion-maned Viking with his square jaw and noble profile was actually in awe of a cuddly Yorkshireman who favours nightshirts and for years has collected the pith of all the oranges he eats, in a Jacobs Cream Cracker tin under the bed.

So I couldn't fathom why I felt so low. Surely it was better to be here making the discovery of the millennium than just on some mad, spur-of-the-moment jaunt? Shock, I suppose.

'Does Mum know?' I asked.

'Say again?'

No. Plainly not. It must be our little secret, I supposed. Well, not that little, really. The biggest ever secret, in fact, in the history of history.

But there was no point denying the facts. I'm not thick, and the Earth's crust hereabouts is thin. Two tectonic plates collided here, leaving tiny perforations: TEAR HERE TO OPEN Somewhere near the North Pole, and somewhere down here, too, there are portals in the Earth that open on to a subterranean labyrinth: worlds within worlds. Somewhere near here—out on the Barrier or up on the Polar Plateau itself—lies a geographical soft spot, like that hole in a newborn baby's head. Soon we would push in our thumbs and prise open the secret.

'Why has no one found it before, uncle?'

'Oh, but they *have*, lass! Any number! Think of all those men who've disappeared near the Poles! North and South. Not died, not succumbed and got brought home rigid: *disappeared!* Hudson and his son, for one! *Disappeared*. By! You've read enough about them, girl! I bought you all the books, didn't I? By my way of thinking, they got lost—happened on the Holes—found their way inside— met the Insiders . . . Just that they never came back to tell of it, that's all! Franklin! He's one! Oates! There's another for-instance.'

'*Oates?*'

'Brains on, Sym. Captain Scott's man! Titus Oates! Searched high and low for his body, didn't they? Fine-tooth comb, manner of thing. Found nothing. And this in a place you could find your ski six months after you lost it? Never believe it!'

I searched and searched inside my head, but found

71

nothing there either; nothing, no one—only a series of nesting spheres and all of them whirling like gyroscopes. It was such a lot to take in. A cavity in the Antarctic wilderness? A sanctuary where the lost and dying found succour, down in the deep, dark places?

It's a lot to take in.

A place with my name.

The entrance to a hollow planet.

Worlds within worlds.

And inhabited.

But if Uncle Victor says so, it must be true. Mustn't it?

# Chapter Nine
## Solar Corona

It must be true, if Uncle Victor says so.

Anyway, Manfred Bruch had proof.

He had come across Uncle Victor through an internet chat-room site called Thoughtisfree.com and been quickly convinced by Victor's arguments. Being a film director, his onc desire was to film the discovery of Symmes's Hole and whatever breath-stopping marvels the interior revealed. Fame held no interest for him—'in my work I see this "fame". It is a nothing'—but the desire to capture the discovery on film had become his sole ambition.

He had mortgaged his house, cashed in insurances, cancelled film projects, lost his wife, all in furtherance of the truth, all the while urging Victor to let him help in the search. How to find the precise co-ordinates? The exact sites at Earth's either end where the Holes lay. The precise position where open portals allowed sunlight to slide obliquely in and illuminate the cogwheel-workings of the world.

'First there was that dinosaur—whole and complete. You saw it in the news, yes? Two years back, yes? Then your uncle found the fossil,' said Manfred.

'You put me on to it,' said Victor generously. 'I was at a low ebb after Iceland. Getting downhearted. Getting messed about by idiots. Then I tied up with Bruch here, and things started to come together. Like he says, it was just after they found that dinosaur—entire, intact dinosaur, eh, Bruch? And there was a discussion about it on Thoughtisfree. I knew it was significant. I told them: sooner or later there'll be a better find than that, gentlemen! Sooner or later there'll be fossil evidence of *INTERIOR LIFE*! I was beating my head against a brick wall, though . . . till Bruch signed in. He saw where I was coming from. I told him, sooner or later there'd be fossil evidence found near the Portals. Subterranean species unknown on the surface . . . Fossils of the *ONES INSIDE*! Didn't I say, Bruch? A fossil would be the first physical proof? And it was! Bruch found it! I told him it must exist, and damn me, he found it! A *mammalian fossil*! On eBay. Some Chinese tourist picked it up east of the Dry Valleys. Didn't know what he was looking at. Advertised it for sale on the Net! You got all that oriental scribble translated for me, didn't you, Bruch?'

'I cannot afford to buy this treasure myself,' Bruch interjected, 'but your uncle . . .'

'What a coup! What a thing to own! By! I'll never fathom why the boffins hadn't snapped it up.' He leaned towards me, showing me his palm, drawing on it tenderly with an index finger. 'A hand, Sym! The fossil of a primate's hand! I bought it! I own it! Nothing like anything ever found before! And on the *eastern* side of the seam! All the other fossil beds are on the western side. Only one explanation! Must've come from Down There! From the *Inside*!'

I studied his quaking palm, imagining a baby-size hand. 'On eBay,' I said. He had never shown it to me, this most prized possession of his.

They were fellow enthusiasts, the two of them. Like train spotters or football fans, they rejoiced in shared memories of triumphs, setbacks, and strokes of luck.

'Bruch has this chum at NASA,' said Victor.

'I learn photography with this man at college when I am young,' Manfred explained. 'Managed to sneak looks at satellite photos of The Ice. Big scale stuff. Really big scale stuff.' 'Your excellent uncle tells me where to look . . . And I look . . . And there it is! Symmes's Hole!' His blue eyes were wide, his lashes so blond that they were almost invisible. As he spoke, he swept his hands back over hair brindled blond and grey, and he looked from one to other of us as if dealing cards for a game on which a fortune depended.

Sigurd meanwhile was opening and closing one of the Velcro loops on his ski suit over and over again with a flick of his finger.

'Let's be having it, then,' said Victor in his bluff, most matter-of-fact Yorkshire, but one fist was clenched tight around the toggles of his hood: he was a man in freefall, about to pull the ripcord of his parachute; about to see his salvation. 'Let's see this photo then, Bruch. And the co-ordinates.'

The Viking unzipped his suit and took out a photograph, which he laid face down on the table under the flat of his hand. Victor leaned towards it so that his zip made a scraping sound on the table edge: a photograph, taken from Outer Space, of Symmes's Hole.

'My dear friend,' said Bruch quietly. 'If persons find me with such a photograph it is . . . what do you say— "all up" with me. And with my spy friend at NASA. So, please . . .'

'Yes, yes,' said Victor irritably, looping the wire stems of his reading glasses over his ears. 'Who am I going to tell?'

We saw it then—an indistinct mosaic of pixel squares showing a crater or a vortex. Black at the centre, it looked like a whirlpool spinning, a Charybdis coiling itself into a dark and terrifying pit.

'You look here at Symmes's Hole,' said Manfred reverently. Uncle Victor's eyes filled with tears. Seeing that, so did mine. Even Sigurd, whose face had been turned away since the mention of his mother, gazed fixedly at the photograph.

Victor tried to pick it up, his nails scrabbling at the trimmed edges, trying to slide it towards himself across the table. 'Where are the grid references? Don't these things . . . You said there were numbers!'

Bruch reached into the breast pocket of his suit and fetched out a fold of paper small as a bank pin-code. Again he pinned it to the table with the flat of his palm. 'The co-ordinates.'

Their fingers touched as Victor reached out for the solution to his life's work, but Bruch did not take his away. They sat for a moment, like chaste lovers, hand-on-hand. 'One small matter,' said Bruch, leonine head erect and regal. 'I regret to mention it . . . But the money?'

Manfred Bruch had sunk his all in proving the existence of the Symmes Portal. He did not ask for the credit. He did not ask that the place be named after him, that the historians spell his name right. All he asked in return was the loan of money to finance his film.

'I repay you one thousand times over, when the film it is released,' said Manfred.

Uncle Victor seemed vaguely bored by the mention of money. (I wasn't. It reminded me of Mum weeping in the bank manager's office while he poked millet through the bars of his budgerigar's cage.) 'Let's do it, then. Let's be done with the money side.'

He fetched out a banker's draft, folded almost as many times as a paper aeroplane, so I did not see how much it was costing him: that code, that password, that strongbox combination, that secret formula, that key to Symmes's Hole.

'So when do we go there?' I asked.

'As soon as film crew flies in,' said Manfred. 'Thursday?' He was so calm, so collected, so Slav, slipping the bank draft into a breast pocket.

The door opened. It was Jon saying we ought not to get into the Hagglund—even the rear van—without permission. (He was still mistaking us, you see, for simple tourists.)

Manfred lifted his hands to indicate we had been on the point of leaving. The little slip of paper containing the co-ordinates caught the draught from the open door and flurried into the air. Victor's dangling gloves banged me in the face as he went thrashing past me, snatching and grabbing at the scrap of whiteness. It fluttered to the floor of the van and rolled closer to the doorsill, to the Antarctic wilderness beyond. Then it lodged under the rim of Jon's boot. Victor, bulky in his suit, crawled and strained after it, slapping Jon's toes. He pinched it up; his lips moved as he read the co-ordinates, memorized the co-ordinates, poked the sliver of paper deep into his pocket.

Manfred had not moved from his seat meanwhile. He looked down now at Victor on his hands and knees, and it seemed to me—just for a fleeting second—that there was contempt in the arch of his eyebrow; as if even an Easter-egg planet full of sugar-almond worlds was not worth the indignity of going down on all-fours.


No one was feeling very well. The whole of the Pengwings Expeditionary Force was distinctly off-colour. Jon had forewarned us often enough that we might feel poorly for a while, but people were put out to find just how ill that meant. The American journalist, for instance, was being violently sick anywhere and everywhere.

It annoyed the staff. They couldn't say so, of course, because the man had paid so much money to be there, but you could tell they resented it. It was bad enough having to parcel up the contents of the toilet and fly them out to South America, without having to parcel up the contents of the journalist's stomach too. And Ms Adolphus's. And Clough's.

Mr Pogsbaum complained, on the other hand, that it was bad enough to have to share a tent and do without a proper bed and drink Japanese whisky, without getting the squits as well. Madame Doorbell-St-Pierre lost her creative Muse, driven out by a permanent headache, and couldn't get on with her novel.

Jon kept insisting that our bodies would soon adjust— and then he got ill, too, and conceded that this was not quite what he had meant by 'adjusting'. Hue Fah, anxious for her ailing husband, began asking, in her gentle little whisper, 'What would happen if something . . . you know . . . happened?'

Mike was bright with reassurance. Bacteria could not survive here, so it could not be a virus. Here even the Common Cold germ is put to flight by the uncommon cold. (Seems Antarctica is freer of germs than our guest toilet that no guests visit.) Besides, Doctor Hugh was in residence—rather more accustomed to treating broken bones, Big-Eye sleeplessness, and minor frostbite, true, but perfectly qualified to treat nausea, diarrhoea, and headaches. 'Doctor Hugh is rather unwell right now, but perfectly qualified . . .' said Mike.

Even from his sickbed, Dr Hugh could make a diagnosis. What else could it be but food poisoning? Some people started to murmur about refunds. Mr Pogsbaum said he could have gone to Bali if he had wanted to get food poisoning. Colonel Oliver reminisced about seeing men die of eating bad shellfish in Bombay. Madame Boomerang-St-Phew entertained us to the story of Augustus Caesar, poisoned by the figs on his own fig tree, because his wife had painted them with poison. I don't think it helped, that.

I was perfectly fit, me. I wasn't sleeping any better than the others, my brain confused by perpetual daylight. But I wasn't sick. And I didn't mind not sleeping. I've never minded not sleeping. It was a chance to wander the camp undisturbed, pulling The Great Secret behind me like a badly laden sled. It was a chance to think.

One thing was absolutely clear to me. This one thing, this one certain thing kept arcing through my brain. *I must tell Mum.* Before we set off to make history, before we encountered the subterranean alien and his alien dog Spot; before we boldly went where no man had gone before (except perhaps Oates); before we entered into the Underworld of Odysseus and Aeneas, *I must tell my mum.* I'm sure it never crossed the minds of Aeneas or Odysseus, but they weren't fourteen. Victor said he told Mum everything when he emailed (or rang?) from Paris. But what if he just said 'Antarctica'? Or that we were 'going south' for a couple of weeks? Staying on a few days longer in France was one thing. Going south was understandable. Going to Antarctica, even, was forgivable. But venturing to the door of a hollow planet and penetrating an alien world was not something to be kept secret from your mother. Nor was it the stuff of postcards:

| | |
|---|---|
| *Having a wonderful time.* | ☐ |
| *Wish you were here.* | |
| *Rewrote science today.* | _____ |
| *Also history.* | |
| *Met a subterranean monster* | _____ |
| *and several dead explorers.* | |
| *Hope all is well with you.* | _____ |
| *Weather continues chilly.* | |
| *Love . . .* | |

79

I looked into the distance until my eyes ached: trying to distinguish white shapes from a white background; looking for the onset of proper dark in a country where night stays away all summer. Then I lay down on my back and looked at a pink sky instead. Solar coronas sprinkled the pink, as though God had ripped up a rainbow and tossed the pieces to the wind. Nearby was an ice grotto the shape of a giant cello, strung with glistening icicles; its interior continually changing colour as sunset lingered on and on. Even Mum would have had to admit that such things are worth a million pounds a blink . . . But she was never going to see them. Neither was the bank manager. Not only had we cheated Mum out of all this, but there wouldn't—couldn't—be a penny left to ease her money worries by the time we got home. How had Uncle Victor scraped together so much money? And could he not have paid Mum some rent before he agreed to finance a movie?

'I can't afford for Mum to hate me too, Titus. Not her, too!'

*'From my own experience of mothers, I think I can say . . .'*

But before the man in my head could supply reassurance, Sigurd Bruch was standing over me.

'Rainbows. At two of the morning!' he said.

'Do you think it's really true, Sigurd?' I asked—which was astonishing, because right up until that moment I hadn't known there was the smallest doubt.

'It is true,' said Sigurd peaceably. 'No question. Your uncle is a very shining man. A genius man.'

His faith made me ashamed. 'But why does it have to be such a big secret? Why can't we tell Jon and everybody? We can't very well get there without him, can we?'

He sat down beside me, leaning back on his gloved hands. 'When this secret it break loose, everybody will come! With cameras and guns. The armies they put a fence around it and say "Top Secret". The Americans say it is belonging to them, or who knows? maybe they bomb it—pchhhneow! Then there is war to decide who is King of this Underground. The United Nations they say, "Nobody must know about this: it will make big panic. Shut out the cameras. Shut out the ordinary people. Shut the Holes." It is hush up. But us . . . we tell whole world! We make them to see with their own eyes! Our film it makes *Lord of the Rings* look like Mickey Mouse. Until the film crew come we must tell nobody. Yes?'

I considered this. It made sense. But it did not change my resolve to tell Mum. So I confided that, too. (It felt awkward, mentioning mothers when he had just split up from his, and he did flinch tremendously when I said it.) 'I've got to phone her, Sigurd. It's only fair. It might get dangerous.'

Sigurd was silent for a while, then he said, in his sing-song Scandinavian lilt, 'You tell your mother all things? Always?'

'She thinks I'm in . . . I don't know if she knows I'm . . .'

'You tell her all your secrets? When you meet a boy? No, sure!'

'But I don't—'

Bending one elbow, he leaned over and looked into my eyes—the only bit of my face left showing with my hood cords pulled up tight. His eyes were very, very blue, with a rim of grey around the iris. 'You tell her about me? No, sure!'

'You wanted to skidoo!' I said, on the spur of the moment, and sat up sharply. 'Let's skidoo.'

'At two o'clock in morning?'

'Why not? The sun's out!'

So that's what we did, Sigurd driving, me riding pillion, skirting the tents, shushing through the loose snow, slaloming between the safety flags, then speeding out on to the sastrugi. On the concrete-hard corrugations the machine bucked and bounced, pecking into the dips, lurching out of them again and taking off at the crest so that the engine gave a howling shriek of excitement, and so did we. I had to wrap my arms tight round Sigurd's waist and hang on with all my strength, as my seat lifted clear of the saddle then thumped down again, compressing the spine to the length of a clarinet.

Our helmets clashed. Our hair tangled with each other's Velcro loops and straps and buckles.

On our way back, we could see the camp staff all standing by their tents beckoning, but Sigurd steered in a wide arc and brought us in across the landing strip. The driving-bands rasped horrendously over the blue ice then lost their grip so that we waltzed round and round, out of control, skidding, sliding, spinning, yelling.

It was terrific.

After we had been shouted at by Jon and Vicenzo, and before we went to our different tents, Sigurd looked me steadfastly in the eye, his golden curls making a sun's corona around his head. 'Remember, Sym. Your uncle is a very shining man.' Then he kissed me on the mouth and told me again not to tell my mother.

About the kiss?

About Symmes's Hole?

I don't know: the two things blurred.

And I couldn't even tell Titus about the kiss. For some reason he was nowhere around that night. Out counting ghosts, maybe. Or I forgot to look. It's a shame. I could have asked him if it was true that, instead of crawling to his death, he had found Symmes's Hole. There again, how could he possibly have told me?

Titus never says anything that I don't, in my heart of hearts, already know.


In the end, I left it too late to phone Mum on the camp radio. Next morning, it was out of action. Bob said it looked as if a glass of Japanese whisky had been stood on top of it and had spilled down the back, on to the circuitry. There was a good deal of ill-will expressed towards whoever had done it, but nobody owned up. I thought of asking Madame Dormiere-St-Pierre or Jon if I could use their fancy Iridium satellite telephones, but Uncle Victor says you should never ask favours of strangers because it places you under an obligation to them.

Anyway, I'm too shy.

# Chapter Ten
## A slight change of plan

*Hi, Nikki!*

*Not Paris after all—u'll guess from the penguin pic on the front. Antarctica, hey? Even Maxine might be impressed. Uncle V. is making a scientific discovery and he wanted me here. U'll prob. hear about it before I get back. Penguins stink, but not as much as fur seals. Everything else is too big to fit on here—icebergs, sky, glaciers. All except people. Went skidooing last night with Sigurd who's 16 with hair. Even Maxine would etc. etc. His dad is filming V's discovery. If I die, watch the film, will you? And go and see Mum. She'll be stupendously fed-up. XSymX*

There are Antarctic postage stamps. No post boxes or postmen, but there are stamps. (I think the design should be white snow on a white background, surrounded by white perforations: set the philatelists a challenge.) Jon doled out free postcards and encouraged us all to have them ready for the weekly plane: proof for our friends that we had truly been to the end of the Earth. So I wrote to Mum and I wrote to Nikki. The postcards would take weeks to get home, but they would be proof. No word of a lie.

I was propped up in my sleeping bag, before dawn (if

dawn existed, which it doesn't), thinking everyone else around me was still asleep. Then I heard the sound of crying outside—not wild lamentations but a sort of choked sobbing. I peered around the murky women's tent for an empty sleeping bag, and sure enough, Madame Dormiere-St-Pierre was outside.

She was in the toilet—a G-shaped enclosure with no roof on it—and looked like someone stuck at the centre of a maze, who despairs of getting out. If you are more than five feet tall, your head sticks up above the wall while you are using the toilet, so I could see her horned Sami bonnet bobbing to and fro. I didn't think I could very well disturb her, but she saw me standing there and wailed, 'Oh, honey!' so distractedly that I went inside. She had finished using the toilet, but the zip had stuck on her snowsuit, catching on the clothing inside. As I crouched down to try and free it, she continued to weep inconsolably, big tears splashing down on to my hands.

'You really shouldn't cry,' I said. 'Your eyes might freeze up.'

'Oh, but this place, honey! It's this place! It scoops you out, kinda thing. Crabmeat outa a crab! It so smalls you down, don't it?'

'Pardon?'

'It so makes you small! So much nothing. I'm good, me. At what I do, I mean. Don't get me wrong, but I'm real good! Eighty-seven thousand I did on my last title—inside of a year! But here? Nobody. Nothing. Piecea grit in the Himalayas. Dead soon. Flick, just like that. Shops! Where's the shops!'

'You were expecting *shops*?'

'Naw. What am I, stupid? When I'm down my place in Florida do I miss the shops in New York? Hell no! Do I think *Where's my friends: I gotta get back to my friends?* My mom? We don't even get along! But here! This place, I just miss everyone and everything like I'll go crazy if I don't see them *right now.*'

'Why don't you phone them? I would if I had a nifty phone like—'

'Well, that's just it, though, honey! I lost my phone! Musta put it down some place to take a photograph—or on the whale-type boat, maybe! And the camp phone's busted! Just picture if you were in this place and no one knew it and you couldn't get a call out to them . . .' And there she sat, on the closed portable toilet, missing Manhattan and her friends—'Oh God for a tree!'—and sobbing her heart out, the bells on her Sami hat jingling heartlessly. So I wrapped my arms round her, because I couldn't think what else to do, and she put her head on my shoulder and her make-up on my white neoprene, and told me to call her Mimi in future. 'It don't seem to get to you the same way, honey.'

'Do you know, there are mossy things living here called lions because they're as big as the wildlife gets. Ten millimetres tall.'

'They got a head start on me, honey. I'm shrinking every damned minute I stay here,' said Mimi.

'You should go home, then. On the plane. Tomorrow.'

She shot me a look of desperate disbelief. 'Could I? Could I really? I'm supposed to be here three weeks!'

'Big empty aeroplane. Who's going to stop you?' You would have thought I had personally freed her from Death Row. 'I don't think you'd be on your own. So many people are feeling wretched.'

She stroked the fur round the rim of my hood with a trembling forefinger. 'Not you, though.'

I shook my head. It did not seem any time to start explaining.

'He sure is cute, that Sigurd.'

'Oh, I didn't mean—'

86

'D'you know what? His pa's planning on making a movie outa my last book: *The Crimson Slippers*. Gonna collaborate, him an' me. Hey! I can invite you out during the shooting! Spend some time with blond-boy. Manfred's pretty cute, too, wouldn't you say?' She giggled girlishly.

I ran the mended zip up and down a few times, and Mimi kissed me on the forehead with her glossy lip-balmed lips. 'That Sigurd's sure got the hots for you, babe.'

'Oh, I don't think—'

'You be sure'n fix to meet up with him some place warm next time. This frigidaire is enough to cool any guy's ardour.'

'I LOVE it,' I said, with more emphasis than I had intended.

Mimi flinched, then shook her head in bewilderment. 'And it don't make you feel small like a piecea grit?'

She's right. It does scoop you out, this place. Crabmeat out of a shell. Shrimp out of its pot. Tears out of the bottom of your lungs. Laughter out of your knees. But being bad with words, all I could say was, 'I'm bigger here.' As she hugged me to her mended zip, though, I did slide my post-cards into the rear pocket of her snowsuit. 'By the way, that nice American journalist man has a satellite phone, I think. So does Jon. You could ask to borrow.'


'Is it true, Titus? Do you think this place is magic enough? Do you think I could rise above myself? Go home new? Bigger?'

'*People change,*' said Titus warily. '*Look at me.*'

'You don't, Titus. That's the whole point with you. I always know how you'll be.'

He drew his knees up to his chin, eyes twinkling in the lamplight, making fun of me. '*Sometimes I'm startled by how much I've changed since you took me in hand.*'

I don't like being made fun of by my own imagination. 'I never stopped you smoking your pipe!'

'*Only the cigarettes.*'

'Cigarettes shorten your life.'

'*Not if you're already dead. And I know memory plays tricks, but I don't recall being an abstainer either, in my previous life. In fact when I was abroad for my twenty-first birthday, flat on my back with a bullet in my thigh, I recall I dreamt of English draught beer and woke up crying.*'

'But why drink? Why would anyone want to drink? You saw what Dad was like when he drank!' I protested.

But no. He hadn't. Of course he hadn't. Strictly speaking. The timing of the two things—Dad's death, Oates's arrival in my head—suddenly tripped me up, and my concentration faltered, and I lost sight of Titus, and found myself alone. Found myself in a tent full of sleeping, snoring people, my head full of times I did not want to remember: Dad drinking his way through the Christmas wine, the chocolate liqueurs, the cider vinegar. Trying to drown the rats he said were nesting in his skull.

Inside my snowsuit, inside my sweatshirt, inside my thermals, under my plait, the short hairs on my neck stood on end.

'*People change. That's all I meant,*' said Titus, stroking them down again.

'Even me?'

'*I dare say. I'd hate to bring untimely death on any fairies, but I don't believe in Neverland.*'

'But *you* mustn't change, Titus. You're not allowed to change. Not here. Please! Everything's fine. Make everything stay like it is.'

'*We'll see,*' he said, for all the world as if he was miles older than me, and not just the odd ninety years.

\*         \*         \*

This is how I made sense of it. What Sigurd really admired was Uncle Victor's genius. But because Victor makes people nervous, Sigurd was being nice to *me*, instead. Admiration-by-association, sort of thing. Not the hots. Definitely not. That would be ridiculous.

But anyway, Sigurd certainly seemed keen to spend time with me all of a sudden. Every time I looked round, there he was. Admittedly there was no one else remotely his own age on the trip, but he could have hung out with Mike and Bob, with Jon, or with his sporty father. Instead, he sat down beside *me* at mealtimes. He took the seat beside *me* on the twin-Otter when we flew to see a colony of fur seals, and he wanted *me* in his photographs. He began teaching me how to shush on skis.

And it wasn't the red silk skirt and camisole misleading him, because there was no chance to wear them. We were forever bundled up in snowsuits.

I mean, I wasn't sorry. I don't mean that. It was just . . . odd. As if the Pixar lamp had come boinging over to shine in my face. It felt . . . odd.

It put me in mind somehow of Maxine's practical joke.


One day after school a boy stepped up to me at the school gates. He only came as high as my armpit and wore studded leather cuffs round each wrist, but that's not enough reason to be rude to a person, so I stopped to see what he wanted.

'Maxine says you're up for it,' he said. 'Wadya say? Wanna do it? My bruvver's got a car.'

I turned round so sharply to get away that my schoolbag hit him and knocked him off the kerb and one of the bikes turning out of school very slightly ran him over. So I even had to apologize to the little . . .

Not his fault, I suppose. Maxine had put him up to it.

Just to see me run. Bear baiting brought up-to-date for today's modern audience.

What's wrong with me? Do I lack curiosity? Should I want to know about this thing Maxine so loves talking about? Am I supposed to crave the touch of acned cheeks? Am I supposed to lie in my bed at nights hungry for the caresses of inky fingers with bitten nails? Maxine says so. Nikki does. I just . . . can't. To me it's like that party game where you push your hand into different bags of vileness and have to guess what you are touching. If sex has anything to do with . . . with that word Maxine likes so much—the f-word—she can keep it. It must be violent and angry and scary and crude. The yobs are welcome to it—the kind who shout it at each other in the street. And what did his brother's car have to do with it anyway?


Not that Sigurd was like that boy, of course. Just . . . unexpected. In point of fact I was very glad of someone to talk to about the Great Quest. How would we get there? What if Vicenzo wouldn't fly us to secret map co-ordinates up on the Polar Plateau? What if it was dangerous—treacherous—somewhere the plane could not put down? Would the two men want to climb down into the Hole when we got there? What if the weather changed and we could not set off at all before it was time to go home?

Not that Sigurd could answer any of my questions, but it was a relief just to ask them. He seemed to know almost as little as I did. All he was sure of was that I shouldn't call my mother. In fact every time I mentioned wanting to call her he changed the subject, and that usually involved kissing. I must say, it was a very effective way of changing the subject: Mum went clean out of my mind. It was really rather nice, too—except for the slight feeling

Sigurd was *being kind*—doing me a kindness—like a neighbour who volunteers to teach you to drive for free. And while we kissed, I couldn't quite help thinking, 'Well, that's GCSE Kissing out of the way,' and 'This'll get Maxine off my back,' and 'If my friends could see me now!'— which seemed a bit scummy of me.

I'm not sure kissing ought to be a thinking kind of a pastime.

Stupidly, I was still hoping The Quest for Symmes's Hole wouldn't interfere with the scheduled trip west across the Ice Shelf to see Scott's hut at Terra Nova Bay. I know: all that stuff is just history, dead and gone, whereas Symmes's Hole is here and now and about to change the entire future of the world. Even so. To have seen where they all slept, ate, kept the ponies, read books, played bagatelle, and sang to the music of a pianola . . . to have flown over the very spot where Titus died . . .

*'I won't come on that one, if it's all the same with you,'* said Titus, with Sunday school politeness. *'I went once before and I didn't enjoy it.'*

The wind dropped briefly next day. There was brilliant sunshine. Sigurd and I were in T-shirts and sunscreen, messing about on the skis, snowsuits rolled down to our hips, like skinny moths emerging from chrysalises. Manfred and Victor were pacing the perimeter of the camp. There was no longer any need for them to pretend they were strangers, unacquainted. (I couldn't see why there ever had been a need.) Now, no one was the smallest bit interested.

For everyone else in Camp Aurora was ill. The scheduled excursion to Byrd Base was cancelled. With the radio out of operation, there was a palpable sense of unease among the Pengwings Expeditionary Force. The reporter from Maine did have a satellite phone; Jon had one, too, but with everyone wanting to use them, the batteries were getting low. And the Siple Coast was no place to get ill. Early that morning, people began searching the sky, straining their ears for the approach of the weekly DC-6. There was a feeling that everything would be all right if only the plane came, offering an escape route; if only they were no longer totally alone at the bottom of the world.

I had guessed rightly that Mimi was not the only one wanting to cut short the holiday. The Pogsbaums, the journalist, the honeymooning Colonel and Hue Fah, and Ms Adolphus all had their cases stacked beside the blue-ice runway. Talk of lawsuits and refunds had tailed away; they had no energy left for outrage.

Noise travels vast distances through super-cold air. We heard the plane ten minutes before it became visible. As Clough watched it through his bird-watching binoculars, I thought I saw the same look of joy on his face as when he first glimpsed a snowy albatross.

It approached, one-wing-forward, battling high-level winds, tiny and frail at a distance, putting on weight as it came in for its inelegant, slippery landing. The groggy Pengwings Expeditionary Force, hands raised to shield their faces from the snow-blow, looked like devout pilgrims whose prayers had brought deliverance and a big grey steel chariot winging out of the sky. The camp doctor crawled out of bed to lay hands all the sooner on the medicines he had ordered. The journalist from Maine leaned aside to be sick yet again, but with the air of a man who knows his sufferings will be rewarded soon, in a better place.

Manfred and Uncle Victor were there, waiting to greet the film crew. The contents of the toilet and the litterbins were bagged up for shipping out: as if Antarctica was some pristine sheepskin rug to be kept clean.

'No pollution allowed, you see, Titus. These days there's

a Keep-Antarctica-Tidy rule. You don't drop your chocolate wrappers or juice cartons or paper tissues . . . You don't pee on the snow. You don't vomit. You don't . . .'

'*You don't say?*' said Titus. '*And there's us, we made such a mess. All those food dumps. All that abandoned equipment. All those butchered ponies. And dogs. And dead explorers.*'

'No. Not dead explorers. Not according to Uncle Victor.' I said it tentatively wanting some hint from him. 'Not you, anyway. Victor says you found Symmes's Hole. Victor says you found help.'

'*Really?*' said Titus with that slight sardonic inflection in his voice. He picked a crumb of tobacco off the tip of his tongue. '*Well, that's all right, then.*'

Manfred and Victor helped push the steps into place for the passengers to disembark. A party of four mountaineers descended, come to acclimatize before going climbing in the Victoria Mountains. There was an Otter pilot, come to relieve Vicenzo. There was no one else.

Calor gas for the stoves. Newspapers. But no cameras. Potted shrimp and smoked salmon. But no film crew. Manfred climbed into the plane himself to look, as if they might be too airsick or shy to emerge, but there was not so much as a reel of film aboard.

'I cannot imagine . . .' said Manfred, stamping about, clawing at his hair, swearing at the sky. 'I am so sorry, Victor! I cannot guess what has happened!'

Uncle Victor, if he was upset, showed no sign of it.

'I fly back to Punta and see what is happened!' Bruch insisted.

'Please yourself,' said Victor with a shrug. It seemed to trouble him very little either way.

'One whole week gone! Wasted! I am pained to my soul!' exclaimed Manfred Bruch. 'But what can I do?'

Victor shrugged. 'Catch me up.' He pottered away with his distinctive rolling gait, whistling tunelessly. His nose, cherry red from sun and cold, gave a misleading impression of jollity. There again, I don't think he was angry; he simply had no brain space or thinking time to spare for minor changes of plan.

Manfred ran after him. 'What? You will not start without me, I think? You will wait one week? I go; I come back on next week's airplane. One week is small time to wait!'

I don't think Victor even heard him. He certainly did not hear Jon announcing the meeting in the Leisuredome. I had to run after him and fetch him back, like someone with Alzheimer's wandering off. Like some old person. 'Uncle Victor! There's a meeting!'

Inside the Leisuredome, Uncle Victor took a chair near the door, but I looked around for Sigurd, so as to sit next to him. He was not there. So I walked back to the men's tent to look for him.

It smelt quite different from the women's tent—less perfume and more sweat. Everywhere at Aurora had the slight smell, too, of unwellness. My eyes groped at the dark—and there he was, rolling up his sleeping bag.

'Guess what. There's a meeting.' He looked up sharply and groaned—just for an awful moment I thought he was groaning at the sight of me, but it must have been the prospect of yet another meeting. Soon I realized he was not going to get up and come—could not be bothered to attend. 'What if it's important, Sigurd?'

'Someone will tell it to us.'

The dark interior of the conical tent was still for once, with little wind to rattle it. A gimballed lamp hung from the apex glimmering dimly, lending a sacredness to this shrine of socks, thermal underwear, guidebooks, and cameras. It was easy to see where Uncle Victor slept: the oblong of his sleeping bag was completely immaculate, decorated with serried lines of possessions: compass, keys,

94

notebook, pencils, vitamins, three passports . . . I was touched to see a dozen packets of batteries for my hearing aid. However many did he think I got through in the course of a month? I opened the notebook to see if it was a record of his dreams—'*Columns. Black-and-white or colour. Pleasant or not. And the setting. That's all you need.*'—but it was simply crammed with page after page of mathematical calculations: graphs, etas and thetas, cosines, geometrical shapes and asterisks, logarithms, fractions, and equations. The writing, sprawling at the start, became smaller and smaller from page to page, as if Victor realized he might run out of space. There was a newspaper cutting, too, about the discovery of Antarctica's first complete dinosaur.

There was too little headroom to stand up, and something very kindergarten about the two of us on our hands and knees. We looked as if we were playing dinosaurs. I wondered whether I should tell Sigurd that Madame D-St-P thought he was cute—thought his dad was even cuter. The dinosaurs nosed closer. Another week's wait, and his father back in Punta Arenas, and here we were at the end of the world. Sigurd's rolled sleeping bag gradually unrolled itself between us like a lolling red tongue.

Then I saw his rucksack hunched against the tent wall. 'You're packed!'

'Of course. My father and I we fly back to Punta to find the film crew.'

'But why do *you* have to go?'

For a second he looked like an actor who has forgotten his lines. 'My father and I we do not travel separate. Never.'

'Are you very disappointed?'

'What?'

'About the film crew.'

'Oh. Yes. Naturally. But it is small delay only. Nothing to worry.'

'You're a quick packer,' I said. Not ten minutes could have passed since Manfred climbed down from the plane fuming and apologizing. And here was Sigurd already packed, his sleeping bag the last thing to stow. And why did he need to take all his kit with him if he was coming back in a week?

Twin diplodocuses, we knelt there looking at one another, me waiting for him to say something, he not saying it. In fact, he didn't say a word. He simply advanced, nylon leggings whistling as they brushed the ground-sheet. I backed up, disrupting Victor's tidy, tidy belongings with my boots.

Get out of my head, Maxine, with your dirty words and your dirty jokes. Get out of my head, cosines and co-ordinates. Get out of my head, Nats, with your sensible advice. Get out of my head, killjoy questions about rucksacks and eBay and *The Crimson Slippers*. I want to take all my dead-balls back and shoot them again and again until they all . . .

Sigurd moved closer, smiling, stretching out his neck, turning his head on one side.

Suddenly the flaps cracked back and Manfred's blond bush of hair burst into the tent. He shouldered his way indoors saying something that must have been Norwegian, though it sounded like Maxine's favourite swearword. His eyes unaccustomed to the dark, he called Sigurd's name twice before seeing the two of us, nose-to-nose on our hands and knees. Then his face resolved itself from Viking raider to film director as he recognized me.

'Time to go,' he said, and Sigurd reached almost eagerly for his rucksack. 'Time for *everybody* to go,' Manfred added hastily. 'At this meeting it is said all people must leave. Because of the sickness. You should go pack, Miss Sym.'

A slight change of plan. Most regrettable, but there it was. Pengwings had decided to cut the tour short, on grounds of health and safety. In a matter of hours we would all fly out of Aurora Camp aboard the DC-6.

One week instead of three. Highly regrettable.

Albatrosses instead of aliens. Most unfortunate.

Health before heroics. Such a shame.

A slight change of plan.

Sym's Home instead of Symmes's Hole.

Like rogue fireworks, relief and disappointment tore through me in opposite directions: relief and disappointment at Manfred Bruch's sudden return; relief and disappointment at the thought of going home and of leaving this place; relief and disappointment at the collapse of Victor's plans.

I tried to imagine the terrible journey home alongside him, his hopes in rags thanks to a bout of food poisoning. I looked for him, to say how sorry I was. I looked for him to ask where he had stowed the big suitcase. I looked for him to ask if we could possibly come back again soon. I looked for him to tell him there was a farewell party beginning in the Leisuredome. 'Mimi! Have you seen my uncle?'

'Saw him leave the meeting before the end, but . . . sorry, honey, no.'

Finally I caught sight of him, outside the confines of the safety flags, a tiny figure in the vast white landscape, moving like an emperor penguin on its long arduous trek between the teeming sea and the gaping mouth of its hungry chick.

'I heard,' was all he said when I told him the holiday was at an end. But when I tried to sympathize, he just laughed—fondly—affectionately—and hooped his arm around my neck. 'Don't fret, lass. Never you fret. All's on course.' His bare hands were deadly cold. I put my mittens on them, and since the mittens were attached to my snowsuit, we had to walk back to camp as if we were dancing the Gay Gordon's, promenading over the sastrugi.

Just then, there was a huge thud. The ground moved under us. A nearby corniche of drifted snow collapsed and smashed, like a wave hitting shore. The snow all around changed colour, swallowing the glow of the explosions just then ripping through the DC-6. Within the transparent rag of red flame, the huge metal shape of the aircraft began to move, subsiding, settling, sashaying across the melting ice until the runway was too liquid to any longer support its weight. Then it keeled over on to one wingtip.

Smaller explosions sent fire washing outwards in lavish swags that engulfed the piles of luggage, the bagged litter, a row of safety flags, and a skidoo. The petrol tank of the skidoo itself exploded, tossing the machine high into the air to crash back down on the kitchen-tent. In the heat from the fire, the surrounding wall of the toilet, built from blocks of ice, leaned outwards and fell. One leg of the radio mast melted, it keeled over and, with night-mare slowness, fell across the parked-up Otter ski-plane. The tents filled with the blast of hot air—swelled up, bloated, straining at their guy-ropes. The red plastic of the Leisuredome, though eighty metres away, lost its shine and went brown, like an apple rotting.

The wind, which had left Aurora in peace for half a day, chose that moment to pick up again. It gave a whistling murmur of interest and scurried through the camp, fanning the flames, whipping up loose snow, sending the black smoke spilling and swirling between the running figures, worrying at the clothing of those too shocked to run.


Only one person was killed. The American journalist from Maine, who avoided meetings and parties, had gone to the luggage standing stacked beside the runway, to stow his laptop, and had been caught by the first explosion.

Perhaps a flying chip of ice, perhaps metal fatigue, had holed the wing and allowed aviation fuel to trickle out of the tanks. Perhaps some spark, some fault in the complex membrane of electrical cables had ignited it. It was an old plane. But it would take aviation experts to account for exactly what had happened. In the meantime, the Pengwings Expeditionary Force stood gaping at the charred remains of the chariot that had come to carry them home and had only succeeded in returning one man to his Maker.

Ten minutes later, Mimi was still hysterical. Ms Adolphus had fainted twice. Colonel Oliver was prostrate in his tent, while Mr Pogsbaum sat in the snow as if it were a beach in Florida, and absently hacked away with an ice axe until he had made quite a trench. Tillie and Brenda were covering up the remains of the journalist using two bright orange litter-bags; his Iridium phone lay nearby, melted into a chunk of tar. Bob was trying to contact McMurdo Base on Jon's phone, but the battery was flat. Jon himself walked up and down, arms wrapped tightly round his aching stomach, weeping like a little boy. The warning flags were still burning at the tip like eerie candles.

Silence laid siege to Camp Aurora: an implacable army of silence pressing in, standing too close, leaning too hard against the compound, breathing menace. Black petroleum smoke, still belching out of the carcass of the DC-6, scattered black smuts over the white landscape, offending the snaky horizons which promptly crawled away. Colour drained out of the sky, and detail blurred. Soon there was grey in every direction, grey that the eye struggled to make sense of and failed. Only the arrowhead shapes of the tents in the foreground said: THIS WAY UP. The

99

weather was trying as hard as we were to rub out what had happened. Or was it trying to expunge us: us puny, noisy, troublesome, destructive interlopers?

I put my arms round Uncle Victor and he put his arms round me.

'It'll be all right, uncle, really it will,' I said, thinking what Mum might say to comfort someone, thinking: *He doesn't have Titus, like I do. He only has me.*

He sighed deeply and treated me to a smile of pure joy. 'Grand, lassie. It'll be grand. Let's make everyone a nice cup of tea!'


Fear must be very tiring. Within a couple of hours, people hysterical with fright, isolated and unable to escape a desolate, hostile wilderness, were all sleeping peacefully. The long pink hours dyed the cloth of the tents and made them glow. The wind rattled at the skeleton of the dead plane, tearing free the odd strut or piece of steel cladding to fall with a clanging clatter through the wreckage. And yet everyone slept. No radio contact had been established with McMurdo Sound, Scott Base, Patriot Hills, or the outside world. No help was on its way. And yet everyone slept.

Everyone except me. The women's tent, which a short while before had been like a theatre set for *The Trojan Women*—all weeping and wailing—was peaceful now. Even Mimi was curled up in her sleeping bag, both arms clutched tight around her handbag, eyes flickering behind her lids. (Are dreams here in white-on-white, do you suppose?) The comforting cups of tea stood empty by each bed. Perhaps I should have had one, but Victor did not offer. He forbids me to drink tea—says it over-stimulates the hypothalamus. I could have done with some comfort, though. For the first time since getting to Antarctica, I was afraid.

100

Oh, we were bound to be all right: that wasn't it. A party of tourists in trouble on The Ice was not going to be overlooked. Mike and Bob and Jon all said that the very lack of radio contact would soon bring ski-planes over from Byrd Base to check on us. No, that wasn't it. Mine was a nameless, shapeless fear. The singing, raging happiness inside me—at the vicious beauty of this place—had drained away, and I liked me better when I was the one person not afraid.

At home, I could have shut the book and put it back on the shelf. Now somehow Antarctica had overspilled the binding, overrun the bounds of safety. (It even seemed to have got into the tent, because it was unusually cold. You would hardly have thought the stove was working.)

I rested my head on the pillow and pulled a down-filled imagining over my head. Sigurd.

No! Not Sigurd! I sat bolt upright again, sweating despite the cold, and even more namelessly afraid than before. What's wrong with me that the thought of Sigurd-son-of-Beowulf sets the stupidity alarms ringing overhead?

Lying back, I shut my eyes and summoned up Titus—apologized for neglecting him. He did not seem to have noticed: women's company he could always take or leave. You know where you are with a man like Titus.

'Why did you come here?' I asked him.

*'You brought me,'* he said brightly.

'The first time round, I mean. Ninety years ago. Why did you volunteer to try for the South Pole?'

*'Guaranteed promotion,'* he said, turning the page of his book without looking up.

'Don't believe you.'

His eyes glanced over the top of the page and I refused to let him look down again. *'India was palling, what with smallpox and bad tinned fish.'*

'Don't believe you.'

'"*The climate is very healthy, although inclined to be cold*".'
'That might have convinced your mother. Try again.'
'*It caught my imagination, then. New horizons. That's as far ahead as a man like me can see: the next horizon. I bore easily.*'
'Did you ever think you might die?'
'*Any number of times. India. South Africa . . .*'
'Don't be obtuse. Here, I mean. Did you ever think, This trip might kill me. This is the place I might die?'

Titus shrugged, his eyes elusive, evasive. I could have read every book that was ever written about him and still not know what answer he would come out with. Because nobody ever knew. Nobody has ever known. So even when he threw his book at me, I refused to blink, to relinquish the smoky brown of his eyes; *The Peninsular War* simply melted away in mid air.

'*Enough of the doomed hero tosh!*' he exclaimed. '*I'm the great survivor, me! Think about it!*' And he began to count on his fingers. '*I was a sickly child but I made adulthood, look! Got enteric fever in South Africa. Some other kind in Turkey. Got shot at by my own men (understandable mistake: it was dark). Got shot in the thigh by the Boers. Interesting. Got yellow fever, smallpox, and food poisoning in India. Ran aground in a yacht off Belgium and nearly drowned everyone on board. Fell off any number of horses, any number of times. Crashed my motorbike . . . Surprising I ever made it to thirty-two, if you think about it. On nodding acquaintance almost, Death and I.*'
He looked across my shoulder—beyond me somewhere— frowned momentarily, nodded his head once, then glanced down, all the stubbornness gone from his mouth: '*Still startling though. In the end. When Death won't take no for an answer. When He's finally there in front of your . . .*'

I opened my eyelids and there, a few centimetres from my eyes, was a scarlet face, papery wrinkled and grotesque, with holes for eyes and a slit for a mouth. Its cheeks rattled loose and its nose was no more than an obscene bulge distorting the other features. I made to scream, but the air I snatched in was so cold that it wedged in my throat and choked me.

'Time to go,' said the face, and its tissuey lips flapped quite away from the bone white of teeth. A flayed face? A burned face? A deathmask?

A mask.

Uncle Victor was wearing one of the face-masks that the technicians use if they have to go out in a blizzard. Faceless. Featureless. There was no telling what expression lay behind it.

'Where are we going?'

His voice skittered between low and piping shrill, on the verge of hysteria. 'To find Symmes's Hole, of course!' How often he must have practised saying those words: *To find Symmes's Hole, of course!*

# Chapter Eleven
## The Heart of the Barrier

*Dear Nikki, Today we stole an amphibious truck and drove out of Aurora on to the Ice Shelf. We are going in search of a hole in the Earth's crust and if we find it Uncle Victor says no one is going to care about one little truck. I think I must be asleep. Or maybe mad. I've often wondered: is madness hereditary? Or can you catch it from dirty toilet seats? I know you don't believe me. I don't believe me either. Don't worry. They will come after us. You can't lose a big, articulated red van in a white country. And Sigurd and his dad are on board, too. So as long as someone comes after us—and catches us—we will be fine. Give my love to Mum. XSymX*

'Did you leave word, uncle? Say where we were headed?' I shouted above the noise of the engine.

'Say again?'

I tried to picture us from above. A ladybird on a sheet of white paper. A slice of tomato on a tablecloth. The Hagglund has huge caterpillar treads that leave tracks across the ice like the teeth of a zip. People were bound to find us.

But snow, like TV interference, was falling across our path and pattering against the windows so thick and fast that I couldn't even see in the wing mirrors let alone what tracks we were leaving in our wake. Our red roof was piled high with grey diesel cans—and by now a deep layer of snow, as well. So how easy would we be to spot from the air? And what plane would come looking for us? Not the twin-Otter sitting crushed beneath the radio mast at Aurora Camp.

Inside the Hagglund, we were sealed in so tight I could almost persuade myself it was a theme-park ride, a flight simulator, with computer-generated pictures in place of windows. After ten minutes, the doors would open, dreary English daylight would stream in and a bored attendant would tell us to take all our belongings with us. Except that time went by and there was no end to the neck-wrenching roll and dipping of the Hagglund clambering over ridges of ice as high as breakers. The multitude of curly cables hanging from the roof thrashed to and fro; a pencil on the floor rattled up and down, up and down. At first there were flag corridors, red rags flickering past the base of the windows, occasionally scraping the side of the van. We seemed to be driving some hellish slalom. Then the flags were fewer and farther between. Then the flags stopped. The Hagglund careered on, though, nose tipped down. We had negotiated the steep downward incline into a vast, stark, empty whiteness like a dish of smoke. I was pitched forward against my seat belt, head close to the windscreen. Then we levelled off, because we were no longer crossing the union between dry land and sea. We were well and truly out at . . .

No, I didn't know about this place. I didn't want to know what I knew. I'm stupid and the victim of a second-rate education, and Uncle Victor has an IQ of 184. If he had planned this, he knew what he was doing.

He was driving us over the sea.

I knew that for certain, because there was a GPS satellite navigation system positioned between Victor and me, faithfully recording our progress over a splendid map, and the dot that was us had crossed the outline of Aurora Island and moved out on to the Ross Ice Shelf.

Always wanted to do it. The Ross Ice Shelf. Did you know: some of the ice is a kilometre thick?

Except where it isn't.

It's a big bite taken out of the coast. It's the chip in the edge of God's dinner plate that he mended with a slab of ice the size of France. It would be a giant bay, but the ice spreading out from the plateau reached Ross Bay and just kept going, pushing a lid out over the water one thousand metres thick.

Except where it isn't.

All noise was shut out by the ear-protectors clamped over my head. And since the electrical feedback stopped me using my hearing aid, I was sealed inside my own personal silence as well. The only voice I could hear at all was Uncle Victor's, whose headset had a microphone attached. There was a tape deck in the dashboard in which someone had left a cassette, and clearly that reached the driver because, like it or not, I had, in the centre of my brain, Victor singing along to Lee Konitz and 'I Love Paris in the winter, when it's snowing . . .' as he drove us out to sea.

He had fed the co-ordinates into the computer and the computer hadn't objected. The course it plotted was dead straight—as the crow flies—so perhaps, like Dorothy inside her tornado, we'd be carried clean over all obstacles—pressure-ice, crevasse, mountain, and glacier—to the Land of Munchkins. Unless we ran out of fuel.

'How far is it, uncle?'

He couldn't hear me, of course. I had no microphone on my headset. I could hear him but he could not hear me. That had a familiar feel at least.

There was even television—every luxury—a closed-circuit

106

system to show the driver what was happening in the rear van. That was how I realized—finally—that Manfred and Sigurd were travelling with us. We were five miles out of Aurora before Victor turned it on and I saw them, strapped in tight, in the rear section of the articulated Hagglund. Manfred was hanging on grimly to one of the hand-straps that dangle from the roof, trying to brace himself against the pitching of the van. But Sigurd was clearly unconscious. Every sickening roll of the vehicle jarred him against his seatbelts and snapped his head to and fro. His eye sockets looked too deep and his face too white, and his lips too loose. At one point he cracked his head against the window, and a pain went through my own skull, feeling it for him. Manfred reached out and pulled Sigurd's hood up to cushion his head, but his manner was oddly detached, like a man re-stowing his luggage more safely.

I didn't want to think of the others, lying in their tents, back at Camp Aurora, but I could not fail to recall the dreadful hours spent loading the Hagglund amid the eerie, unnatural quiet of a community put to sleep.

Crawling between them, stepping over them, packing my belongings, no clumsiness of mine had roused the women whose sleeping bags encircled mine. Furtively, while Victor was carrying luggage and provisions to the van, I tugged at Madame D-St-P's sleeve—'Mimi! *Mimi!*'— trying to rouse her so that I could whisper where we were going—leave word where we were going. But she only rolled on to her back, mouth falling open, eyelids not quite shut, like a baby sound asleep in its cot. So much for the eccentric Englishman and his harmless supply of teas. There was never anything scones-and-cream about Uncle Victor's home-made teabags.

Then Victor came back, and I was his loyal apprentice again: part of the Great Quest, rolling fuel drums and filling the water tanks.

107

As we heaved the huge suitcase into the back seat, dismantled a field-study tent and crammed that too aboard, I kept expecting Jon or Mike or Bob or *someone* to burst from the men's tent or offices to bawl at us and wrench the stolen property out of our hands. But the whole camp was silent, except for the rattle of flags, the groans of the burned-out plane, the crackle of wind-blown snow against the Hagglund. The slam of its doors, the revving of its engine woke no one.

'*DRUGGED??*' I wrote in the condensation on the windscreen, but Victor said he had not got his reading glasses, and kept on driving. He was very, very happy.

After an hour or so Sigurd began to rouse up, groggy and afraid. I watched him, spellbound. He no sooner opened his eyes than Manfred Bruch began talking to him. No, not to him, but talking—looking straight ahead, looking out of the window, not looking at Sigurd's face.

At first Sigurd kept shouting, gesturing, raging at him—but of course I couldn't hear the argument. Angry goldfish in a slopping bowl. At least he was awake. Perhaps by now the others were, too. Soon they would see who was gone, what was missing, and they would come looking.

On what? In what? And did I really want them to catch us?

Behind the stolen Hagglund, towed along on stolen rope, was a stolen Nansen sled and two stolen skidoos. One of the skidoos had long since fallen over and was banging along on its side, leaving a trail of fuel, pedals, dials, and sparkplugs, buckling and denting, gouging at the snow like an anchor failing to wedge in the seabed. In the end, Victor stopped to cut it loose. Mustn't mar the fuel consumption, he said.

I took the chance to open my door, climb down and

stumble as far as the rear van. The light outside hit me like a train and I realized that the windows must be tinted, keeping this aggressive whiteness at bay. The snow settled on me, big as leaves. As I stood there pulling at the door handles, Sigurd's face loomed on the other side of the window, one cheekbone bruised, snarling with anger. The doors swung open in my face, and Sigurd pitched out on to the ice. It was a long way to fall.

'This is mad,' he said unable to stand up. (We were all unsteady on our feet after the rolling of the vehicle; no Ross-sea-legs.) 'This is mad,' said Sigurd again and again. His father took hold of the back of his snowsuit to help him up—took hold so tightly that he actually lifted Sigurd clear of the ground.

'Now, now, boy of mine,' said the Viking between gritted teeth. 'Remember we go to find eighth Wonder of the World!' and he stood Sigurd back on his feet, like a man sinking a fence post. One hand kept hold of the suit. It puckered against Sigurd's body, creased tight in the groin. Perhaps Sigurd was being reminded of his manners.

Certainly he seemed to think twice. His voice recovered its sing-song inflection: 'Should I not stay at Camp, I mean? Wait for film crew? Yes! I will go back to Aurora!' He was ignored.

'How far is our journey?' said Manfred, as if only mildly curious to know.

'Ooh. Three hundred mile give or take,' said Victor cheerfully. 'It's nowt. A jaunt! You've seen the co-ordinates! It's nowt! Walk in the park.'

'Ah yes. The co-ordinates.' Manfred gave an odd bark of laughter. 'What a stroke of luck. Fate, for sure, that it should be so close.'

Uncle Victor is not a great believer in Fate. He is more a man for pulling himself up by his own bootstraps, but fortunately he did not choose now to argue the point. If

109

you stand still for too long here, the cold clings to you like a wet shower curtain on a bare body. My clothes rattled round me—cotton and shell silk and neoprene. The channels of my ears contracted around the earpiece of my hearing aid in painful spasms that joined up into a perpetual ache, as I watched Victor putting diesel into the tank. He used a plastic funnel, like a bigger version of the mobile phone safety device, and in my odd frame of mind it seemed to me that he was pouring pain in at my ears.

'I'll ride in the back with you this time,' I told Sigurd, as Victor discarded the empty can.

'No. No, I'm not going. It's mad.'

I could see the punch coming, so I don't know why I chose that moment to step between Sigurd and his father and hustle him into the van. The punch hit me in the back instead, and knocked the wind out of me. But that was all right, because it served to wake me up. You can't afford to get dreamy hereabouts. Anyway, Mum and I got quite tolerant of Dad and his fists towards the end. You have to be tolerant when people are afraid, that's what Mum said. Still, there was something very odd about being punched by someone so calm, collected, and soft-spoken as Manfred.

Not so charming a Viking, then. Marshal your facts, Sym.

Manfred did not seem to know what to do about having punched me by mistake. When he saw I was not going to say anything, he did not mention it either. Instead, he shut the van doors behind us, put an arm around Victor's shoulder, and steered him away to the front van, enquiring in the gentlest of purrs whether he was absolutely sure we did have everything we would need for such a journey.

Slyly, Sigurd watched them pass the windows, then made a rush for the door.

110

'You *can't* go back,' I said. He ignored me, fumbling with the complicated door lever in his slippery under-mitts. 'Your dad locked it. It's locked. Anyway, you *can't* go back,' I said. 'You've been asleep. We've come a long, long way! Have you any idea what a fluke it is that we got this far?'

Actually, he was probably better off not knowing what kind of terrain we must have skirted or hopped over on the way down from Camp Aurora; how deadly and reck-less our passage must have been once the guidance flags petered out. I didn't want to know it either. Right then I wanted to un-know everything I knew about ice shelves and curl up inside my head with Titus and an imagining. Go to Glasstown. But here was this nice boy who had been so kind to me. And when someone is kind to you, you have to return the favour; stick around; say some-thing helpful.

'You know the story of Hansel and Gretel?' I said.

'Bog off,' said Sigurd slapping the locked door. Maybe he thought I was planning to tell him fairy stories to pass the time.

The van started up. Sigurd flung himself down in his seat again, and shut his eyes. He took one or two deep breaths. Then he appeared to be praying, lips moving ever so slightly. Or perhaps he had just retreated into his imagination, too. Do boys do that? I never thought of it before.

'We should try and leave some kind of trail, was all I meant,' I said doggedly. '*Like Hansel and Gretel*, you know? So that they can find us!'

When he finally opened his eyes, he was Sigurd the Charming again, calm and cheerful and ready for anything. 'Ah!' he said. 'Clever.'

'This wasn't my idea, you know? I never wanted to go looking for Symmes's stupid Hole!'

111

Just then, the crackling voice of Uncle Victor came over the loudspeakers: 'What people fail to grasp is . . .' It was as if he was right there, with us, in the van. What if he had heard me! I sweated at the thought of my treachery being overheard—waited for Victor's crackling voice to reproach me. Gradually, though, I remembered watching the silent CCTV, the angry dumbshow between father and son. No. Victor had not heard my terrible disloyalty. Somewhere there had to be an intercom that would let us communicate with the men in front, but with the van so stacked with fuel cans it was out of sight and reach.

There was an overpowering smell of diesel. Fuel cans lined every wall and were piled up to the roof. On the breakneck career down the ice-chute they had been wedged in too tightly to move. Now, with one gone, the rest wriggled and turned like restless sleepers, their sides sweating diesel where the cap-seals weren't perfect. The floor was taken up by stacks of red boxes with transparent lids—pre-packed provisions for use by sled trekkers. How Victor and Manfred must have laboured to load so much kit, while Aurora Camp lay cocooned in its drug-induced sleep.

Outside, the Shelf was a hollow sphere of a world quite worthy of John Cleeves Symmes. There was no horizon, only cloud and cloud-shadow with nothing to mark where one ended and the other began. The ground was a geometric pattern of lilac and grey and white. Some of the lines were lumps and creases in the surface. Some were shadows cast by the lumps and creases. Some were cloud shadows. Now and then, Victor wrenched on the steering wheel to avoid hitting obstacles that were not there. We were driving through a painting by Escher, a hall of frosted mirrors. I watched it out of the window until it became just a pattern: two dimensions, flat, unreadable.

112

The sun was a burnished silver disc, like a button to press for your money back.

'Does your dad have a satellite phone?' I asked Sigurd.

'No chance. £2000, they cost!'

I thought of Victor pouching the SIM card out of his mobile, chewing on its delicate contacts. Not that it would have been much use to me here. But I might always have spoken to my mother from Paris, or South America. I suppose that's why he did it. Now I might never . . .

The van began snaking and weaving. Manfred must have leaned his head close to Victor's microphone, for we could just hear his voice over the intercom. 'You are sleeping, my friend,' said the voice soothingly. 'Permit me to drive for a while.'

At the best of times the never-ending sameness of the Shelf is mesmerizing. On top of that, I doubt Victor had slept for two hours together since Paris. His voice, even distorted by static, sounded slurred and vague. 'I can sleep to order,' he said. 'Sleep's a state of mind. Habit. Turn the lights out, get into bed: of course you sleep. Sleep out of habit, most folk. State of mind. Nowt better to do with their nights. Me, I've trained myself up . . .'

And on we went, through the hours that should have been dark but weren't, through the trembling, milky miasma of the Barrier.

Suddenly, for no apparent reason, the surface would change to sastrugi or a royal icing of frozen snow. There would be sharp steps up, or one side of the van would lurch over a solidified snowdrift. For the most part it was a shining lake of platinum puddled with mirror-bright patches of platelet-snowflakes—as if a billion sequins had been squandered over the ice. Sometimes—the worst times—there would be a sharp step down, and my internal organs would cram together under my ribcage like sheep in an abattoir, terrified.

113

Once or twice the brakes came on hard as Uncle Victor, dozing off at the wheel, woke and reflexly slammed his foot to the floor. Then the two vans would close up, the fuel slop, the sled cannon into the back step, the skidoo clatter into the sled. Sigurd and I stopped looking out of the window. We looked instead at the fuel cans piled up like some gigantic supermarket display—and starting to shift. Any one of them was heavy enough to crush us if it fell. We stood up, trying to brace the cans in place, feeling the loose diesel run down our arms. The fumes were sickening, and pretty soon pieces of black rag seemed to blow in front of my eyes. My head began to pound. 'STOP! PLEASE STOP!' we yelled. One of the topmost canisters shot over my head and landed on the bench were we had just been sitting.

At last Manfred must have glimpsed our plight on the CCTV, because his voice came faintly over the intercom, urging Victor to stop, telling him about the shifting cargo. Another sharp jab on the brakes. The provisions boxes came sliding along the van, shunting into our legs, sharp-cornered and bruising.

'Have we turned over?' said Victor's voice, quizzical, puzzled, sleepy. The mesmerizing flicker of shadow, the swirl of snow, the lack of horizon had at last defeated him. The harder you look where you are going, the less sense you can make of it, this funnel of light revolving like the inside of a huge pipe as it rolls downhill. Vertical and horizontal lose all their meaning in a place without horizons.

Manfred opened the rear doors, letting in Cold sharp as a hatchet. As he righted the fuel cans, he was muttering under his breath, warning Sigurd to remember what he had been told. (What had he been told, I wondered? To treat the young lady with chivalry?) Sigurd and I climbed down and stood with our heads back, letting the wind

114

blow into our noses, the snowflakes fill our mouths. When I went to look, Victor was asleep over the steering wheel, eyes quivering behind their lids, at the bottom of sockets deep as shell-holes. I stood beside the van watching him sleep, wondering what he was dreaming and whether Mum or I featured at all in his dreams, ever.

Deaf Sym wasn't the first one to hear it, of course. Manfred suddenly lurched up behind me, reached into the van and cut the engine. The Hagglund gave a shuddering sigh. He might as well have turned off a forcefield, for the Silence came at us in a rush, set our ears ringing, came clamouring round us like a shrill swarm of wasps: silence. It was a while before I realized that Sigurd and Manfred were hearing something more. They were hearing another engine.

An aircraft.

At home there is nowhere you can stand—the playground, the garden, the high street—and not hear the drone of an aeroplane. But here in Antarctica it is the rarest of sounds.

We pulled our snow goggles into place and scanned the sky. What direction was it coming from? We cupped our hands round our ears and turned to all four points of the compass, but the sound was filling the sky like a cloth soaking up blood. The whole hollow sky reverberated with engine noise.

I looked at the Hagglund under its white tarpaulin of snow. I looked at our snowsuits, all pastel pale. How would it ever spot us? I looked at Victor slumped over the wheel. Should I want them to spot us?

Was it a routine flight or a search plane? A ski-plane that could set down beside us on the ice? Or an airliner at 15,000 metres, en route for Australia? Was it a military plane delivering personnel to the Scott-Amundsen Base? Or the Law in pursuit of those who had drugged

115

an entire campful of people and stolen away in a half-million dollar vehicle?

Sigurd pulled a red provision box out on to the ground and prised off its plastic lid. He shook the contents out on to the snow.

'What are you looking for?'

'A flare! A flare!' said Sigurd. 'They'll see a flare!'

'That's food,' I told him, and he kicked the box with the side of his foot. It went an amazingly long way, skidding on and on, slowly revolving. Our eyes followed it hypnotically. 'We couldn't let off a flare anyway,' I said. 'The air's full of diesel. The whole van would go up. Flashback. Flashover. Backdraught. Something . . .' He blinked at me vacantly. 'Sigurd, you've got diesel all over your clothes: you'd go up like a torch!'

But despite me saying it—and perfectly loud—the Viking reached into his breast pocket and took out a big gold lighter, thumb resting over the flintwheel. His goggled face turned like an automaton's, as he ran his eyes over the whole length of the Hagglund, from its gaping rear doors, along the roofline heaped with fuel cans, to the front section where Victor lay sprawled over the steering wheel, sound asleep. Seeing the lighter, Sigurd gave a howl of terror. 'No!' he said. 'No, please! What about the backdraught?'

The Viking, mishearing him, patted his breast pocket. 'I have it safe.' He thumbed the flintwheel.

Sigurd looked to and fro between the lighter and the diesel-stained arms of his snowsuit. 'No, please . . .' He stooped to scoop up snow and rub it along his arms, trying to wash them clean.

I know when not to bother speaking. I know when people aren't open to reason. Dad used to light bonfires sometimes, to scare away the jackals he said were looking in at the windows . . . I climbed on to the van steps and

116

began to drag on Victor's arm, trying to pull him out of the driving seat. His seat belt was holding him in place.

*'Please! Mr Bruch, please!'* Sigurd begged. *'Don't!'*

*'What about the Hole?'* I called, as I snapped the seat belt out of its slot. *'Don't you want to find Symmes's Hole?'*

Uncle Victor roused up and frowned at me blearily. 'That's my girl,' he said. 'Not far now.' And his body, which had been spongy with sleep, began to resist my efforts to pull him out of the van. His fists clenched the steering wheel. He's strong, Uncle Victor. I knew I was no match for him once he was fully awake. The reek of diesel was everywhere, like the noise of the plane.

'Uncle, could you maybe get down . . .'

'Say again?' The more I pulled, the more he roused up and resisted me.

Manfred Bruch stood gazing up at the sky, cigarette lighter raised.

*'Mr Bruch! Mr Bruch, sir! Please!'* begged Sigurd, backing out of the lee of the van and into the never-ending rip and rasp of the wind. But the plane did not materialize. In Antarctica sound travels immense distances. It might have been a mile up or a hundred kilometres away; there was no knowing. No knowing, either, what Manfred Bruch was about. Dad used to say jackals were watching him through the windows; there's no point asking what's going on in another person's head.

Gradually the stench of fuel dissipated. So too did the engine noise. The Viking put away his cigarette lighter—though come to think of it, the last time I'd seen it, that bulky, gold obelisk of a lighter, it had belonged to Mimi Dormiere-St-Pierre.

'Bite to eat, lass,' said Uncle Victor rousing up fully. 'Make thysel' useful and fix us a bite to eat, eh? What's today? Thursday? Think on. My day for fish.'

117

I climbed down and walked slowly out to where the red provision box stood on the ice. Its side was dented from Sigurd's kick. Towing it along by one of its cord handles, I turned back towards the Hagglund—which looked suddenly tiny. Even the small distance I had put between me and it rendered the two-ton Hagglund as small as a Dinky toy. A Dinky toy lost on some great expanse of white lino under God's bed.

'*Thursday was always a holiday in India,*' said Titus, coming to help.

'We're in the middle of Nowhere. That's where we really are.'

'*You can't make a melodrama out of a pig's ear,*' said Titus and repeated, '*Thursday was always a holiday in India.*' His hand closed over mine to help pull the provisions box. It weighed nothing once he was pulling.

'So tell me what we did on Thursdays, Titus. In India.'

'*We went after the jack. Took the motorbike out for a spin. Saw to the dogs. Went for a picnic.*'

I suddenly pictured what might have happened if Manfred had flicked the wheel of that lighter, and my legs unaccountably refused to carry me. So I crouched down and ransacked the red box until I found a jar of Swedish sild that looked a bit like fish: it would do for Victor's tea—as soon as I could stop my legs shaking and get it back to the Hagglund.

'Can I come next Thursday, Titus?'

'*That would be ripping, Florence.*'


Sometimes I'm not me at all, you know? Sometimes, when I need to get away further than usual, I'm Florence Chambers.

Oates asked her out, when he was twenty-two—signed himself, '*Your ardent admirer*', but her mother said no, she couldn't go, so they met in secret once or twice and he took her photograph and that was that. He was still talking about her ten years later, in Antarctica.

So sometimes I'm Florence Chambers. And Titus and I meet and change history by secretly eloping, and I follow him from posting to posting: South Africa, Egypt, India, Ireland . . . living in disguise near the barracks, and he confides only to his very best friends how much in love we are; Deighton, for instance, his kennelman and mechanic and army valet and trusty companion. Deighton has a whole subplot.

What?

And I ride pillion on Titus's motorbike, and look after his pet deer and exercise his horse in the cool, misty mornings, and afterwards we curry the sweat from its flanks, the horse in parentheses between us, our arms mirroring each other as we brush, the tail splashing us each in turn, amid a smell of saddle-soap and straw, because if Titus were ever to love a woman it wouldn't be anyone helpless or feeble who cried for want of an aeroplane or out of fright and couldn't make her legs stop shaking or keep her wits about her or marshal her facts; it wouldn't be anyone like that; it wouldn't be anyone like that; no one like that.

What?

The Brontë sisters invented a whole town full of people, didn't they?—Glasstown—and wrote stories about it in microscopically small handwriting. Anything sooner than be cooped up in a gloomy rectory in the middle of a god-awful moor: Glasstown.

Anything sooner than share a school bus-ride with Maxine and her huge repertoire of filthy jokes. Glasstown.

Anything sooner than remember Dad lighting bonfires from my books, to keep imaginary jackals away from our windows. Glasstown.

119

Anything sooner than drive over a frozen sea,
with people who are not what they seem,
towards a gaping hole in the Earth.


'Just you and me on a Thursday in Glasstown, eh,
Titus?'

*'Just you and me, Florence,'* said Titus. *'Though may I make
bold to observe: Sigurd the Golden One calls his father Mr Bruch?'*

'You think I didn't notice?'

*'In that case, let us picnic.'*

'What's sild?'

*'Oh, specialité de la Maison Amundsen, ma chère. Sardines
in formaldehyde. You'd stick with pony hoosh if you were I.'*

# Chapter Twelve
## Glasstown

The Shelf isn't beautiful. It isn't anything. It's like a carpet warehouse where you can go to buy Nothing by the square metre. Broadloom nothingness. But Nothing was so much better than what was coming that I started to think of the Shelf as beautiful—a beautiful vacant antechamber to tomorrow, with nothing to do but sleep and eat and imagine. A sort of Glasstown-on-Ice.

'Somebody built an ice town on the Ice Shelf once, Titus. Thought he'd capture the sublime essence of Life, living on the limit.'

'"Only one step from the sublime to the ridiculous," as my hero Napoleon once said. What did this gentleman "capture" exactly?'

'Major depression. Life was meaningless. God was dead, that sort of thing, I think. Not a successful experiment.'

'I'm surprised it was only God who was dead by the end of it,' said Titus.


Little by little, the huge wall of fuel cans shrank until there was room in the back van for us. We found the intercom, for communicating with the drive-van, but we did not find the reason to use it. Sigurd and I could sit comfortably enough to sleep now, and Manfred and Victor had agreed to share the driving. The Viking seemed to like this

121

arrangement. Maybe he thought if I was allowed to ride up front with my uncle I would mention the punch or the incident of the cigarette lighter. But as the hours rolled away and the kaleidoscopic flicker of sky and ice sucked us down its revolving tunnel of edgeless light, I became less and less sure what I had actually seen earlier on.

This isn't somewhere that you can trust what your eyes are telling you. Maybe Manfred had simply taken a minute or two to comprehend the danger of a naked flame. Or perhaps he had just been teasing. I thought of asking Sigurd if his dad had a really weird sense of humour.

I thought of asking why he called his father 'Mr Bruch'.

I thought of telling him about my dad and asking if he was afraid of his, too . . . But already he was behaving as if nothing had happened. Nothing. He was smooth and cool and charming again, saying all the right things. It was incredible. 'He must have nerves of steel,' I told myself, humiliated by his courage. They were all three so brave: Victor and Manfred and Sigurd! They didn't seem frightened at all, whereas me . . . What a coward! What a gutless, spineless, potted . . .

I tried to forget everything I had ever read about the Ross Ice Shelf—about Antarctica. I wanted not to look— wouldn't look, I decided. I would turn inside and be with Titus. That was best. Wake me when it's over. But even my imagination was rigid with fright. I had trouble conjuring up Titus's face.

So I concentrated on the Hansel and Gretel trail—all those empty fuel cans, caterpillar tracks, splashes of green diesel, sild jars, an empty peanut butter pot, urine stains as orange as Sunny Delight. I held the list in my mind, adding to it, memorizing an aerial picture of all the clues we had left in our wake.

Victor, when I was little and he was training up my brain, used to put two things on a tray, then three, then four, then five, then cover them up and I would have to remember them. He said it 'flexed the thinking muscles'. In the end I could remember thirty-two things. Apparently Victor's record was eighty-eight, though I never saw him do it; he said it would be showing off and anyway it would dishearten me, since I could only manage thirty-two. I remember, Dad came in and I wanted to show him what I could do, but he was on his way out to a job. 'Ah. Pelmanism,' he said. Just that. 'Pelmanism.'

I had to ask Victor what it meant: 'Pelmanism'. Even remembering makes my heart clench up in a ball. 'Time-wasting,' Victor said, translating Dad's contempt into words I could understand. 'It means time-wasting.'

Maybe Courage is like Memory—a muscle that needs exercise to get strong. So I decided that maybe, if I started in a small way, I could gradually work my way up to being brave like the others. In this landscape only the colour of something matters; it need not be big to be visible. A pile of shit from ten metres away looks like a tent ten kilometres away. So I steeled myself to do something useful for a change, and add to our Hansel and Gretel trail.

To do it you have to take off your overmitts, then your big jacket, then your quilted shell-jacket, then your fleece jacket and glove-liners, find the top of your tracksuit bottoms, then the tight waistband of your long thermal pants. The face-mask and the neck gaiter and the body-bib make it hard to look down, so you can't see what you're doing—and by that time your hands are so cold that you can't feel detail or fastenings. The cold bites like a dog and makes your muscles pull rigid. So much toilet stuff is habit, but automatic reflexes stop working in the cold. It's like stepping into freezing water up to the waist. You're a metal pipe bent into the shape of a handlebar, moaning and singing and chanting the Table of Elements or 'The Lady of Shalott', to keep your mind off the cold swilling between clothing and skin, sending your muscles into spasm. Then your hands are too cold to find the edges of your clothing again.

I told myself I was emptying out the fear.

I told myself that Captain Scott and his men did this every day, sooner than be ungenteel inside the tent, in sight of one another. And if Titus could do it, so can I now. It's hardly a Union Flag or some ragged penant fluttering over a heroic achievement. But a pile of shit in the snow can be seen from a kilometre away, and I really want us to be found if we run out of fuel. (Not that we will, of course, because Uncle Victor has planned this all down to the last letter.)

After I came back the first time, I tried to explain to Sigurd what I was doing. But singing and moaning and chanting pump out a lot of wet air and the condensation had frozen my scarf to my mouth with a spaghetti of ice strands. He just stared at me and said, 'Crazy!'

How to impress a boy, eh? I must tell Maxine when I get home. Start a trend. The school caretaker may not appreciate it.

Sigurd wouldn't do his business outside—not even to uphold male prestige and help with the trail. The best he did was to drop a half-dozen paper cups in the snow as we were climbing back aboard after a fuelling stop. They danced in a circle on the ground, then took off and tumbled in slow-motion somersaults away and away and away. It was such a futile gesture—such a dozy, helpless, stupid idea that I laughed out loud. My laugh too was snatched away, just like the cups. This place can do that—steal the life straight out of your mouth.

'Oh, Titus! Titus! It's Thursday! Fetch a pair of horses! Send native servants to check the verandah for snakes and make the bungalow ready for us! Unmoor *Saunterer* and let's go for a sail! Send Deighton with a shovelful of

124

bravery and the route map to Glasstown!'

But every time I thought I'd called my man's lovely face to mind—the long pale plains beneath his eyes, the smile-lines radiating out through the snowburn on his temples—Sigurd Bruch began making civil conversation. And I couldn't very well ignore him. I certainly couldn't ignore the chocolate he extracted from every one of the red provision boxes and lined up on the floor for us to eat. Also, he asked me questions about myself. Oh, I know that's only what people do to be polite, and it's not that they really want to know. Still, it was kind. By now, Nikki would have asked Sigurd his blood type, his sign of the Zodiac, and whether he wore boxer shorts or Y-fronts. Maxine would have asked him for a date. Me, I asked if he smoked.

'Smoke? No, for sure! Do you?'

'What?'

'Do you smoke?'

'Me? Grief, no. I have a friend who smokes a pipe . . . Does your father smoke?'

'No, no. He does not. Oh, I—' I saw him trip over the trick question and pick himself up again smartly. 'Aha! I see! That lighter . . . it is given him by a woman friend. They were . . . you know,' and he rocked his head on his shoulders and put his feet up on the seat opposite, smirking.

'Mimi, yes. She said he was cute.'

He hid the flash of alarm very well. The only hint was the way he put two fingers to his lips and tried to smoke a non-existent cigarette. 'Did she say more?' he asked nonchalantly.

I picked and chose: 'She said you were cute, too.'

Sigurd smiled with pleasure and relaxed again. He wriggled into the horizontal, resting on his heels and his elbows, lifted his hips to resettle them on the soft luggage piled between the seats. 'I wish these words they were yours,' he said, and offered me one of his 200-watt smiles. 'Ah, but there is this friend of yours, I suppose. With the pipe. I have no luck.'

'Oh yes . . . I mean, no, I—Yes. There is him.' I could almost hear Maxine's snort of contempt, her felt-tip squeaking across my file cover:

*Sym Wates—virgin on the ridiculous.*

She's right. I am a coward. About this place. About boys. About everything.

'So, Clever Sym, you know about Antarctic, yes?' said Sigurd. 'The Hole, we will find it soon, you think?'

'I only know what I've read, nothing at all hardly. No. Not this side of the mountains.'

'There are mountains?' He looked out of the window. 'How far?'

'You don't—you know—kilometres are no good out here. It's more, you know, days.'

'How many days so?'

'Or luck.'

*'As in "how long did their luck hold out?"'* said the friend with the pipe.

'Shut up, Titus. I don't want to scare him.'

*'Scare the young Lochinvar? No! For sure!'* said Titus sarcastically.

'About Mr Bruch . . .' I began.

'So. You live where in England, Symone?' Sigurd interrupted.

'Croxley Green. Look, Sigurd, about your fa—'

'I am staying some long time in Norfolk. You know Norfolk, yes?'

*'Very flat, Norfolk.'*

'Shut up, Titus. Oates couldn't possibly quote Noel Coward.'

'I would like to show you some time my beautiful country of Norway.'

'Thank you. Look, Sigurd . . .'

'Yes?'

But my puny courage failed me. 'Oh. I just wanted to say . . . About Uncle Victor. I'm really sorry. And the tea. Drugging you. Sorry. Drugging everyone. I think the fire—you know—I think he must have—you know—been in shock. Sorry.'

Sigurd regarded me with a smile of such understanding and wisdom that he might have been forty-five. 'It is most natural.'

*'As yoghurt!'* said Titus incredulously. *'Natural?'*

'Well, actually, I think it was a bit beyond the pale, actually,' I said to Sigurd.

'Ah! But your uncle he is man in love with Big Idea! Is same for my father also. All is done for the Big Idea. But you? Your love it is not for Big Idea. For what, then? For this friend of yours, yes? With the pipe?'

*''Fraid so,'* said Titus, briskly reefing mountaineering rope into a figure-of-eight around his hand and biceps.

'There's a girl at my school—Maxine—she's going out with a man of thirty called Waldron. How dodgy is that?'

Sigurd flinched from the nervous loudness of my giggle, but he didn't stop smiling for a moment. 'He is rich, maybe, this Waldron. Like you.'

The odd inaccuracy of this rather slipped by me, since Sigurd had moved to sit much closer. As the van hit a step in the ice, our shoulders were jolted together. He slipped an arm around me and took aim on my mouth.

'You're very good,' I said, after the kiss. I meant his command of English! His English vocabulary! So why didn't I say that? 'What's yours?'

*'Complete sentences, Sym. Think on.'*

Oh, please shut up, Titus.

'What's your dream, I mean, Sigurd? What would be your totally—you know . . .'

A quite different look came over Sigurd. It made kissing seem like old gum he'd been chewing only until the pizza delivery-man came. 'I shall be in films!' he said.

'Wow. Lucky your dad's in the business.'

Sigurd bridled. 'I'm good, me! I don't need help! I'm a good actor!' he declared hotly.

*'Except for a certain incontinuity of dialect,'* said Titus, but I shut my ears to him. There was a brightness and sincerity in Sigurd's face now (Heaven knows, it was close enough for me to see) and 'sincere' was better than 'charming'. *'I'll go away,'* said Titus. *'I am clearly not required.'*

*No! No, don't go, Titus! Please.* But I couldn't concentrate enough to keep him by me. 'Sigurd, about this trip . . .' I began to say.

'For you life is one big holiday, I bet?' Sigurd interrupted again. 'Rich is good, yes? One day I also am rich.'

'Oh, but I'm not . . .'

The rear doors opened. I had not even noticed the Hagglund stopping. Sigurd moved sharply away from me as Victor clambered in to fetch another can of fuel. He was wearing the red face-mask. I snatched up the funnel and went to help.

'Can I ride up front with you for a while, uncle?' I asked, steadying the funnel in the filler.

He said: 'I see you two are getting cosy.'

The CCTV. Of course. He had seen the kiss. I couldn't tell how angry he was with me, behind the mask. I'm like a daughter to Victor. Well, while I'm here, he sort of *is* my father, I suppose—honour-bound to keep an eye on me; stop things getting out-of-hand. I remember him signing a form for Pengwings . . . *'parent or guardian'.*

128

That's good. I don't mind. Maxine would. Maxine says parents are as much fun as bull terriers in a nudist camp. But I'm *glad* there's a fatherly eye watching over me. People like to think of God looking down on them, don't they, even if He does tend to criticize.

'That's good. That's grand,' said Uncle Victor pushing his mask up on to the top of his head. 'You and the boy get to know each other! I mean really . . . get to it. No rules out here, lass! Drop the niceties! You have fun, the two of you! Mek the most of it!'

Clumsy as ever, I jerked the funnel and it fell out of the filler-nozzle and rolled under the van, and some of the precious green fluid spilled on to the snow. I tried to reach under the van, but my arms were too short. Victor had to get it himself, huffing and puffing, flooding a sunburned face with a further flush of red. I felt it in my own cheeks.

His head brushed the ground, too, and some of the snow-platelets stuck, sequin-like, to the side of his face after he stood up. I should have reached up and brushed them away: they would burn. In any case, they made him look lizardy, metallic. As if he was turning android.

But I didn't brush them off. I left them there, those mirror flakes of sequin ice. Standing up had made my head spin. And suddenly Victor seemed as far off as the Hagglund had when I walked away from it across the Ice. What kind of an uncle . . .

This place messes with your senses. Optical illusions everywhere. Maybe I imagined it or misunderstood. God and fathers are meant to keep a fatherly eye on you; they're meant to give a fatherly damn.

'Can I ride in the front, Uncle Victor?' I said again, taking particular care to speak clearly. 'Please.'

'Nay. Be told, lass. You and Sigurd stay in't back. Get properly acquainted. Up close, manner of thing.' And he actually winked, so that I could be left in no doubt as to his meaning.

I should not have eaten all that chocolate. Or maybe it was the diesel fumes making me feel sick.

I was not the only one feeling ill. Victor was just screwing the filler cap back into place when Manfred Bruch—making use of the time to stretch his legs—suddenly clutched his stomach with one hand and made to lean against the Hagglund with the other.

'*DON'T!*' I shouted. '*Bare hands!*'

Both mittenless hands came to rest on his abdomen and he gave me a small Germanic nod, acknowledging the warning.

Then the empty fuel can was cast aside—'Lessen your weight, increase your miles-per-gallon. Think on, Sym!'—and our endless odyssey continued. As the giant vehicle shuddered back into life, Sigurd and I could hear over the intercom Manfred asking, 'Now, Victor, you are perfectly sure you have enough of fuel for round trip?'

'You don't have to worry on that score,' came Victor's reply, and he began to whistle under his breath. The red light went out on the CCTV camera; Victor had turned it off so as to grant Sigurd and me our privacy. How kind.

No guardrails on the Barrier—not for a hundred kilometres in any direction; not a thing to hang on to when the world spins too fast. Get a grip, Sym. Victor wants you to grow up. Don't you see the notices written up on the walls of Antarctica?

NO CHILDREN

Sigurd sat down again in the seat alongside mine, smiling his 200-watt smile. I edged away and picked up the manufacturer's manual for the Hagglund as if I might be planning to study amphibious vehicles at university.

Sigurd closed the gap, his neoprene and mine rubbing together to produce a kind of soft wolf-whistle.

'My friend. With the pipe? We're . . . you know,' I said, rocking my head suggestively, as he had done earlier.

'Ah. I see,' said Sigurd. And nice boy, nice, nice boy: straight away he believed me. How excellent is that?

So now we are all liars.

What's wrong with me? Is there something wrong with me? Sigurd's really fit! Sigurd's really . . . you know. When we kissed—you know—it was quite . . . I quite enjoyed it in a Chinese-puzzle-which-bit-goes-where sort of way. What nursery am I locked in that I can't get out and go downstairs and join in the grown-up games? Can't *want* to join in? Am I like those poor kids that wait and wait for their growth spurt and it never comes?

What's wrong with me, Titus? I know *some* things about Love, don't I? Why Leander swam the Hellespont; why people do crimes of passion! I know how one word— 'cavalry' or 'Napoleon' or 'Antarctica'—can make the world suddenly crash its gears and jolt so hard that you have to stop and lean against a wall until you can remember how to breathe . . .

But maybe I've got it all wrong. Maybe 'making love' is just what it says it is—a handicraft. Maybe you have to *make* it before you can *give* it to someone. Like soup or a raffia table-mat.

'*Can't speak from experience in these matters, naturally,*' said Titus, packing tobacco into the bowl of his little white pipe. '*In the army, an officer was not expected to marry until his mid-thirties. We channelled our energies into other pastimes. Racing. War. Polar exploration. Getting killed . . . In my day the words meant—well, wooing. Courting. Walking out. Something a long way short of marital intimacy. I take it "making love" came to mean something other?*'

131

'It did. Actually we moved on from that too,' I told him. 'Nowadays people don't make love, they have sex.'

*'People always had sex,'* said Titus fastidiously. *'It's an accident of birth. Like hair colour. Date of birth: March 1880. Place of birth: Putney. Sex: Male.'*

'Well, now it's more like having fish and chips.' But the tight knots in my stomach had begun to unravel. This was what I wanted: the quaint, chivalric chastity of my beloved Edwardian . . .

*'Oh, if you mean fucking, we had that, too, of course,'* said Titus startlingly. *'But fucking's a continent away from making love. And all-round bad for an officer's career. Never resorted to it myself. Except in regard to swearing. I regret, I did swear on the odd occasion. Unlike the others: all staunch Christian gentlemen clean in thought, word, and deed. The ratings called it my "emergency vocabulary". But Anglo-Saxon is an ancient language and very useful, when your pony kicks you in the shins. Despite appearances, Sym, Love is not a four-letter word.'*

Apparently this was a day for everyone to behave oddly, even the man in my head. But at least he was there at last, and in sharp focus, in his shabby leather jacket and torn trousers. My peripheral vision shut down until all I could see was his face, the good-humoured wrinkle lifting the lower lids, the chevron creases holding his mouth in parenthesis, the contours of his hairline like South America tailing away southwards into the darkness of tomorrow's beard. Safe at last. Now if I could just hold on—if I could just turn away inside my head and be with Titus—go to Glasstown—lace shut the tent . . .

'Why weren't you afraid, Titus?' I said. 'Back then.'

*'Who says I wasn't.'*

'How did you learn to be brave, then?'

*'At bravery school.'*

'Where's that? Eton? Boer War? Edwardianland?'

Titus looked at me, his head on one side, exhaled

smoke re-entering his mouth as he breathed in to speak. *'Right here, Sym. Right here.'*

And I suddenly realized something that had eluded me up to that minute. I knew why Sigurd and Manfred weren't afraid. It had nothing to do with courage. They weren't afraid, because they didn't know anything about Antarctica. They didn't know what was coming.

They thought they were going to make it home alive.

# Chapter Thirteen
## Diamond Ice

When the fog came, I thought Titus had sent it, it came so out-of-nowhere and was so perfect a solution. We had crossed five hundred kilometres of frozen sea without mishap, used up half our fuel, and now, in the nick of time, we could not go on. How can you go forward when you can't see anything in front of you?

The rolling motion was stilled. The noise of the Hagglund subsided into neutral and then, after a few minutes, into silence and everything was so still we could have been at the bottom of a glass of milk. Oddly, we appeared still to be moving forward, like in a dream when you find yourself driving a car and your legs are paralysed so you can't operate the pedals even if you knew how to drive which you don't. But it was only the fog rolling past the window in tumbling, half-human shapes. Jaundice yellow it gurned in at the windows, then moiled on by. In the fog no one would be able to find us, but at least our endless journey into the white darkness was halted. Blinded by the milky miasma, deafened by the silence, Sigurd and I sat stupefied, unspeaking. I laid aside the manufacturer's manual.

'That's it, then,' I said. 'We can't go on in this, can we?' Inwardly I was saying, *Oh, thank you, thank you, thank you for the fog. Thank you for the fog.* Though whether it was to Titus or God or the grinning fog-ghosts, I have no idea.

Poor Uncle Victor: he had taken a wild gamble and lost. It's one thing to arrive back with photographs, with booty, with a hank of alien hair, with Proof. But to arrive back empty-handed; to have to explain petty things like motor-theft and narcotic tea-bags when he should have been explaining about worlds within worlds! Now he and Manfred Bruch would almost certainly have to share the glory of discovery with American geologists and South American tour guides. Or, if they kept the secret to themselves, they would have to leave Antarctica, flat broke, and start saving up for another trip. That's if they escaped prison.

Perhaps we could say we had taken the Hagglund to go in search of help after everyone in Camp Aurora mysteriously went to sleep.

Victor and Manfred came into our van for a food break, and though the Viking was looking wretched, Uncle Victor got on and made tea. He guarded jealously the task of serving us the drinks he thought we deserved: hot chocolate, tea, cordial. 'Drink! Drink!' he would say. 'Dehydration, that's the big danger down here! Driest place on earth! People don't realize.' I went to give him a kiss on the cheek (because inside he was surely churning with disappointment) but he was too busy lining up vitamin tablets on the table, beside his fruit cordial, and he brushed me aside. 'Drink up! What people forget,' he said, pausing between words to swallow another letter of the alphabet—vitamin C, E, B12, 'this place is categorized "desert" . . . water cycle here takes ten thousand year . . . *Water, water everywhere, nor any drop to* . . . Drink up! Drink!'

'It is regrettable, but it seems . . .' Manfred began, face sweating.

'Good cover, this fog,' said Victor.

'. . . half the fuel is gone now,' said Manfred unzipping

his jacket even though he was shivering. 'Sadly we must turn around and go back.' I noticed that the belt inside was unbuckled, his trouser fastenings undone as if he had eaten too big a meal for comfort.

'Uphill going, downhill coming back,' said Victor. 'Travelling lighter now, too. Need less fuel.' And he slapped his knees and stood up, his round belly exaggerated by the many layers of clothing and the bulky ski-suit. The four of us so filled the space that the van from outside must have looked like a tumble dryer crammed with Teletubbies.

'But we can't in the fog,' I said without thinking. It wasn't mutinous. It was just a fact.

'With GPS?' said Victor. 'What's to stop us!'

'Well, the Shear!'

'What's the Shear?' asked Sigurd.

Victor rattled his sinuses in an enormous, scoffing snort. 'Hearken to the ignorance, eh, Sym? Asks what the Shear is!'

'The provisions, also, they are half used up,' said Manfred counting up the red boxes with the transparent lids. 'More than half.'

'More in the Nansen,' said Victor.

'How would we see crevasses? Or pressure ice?' I said.

Victor's brightness was undimmed. 'This crate'll carry us through. Better than a Sherman tank, these items!'

'Crevasses?' said Sigurd and swallowed hard.

'How do we find a glacier in the fog?' I said. 'Let's wait till the fog lifts, at least!'

'A spot less negativity please, Sym,' said Victor curtly. 'What do I teach you always? Positive thinking brings positive results. Now's not the time for getting cold feet.'

Inside my head, Titus burst out laughing. It chimed in with the rising hysteria.

'Glacier?' said Sigurd. 'What glacier?'

136

'Tell him, Sym,' said Victor closing his eyes with Buddha-like patience. 'Tell the lad.'

The Norwegians both looked at me. I felt like Skippy the Kangaroo asked to count by hopping up and down on the spot. Titus was laughing so hard now that he had to sit down on the floor. 'To get up on to the plateau,' I muttered; 'to get through the mountains—we need a glacier. It's like—you know—taking the wheelchair ramp instead of the stairs.' Titus laughed even harder, breathlessly, groaning and sighing with mirth.

Victor beamed. 'Route's all plotted! No time like the present! Time and tide, you know? 'Nough gossiping. Fall in, everyone! All hands on deck!' And he opened the door and climbed down again, shedding nautical bluster like snow.

I went after him. The fog had laid a milky film of ice over the three metal steps and I pitched down them. 'But the Shear, uncle! Please don't go into the Shear! Not in the fog!' Recovering my feet I turned round and the Hagglund was a dark shape devoid of colour, like a cellar door in a house full of smoke. I knew that if I lost sight of it, if I took one step further into the fog, there would be no Hagglund, no gravity, no day of the week, no geometry, no news, no Sym.

The engine started up. The sagging caterpillar tracks engaged with the drive wheels and flexed into life, shedding blocks of compacted snow. Bare hands, Sym, bare hands! In a panic, I slid one glove on the wrong way round—no thumb—felt my way along the side of the vehicle. It throbbed under my touch. The hydraulic link between the two vans gave an exasperated sigh as I passed it. I twisted my glove round and pulled myself up on to the slippery steps of the front van, just as the caterpillars started to move. As I clung to the open door I heard the back one bang shut. I suppose the Nansen sled and the skidoo were stirring into life at the end of their ropes, falling into line between the caterpillar tracks. Falling into line. Not that I could see. There was nothing to be seen in the big wing mirror but the white blindness of curdling fog. Uncle Victor reached out a hand and pulled me inside, into the passenger seat, but he did not lift his foot off the accelerator or stop whistling under his breath.

Sigurd's voice came over the intercom. 'What is Shear?' it said. Sigurd had started to sound like an English language teaching tape:

**What is this?** This is a Hagglund.
**What is that?** That is a mistake.
**How is the glacier?** The glacier is cold.
**Where are the crevasses?** God alone knows.

Victor did not trouble to answer him. I fastened my seat belt before slamming shut my door. The headlamps lit two large cones of fog without showing anything of the way ahead. The fierce bright nothingness of the Ice Shelf had pained our eyes, but this fog? This was a cataract in the eyeball. *Please make the fog lift! Please make it lift! Make the fog lift!* I prayed now, and whether it was to God or Titus or the grinning fog-ghosts I have no idea. The cones of light swarmed with mosquito flecks of ice. The windscreen was full of fog. It came at us like dust-debris from an explosion—clouds and clouds and clouds of impenetrable smoke, or the steam from a steam train about to wipe us out. My eyes strained to see through it—strained and strained and could not be kept from trying to see. I could feel the optic nerves stretch like threads of bubble gum.

So I turned on the closed-circuit TV, just as Sigurd said, '*Tell him!*' I didn't *hear* it, of course. But 'Tell him' makes for a fairly distinct lip movement, and Sigurd said it several times over: '*Tell him! Tell him! Tell him, please!*' Manfred Bruch gave a violent shake of his head. Of course those lip movements might mean something else entirely in Norwegian, but thinking about it, I'd never once heard Sigurd and Manfred talk to each other in anything other than English.

'OK, what's so funny?' I said to Titus who was in the seat behind me now, using his hat to wipe the frozen fog out of his hair and the tears of laughter off his cheeks.

'*Sorry. Just my black sense of humour, hoo-hoo, sorry,*' he hiccupped softly. '*"Now's not the time for cold feet." Is that what he said? Quite worthy of Scott, that. "Now's not the time for cold feet!"*' He was in snow clothes now, I noticed, and his boots were sodden.


Endlessly patient with our stupidity, the dot on the GPS navigation system winked and blinked on and on and on, tracing our progress towards the Transcontinental Mountains and the Polar Plateau. Towards Symmes's Hole. You would have thought fright might have quickened its electronic heartbeat. But it's British, so I suppose it hides its emotions.

Its pulse stayed steady even when we hit the ridge.

We hit at twenty miles an hour. It seemed to hit us, rather, looming up out of the fog like Moby Dick attacking the *Pequod*, ramming us head-on. The impact was so great I thought for sure the Hagglund would fall apart around us. The drive-wheels screamed inside the rubber of the caterpillar tracks. The headlamps blinked out. A crack appeared across the windscreen, with a noise like a pistol shot. The engine over-choked itself and died.

Despite our seat belts, Victor hit his chin on the steering wheel and my hands were flung forward like stones from a slingshot. On the CCTV screen I could see Manfred and

Sigurd gasping for breath where the impact of their seat belts had jarred the wind out of them. I would have breathed on their behalf, but my own lungs were just as flat.

In the fog, the ridge we had hit could have been any height—the same as the van's or twenty times taller—a wave-shaped petrifaction of snow aslant our path, solid as concrete. The Hagglund could no more tackle it than a baby could crawl up a brick wall. For a long time the engine would not restart, and then Victor could not find how to shift the gears into reverse. (Reverse had never been part of his plan.) Finally he manoeuvred us round and drove alongside the ridge—tried to drive parallel to it, though it was impossible to tell ridge from fog, and the big wing-mirror kept gouging and scraping against the wall of ice until its glass broke and its bracket buckled out of shape. Manfred was all the time leaning on the button of the intercom, yelling for Victor to stop, swearing, demanding to know what was happening, what was going to happen.

'No harm done. Built like a tank, these items! No call for language,' Victor murmured into his microphone, jovial as a tour guide on an open-topped bus, still hoping for a tip at the end of the ride.

For ten kilometres we followed the ice ridge, while the surface under us roughened into a jumble of angular blocks and the fog boiled around the windows. Then the front of the van reared up, dragging itself over a clutter of boulder ice like rubble left by the collapse of a wall. A stretch of the ridge had decayed and we blindly reeled and pecked our way through the gap and on to flat ice again. The twin cones of yellow electric light no longer lit the fog, but it was small loss. What good is a torch to a blind man?

Within a kilometre we crashed again, this time into a

140

great monolith of frozen snow like the stump of a giant redwood. Swerving to avoid it, Victor collided with another, even bigger, and stove in a corner of the engine housing. When we got out to inspect the damage, I groped my way along the trailing tow rope only to find the end frayed and the skidoo gone. The Nansen sled had turned over and had been dragging along on its side. We got it back onto its runners—*'Gloves, uncle!'*—but the fuel cans lashed to it had been holed and although the diesel inside was frozen solid, it would all leak out as soon as we thawed it for use.

'We go back. We go back now,' said Manfred Bruch over and over again. 'I'm sorry, but . . .'

Uncle Victor neither argued nor agreed but simply went on whistling between his teeth—*I love Paris in the summer, when it sizzles* . . . trying to kick the bent coachwork back into shape and stop it catching on the caterpillar tracks. Sigurd said nothing at all. He was pasty pale and he had bitten into his lip when we crashed.

'Right, Sympatica!' said Victor, slapping me on the back. 'Let's get this tank back on track!'

'Can we get home now?' I asked—as if the evening had turned chilly and it was time to turn back to a nice warm fire after a ramble in the countryside. What I meant was: 'Is there enough fuel?', but Victor had done his calculations, had allowed for snags and hold-ups, had been planning this for years. He put me in charge of watching the gyro on the dashboard—'just keep us heading South'— while he rectified our course.

Three more pressure ridges and contortions of ice loomed out of the fog. We had become one of those toy cars, bouncing off the walls and table-legs of Antarctica, changing direction at every impact. We were trapped in a maze of dead-ends. The fog itself seemed to be turning into concrete, and the concrete was setting round us into

141

prison walls. In the fog we could not make sense of their geology, what pattern they were following, which way to steer to break free of the maze.

Then Manfred, the toe of his boot on the intercom button even as he strove to see out of the windows, gave a scream of pure terror as he saw the ground give way. It simply unzipped beneath the tank, opening on the left of us, passing under the tracks, and out to our right, dropping compacted snow into the nothingness below it. It can't have taken more than three seconds for the ground to fall from under us.

# Chapter Fourteen

*'What each man feels in his heart,*
*I can only guess'—Scott*

We were left straddling a crevasse, the rear of the front
van overhanging it, all but a metre of the back van supported
by thin air. Manfred Bruch continued screaming: I could
hear him through the intercom, through Uncle Victor's
headset, even, I'm sure, through the walls of the vehicle.

The windows were all sweating with condensation
from our breath. The fog was a kindness. If I could have
seen out—seen down into the dark—I don't think I could
ever have moved my head or hands again, ever have
looked away. As it was, I managed to turn and look at
Victor: he would know what to do. He would get us out
of it: infallible, resourceful Uncle Victor who had aligned
the atoms in his brain to increase his IQ.

His hands were white on the steering wheel. His lips
were between his teeth. His glasses were slightly bent
from the first crash. 'What we're about now,' he said, 'is
an orderly evacuation. Bruch. Listen up, Bruch. Move
towards the back door. If we lighten the vehicle we can
maybe ease her . . .'

'No!' I said, tugging the headphones wide from his head,
shouting into the microphone. 'Don't get out! Manfred!
Sigurd! Don't get out. The footprint of the vehicle's lighter
than a man's. Don't get out.' What a stupid expression:

'the footprint of the vehicle'. But I'd just now been reading the manufacturer's manual, hadn't I? And those were the words! I don't do words of my own. I only do . . . 'the footprint of the vehicle'. What does it mean? How can a two-ton amphibious tank weigh less than a man? Even I don't believe it, but that's what it said in the book. That's what the words said. They're not my words. They're trustworthy, believable, grown-up words. Non-fiction. *'Don't get out of the van!* If it's less than four metres wide we can get over it!'

Four metres. Four metres. Four metres. How wide do you think it is, Titus?

*'Open the door and take a look, dearie.'*

I couldn't get hold of the door latch in my over-large mittens, tore one off, opened the door a crack, just a crack. The fog came in like an Arabian genie, insinuating its way round my legs and face. I could see all three of the icy metal steps so the fog must have thinned; maybe it had been sucked into the crevasse by the falling snow. Maybe it had served its purpose, in losing us. For half their width, the steps overhung the crevasse, for half they were over snow. If I opened the door wide enough I could probably lower myself down on to the brink of the crevasse before the Hagglund jack-knifed backwards into the abyss. How could a little pair of feet weigh more per square whatever than this big, red, ungainly, solid metal tank? How absurd. What rubbish. How implausible. Except that I don't *have* little feet. This is Sym the clumsy, Sym the crass—elegant as a swan out of water. The manufacturer's manual says that the footprint of the vehicle is less than that of a . . . Nothing about swans in the manual. And if the edges of the crevasse are still overhung with snow, I could be stepping on to a bit of brittle snow-crust jutting out over fathomless nothingness. Maybe ten metres deep, maybe one thousand.

144

'I'd take a look for you, Sym, but I don't do metric. Strictly an Imperial man, me. How wide is the crevasse, Sym?'

'I can't tell! The fog! I can't see!'

Uncle Victor jabbed at the button of his seat belt. He was about to get out.

'Just keep driving, uncle! You know what Jon said? It can get over anything, this! Ten metres! Anything!' Positive thinking brings positive results. I didn't want to say what I was really thinking: if we get out and the truck goes down the crevasse, we're dead anyway.

Victor looked at me. He was holding his lips between his teeth and his skin was red and flaky because he doesn't like to wear sun block. He looked like an exotic breed of fish in a broken fish tank: badly done by, bewildered.

So I reached over and slid the gear stick from N to D. It's an automatic. You can do that. The caterpillar tracks went taut. In the rear van, Manfred Bruch gave a roar of horror and made for the door. Sigurd tussled with him in a clumsy little brawl, which ended when his father took a punch in the stomach and dropped to his hands and knees to be sick.

A pat of snow fell from each segment of the rubber track, into the dark beneath. Fog swilled over and round the Hagglund. The transmission whined. Every needle on the dashboard leapt round its dial—except for the gyro which pointed unswervingly south, unmoving; one of the collisions must have toppled it. The tank moved forward, defying gravity, defying physics, finding grip in thin air. Through my open door I could see how the vast noise of the engine was loosening compacted snow into granules, sending them trickling over the brink into the ravine below us. But we moved forward, which meant some few notches at least of caterpillar-track were gripping terra firma at either end of the vehicle.

145

Uncle Victor put his hands back on the steering wheel. He leaned forward, standing up, seat belt undone, to peer ahead into the fog. 'What did I say, lass? What did I say? This crate can get over anything!'

I waited for the rear van to slump into the crevasse and drag us with it. But on we crept, at a snail's pace, easing, easing ourselves over the gaping trench, easing, easing our way back on to the jumbled mosaic of ice blocks into the dizzying swirl of moving fog. The caterpillar tracks found traction again and the familiar rippling jolt picked up.

We had just dared to draw breath again when, with a jarring shock, a giant hand grabbed the Hagglund and wrenched it violently backwards. Everything loose in the cab flew forwards—pens and ear-protectors and the case of the Lee Konitz cassette . . .

At the end of its tow rope, the Nansen sled had just reached the crevasse and plunged into it, yanking the bracket half out of its rivets. Now it dangled and twisted on its rope-end, swinging to and fro. Like an anchor it pinned us to the spot, then Victor revved up the engine and we countered its weight, overcame its weight, hauled it up out of the crevasse. The sled re-emerged like a stretchered patient, its tarpaulin still neatly laced from end to end. Face down it lay in the snow on the brink of the ravine, and I knew it was recovering its nerve, offering up prayers of thanksgiving, steeling itself for worse to come.

Manfred Bruch sat on the steps of the van breathing hard, head in his hands, fingers in his thick, straw-like hair. Sigurd took a few steps into the fog to relieve himself then, panicking, called out to ask where we were. *'Shout out! Make a noise!'* he called. *'Shout out so I can find you!'* I called; Manfred did not stir himself. He seemed exhausted, spent. Every few seconds he looked at his watch, as if Time was of the essence, as if his watch would tell him

146

when the point-of-no-return was past. He did not ask Victor to turn back, because to turn back would mean crossing that crevasse again, wandering to and fro among the pressure ridges in a wilderness of mazes and cul-de-sacs. 'We should camp here,' he said, jerking his hands at the ground. 'We camp here,' but he said it to himself, locked up inside himself. Trouble had gone to ground in his guts, installed itself in his abdomen.

The GPS blinked, telling us we were stationary, but the map showed nothing to account for what we had just gone through. In fact it showed nothing very much at all: just a coastline: the edge of the Ross Ice Shelf, the end of the Barrier. Geographers can't map the chaos of the Shear Zone; it is always changing. This is where the Ice Shelf hinges against solid land, flexing, blistering, and gaping, like a scar that won't ever heal.

'Onward and upward!' said Victor, but nobody stirred. We were all thinking our own thoughts, and onward and upward didn't figure in any of them. It was not until Victor ordered Sigurd to walk ahead of the tank that he got our full attention. We all stared at him. 'What's up? Reconnoitre for crevasses! Rope round his waist. Put him on a safety line. Piece o' cake.' He asked Bruch to back him up. The Viking shrugged, said nothing. He had the look of a man doing mental arithmetic during an exam. Sigurd, though, screamed his refusal—nothing would induce him—nothing! Victor laughed. 'Buck up, lad! Want to find the Portal, don't you? Can't sign up to these jaunts and then not pull your weight! Am I the only one with his mind on the job?'

Fleetingly I wondered whether Victor was punishing Sigurd for kissing me. In sitcoms fathers always hate their daughters' boyfriends, don't they? And Uncle Victor has always been like a father to me.

'If you don't like the work, blame Sym here,' Victor

confided jokily. 'It's her who broke the gyro. Tuh! Lasses and technology, eh? It's her navigating got us here!' and he looked round him at the smoke-filled bowl of the world to which my stupidity had brought them. 'No harm done, though. Off you go, lad. Walk on. Shoo, shoo! You're roped on. Safe as houses!'

He had tied one end of a long, long rope to the rails that frame the front of the tank. Now he advanced on Sigurd with the other end. Sigurd put up his fists.

*'Oh, ripping! A boxing match. I can referee,'* said Titus. *'It's like India all over again.'*

I went and untied the rope, fed it through the rails, tied the end round my waist. 'I'll walk with you, Sigurd,' I said.

You have to do things sometimes to strengthen your courage muscles.

Anyway, I've never been able to stand arguments. I'll do almost anything to avoid a scene.

Anyway, we can't afford for Uncle Victor to get hurt; we need his cleverness. His planning. His mind. His knowing things about fuel consumption. His confidence.

Anyway, Manfred may be a very good film director, but he's got the Aurora stomach bug, and he doesn't know spit about Antarctica.

*'Anyway, you're bloody angry,'* said Titus, amused.

'Well, I *didn't* navigate us here!' I said.

*'You did not.'*

'And I *didn't* break the gyro!'

*'You did not,'* said Titus.

As an afterthought, I went back to the cab and got out two of the ice axes. If we lost our footing on an ice slide or went over the edge of . . . something . . . we might need them. And if, behind us, the tank went down a . . . something . . . we might just be able to cut the rope before it dragged us down with it.

148

Titus looked at me with his head on one side and a look I could make no sense of.

'What?'

A full-in-the-eyes look, no longer amused, no longer the impartial referee, no longer Titus, in fact, his features resolving into those of Sigurd holding the ice axe I had just given him.

'How much do you weigh, Sigurd?' I asked. (Well, you have to muster your facts, don't you, and when you're tied on to either end of a rope with someone, it's the sort of thing you need to know.)

We held hands while we walked, looking for the telltale signs of a dip in the surface, a change in the colour of the snow. Absurd. The fog was so thick we could barely see each other, and we were holding hands.

> *Dear Nikki, Sigurd and I are going out together, you could say. You don't get more Out than here. I have all the right fashion-accessories for a date: an ice pick and goggles, nose-wiper mittens, and a ski-pole to prod the ground with, like a blind man's white stick. My cheeks are just the right shade of blue. We don't talk much—just commune with Nature. Nature doesn't say much either. Tell Mum she mustn't worry. She mustn't be scared. We'll be all right.   XSX*

'This place is "The Shear"?' Sigurd said eventually.

I explained how wherever Ice Shelf meets land they don't quite form a perfect seal with one another; how the sea—way, way down below—keeps pushing the ice up and down, up and down, so that it cracks, and screws itself into great welts and folds. I couldn't tell if he was listening. He had put on one of the grotesque red masks and his goggles. He might almost have been Uncle Victor. Or an Amazon tree frog.

149

'Your mother and father, they name you for this clever John Cleeves Symmes?' Sigurd said later on.

'No! Oh no. A coincidence. No, I'm Symone, that's all. Coincidence.'


Of course, it is nothing of the kind. Unofficial uncles don't name a child. The parents do that. Fathers do that. So Dad must have been part of this lifelong quest for Symmes's Hole too. Looking back, all kinds of things make sense now. When we went to Iceland, the one place Dad and Victor made a beeline for was Snaefellsnes. I remember the excitement in Dad's face as he told me, 'This is where it begins, love! In the book! In *Journey to the Centre of the Earth!*'

Maybe they thought Jules Verne knew something the geologists didn't, and that Iceland really did contain the northern portal to the hollow planet. I recall how the holiday mood suddenly went out of the trip. Snaefellsnes and Jules Verne must have let them down. They found no Hole.

Oh yes, Dad was in this from the start. Dad knew about the Earth being hollow. And he was so grateful to John Cleeves Symmes for the knowledge that he named his baby daughter after him. Symone. Sym. Maybe he hoped I'd have the genius to match. I always knew I was a disappointment to him—just not how much of a disappointment.


Quite suddenly the fog changed substance over our heads. In a matter of moments, the fleshy grey mist resolved itself into a frozen dew, a precipitation of crystals, a burden of ice particles that fell twinkling out of the air like rice at a wedding, sunlight splitting them into all the colours of the rainbow. We were bombarded with rainbows falling from an infinite height, dazzling us with iridescent spears and darts and cataracts of cascading colour. Some of the particles were so sharp that they embedded themselves in our suits like Lilliputian arrows. I didn't know whether to be afraid or amazed. The fog was gone—a magician's cloth deftly whipped off a table of marvels. In the sky, the sun was a hub of dull aluminium spoked with strands of light, and at the end of each spoke— another sun. Cloned suns.

'Oh, my God!' said Sigurd. 'Look at that!'

Black puddles of no-light oozed and smeared the sky between the suns—drops of molasses all the time changing, taking on outlandish shapes: a harp, a hand, an eagle, a dinosaur.

The tank had stopped, but we did not notice until our rope tethers pulled us up short. And when we turned, we were dumbstruck reindeer drawing Christmas in our wake. The Hagglund had grown a phantom duplicate of itself, upside-down, hanging in the air nose-to-nose with the genuine article. At our feet the mirror crystals had joined into long shining strands, and hoar-frost had woven patterns over them, white-on-white embroidery.

'Oh, my God!' said Sigurd.

Why so beautiful? It can't be for our special benefit. I never understood about 'beautiful'. I can see why running water is beautiful, or a tree full of apples—something that meant good things to our caveman ancestors. But I've never understood why lions and tigers and deadly nightshade and sand dunes and lightning are beautiful. Or this. We turned round and round, just staring, hands cupped around our eyes to fend off the ferocious, bludgeoning light.

'Oh, my God!' breathed Sigurd.

Next time we looked back at the van, Manfred and

151

Victor were struggling over the wheel. Manfred (who was in the driving seat) was leaning forwards pointing, spreading his hand against the windscreen as if to lay hold on something. Following his gaze, we saw—it was true—a sight worthy of the Arabian Nights rather than an icy wilderness.

The horizon, for the first time, was sharp as wire— sharp as three wires, in fact, because the horizon had tripled. And there, floating just above it, with a hand-span of sky for a moat, hung a jet-black palace. Turrets and minarets, crenellations and stockades, were all picked out in perfect detail.

'Yes!' cried Sigurd, ecstatic with relief.

Seeing it, Manfred steered towards it—took off the handbrake, put the gears into Drive. Rather than be run down, we had to grab hold of the corner rails as the tank came by us, and hang on with all our might, reefing in rope before it could catch in the wheels and drag us under the tracks. I beat on the metal with my free fist—*pad pad pad*—softly clad in its mitten.

'*It's a mirage,*' said Titus.

But I didn't want it to be a mirage.

'*It's a mirage,*' said Titus. '*Mountains a hundred miles away.*'

But I didn't want it to be mountains a hundred miles away. I wanted there to be people, sentries, Martians in a flying palace of a ship; a secret US establishment we had stumbled upon by chance. I wanted it to be Aeolus, brass-walled home of the King-of-Winds, shipwrecked here in the days of myth. I wanted so much for it to be real. In a place where 'real' puts five suns in the sky and slices rainbows into sushi, why shouldn't there be a palace adrift on the Ice?

'It's a mirage!' I yelled at Sigurd.

The triple horizon became a five-bar stave strewn with music. The castle loomed to a prodigious height and leaned

152

towards us, its turrets rounding their shoulders, stooping because of the lowness of the sky. Lurching over the terraces of sastrugi, the tank tried to shake us off. The crack in the windscreen grew longer.

'*It's a mirage!*' I yelled over and over again.

But Manfred Bruch, eaten up with stomach-ache and ghastly imaginings, thought he had seen his redemption. Not until the sun progressed, and the five suns joined like blobs of mercury into a single blinding silver; not until the refraction failed and the castle blinked out did he take his foot off the pedal and loosen his grip on the wheel.

It was gone—a picture stolen from a gallery, white-washed out, a trick of the light. No manna in the wilderness: just more wilderness. Manfred got out of the cab and sat on the steps, head down, forearms on his knees, hands drooping. His lips flapped loose from his teeth as he wept.

Sigurd and I stepped down from the front bumper and untied ourselves from the safety ropes. We unpicked the knots around our waists, coiled the rope, and hooked the coils on to the radiator. My legs were shaking uncontrollably, my shoulders and pelvis aching from the effort of clinging on. 'Sigurd, we should get warm. We should get warm *now*.' Sigurd pulled off his mask and flung it on the ground in disgust.

I wondered why Sigurd didn't go and comfort his father. 'Go on,' I said. But though he did go and stand over the weeping man, all he did was utter an inarticulate snarl, pull off a mitten and hit Bruch around the head with it. The spikes of frozen moisture on the nose-wiper scratched Bruch's face, and his head jerked, but he hardly seemed to notice.

Little by little, he recovered himself. It was like watching a man pull himself out of a well, shake himself dry, breathe in, test his ability to flex his fingers, to speak, to smile, to win.

'I'm sorry to break it to you, Victor old man,' he said loudly, calling from where he sat on the metal steps, 'but I'm afraid I've been keeping you short on a few facts.' There was not a trace of Norwegian in his accent. 'Sorry to tell you this, but your damned Hole's a mirage too. A hoax. A wind-up.'

'A quick drink,' said Uncle Victor, brusquely—annoyed at Bruch for his stupidity over the mirage but ready to forgive. 'Cup of something warming.'

'How can I put this so you'll understand, you clown, you dingbat?' said Bruch. 'It was a sting. A scam. A con.'

'A swift drink. That's what we all need. Then we must get back on track.'

'Get back. Get back, yes,' said Bruch, picking up on the only words that made sense. 'Did you hear me, Briggs? I'm calling it a day. You can have your money back. Here. Fact is, I've had you over. Fleeced you. Taken you for every penny I could wring out of you. I hold my hands up. Some of us have to earn a living. We don't all have spare millions swilling around in the trough. It's my calling. It's what I do. I'm good, me. I find an obsessive with money to burn and I take it off him. It's what I do. I'm good! We'd've been out of here altogether if the plane hadn't burned, wouldn't we, boy?' He said it to Sigurd. (I think it was the closest Sigurd ever got to an apology.)

Furtively Manfred picked up a fire extinguisher from inside the door of the tank. Clearly he thought that when Victor understood, he would be attacked, and he was not at his Viking peak of fitness.

But far from attacking him, Victor trudged off round the vehicle to the rear van to make refreshments. Manfred had to go after him, lugging the fire extinguisher. 'Did you hear what I said, Briggs?'

Victor busied himself with the primus, arranged the bottles in order of size, the cups in alphabetical order: Manfred, Sigurd, Sym, Victor. He adjusted the spaces between them to be exactly equal. He checked the level in the kettle and added a trickle of water for maximum efficiency and minimum waste of butane. (He hates to see power go to waste.)

'Do you hear me, Victor?' said Bruch. 'That Thoughtisfree website—it's a great place to find obsessives! That's why I use it. First I sounded you out to see if there was any cash . . . Then I fed you what you wanted . . . Made you a happy man, Briggs, admit it! For a while I made you a happy man! But, all right, you were out of my league! You're a thousand kilowatt, Born Again flat-earther! Away with the fairies!'

Uncle Victor put a teaspoon into each cup before filling it, so that the heat would be conducted away from the delicate glaze of the china. Except that the cups were made of melamine. I thought: if I keep my eyes on him, I'll see when he caves in; I'll see the moment when the realization hits him that all his dreams have come to nothing: that he's been bled dry by a crook. I thought, *Why didn't you just shoot him, Viking? You didn't have to rip the heart out of him first.*

Confused by the merry chinking of crockery and the bubbling of the kettle, Manfred grew more and more agitated. 'Everyone wants to be in films! Everyone's secretly hoping they'll meet a film director one day and he'll say "Let me film you! Let me make you famous!"' He gave a rasping laugh. 'I had that Mimi woman begging me to take the money off her. "Joint venture," I tell people. "I'll put in my last cent if you'll put in yours." That's what gets them. They pay out because they think you're risking everything as well. And it *is* a joint venture, it is! You pay: I spend! Hey! Nobody dies!' The grin stayed on his face as if fixed there with drawing pins. In a way he was still playing a role: the loveable rogue, the wide boy, bad but clever, a tireless servant of Free Enterprise. Victor's failure to react was a bit like an audience refusing to hiss the rakish pantomime villain. Manfred squirmed in his seat. His upset stomach thundered.

'Don't you know anything? You can get satellite photos off the Net any day of the week! Any number of 'em! Take your pick! Blow them up. Enhance them. That pit I showed you—it's an open-cast mine in Siberia. Nothing! Anything! You can show people anything: they see what they want to see!' He might have been coaching an apprentice in the ancient and venerable profession of the confidence trickster. This was how he must have coached Sigurd.

'Look, I could have killed you, back there,' he ranted on. 'I had the bank draft—there was that plane over-head—I could have burned the lot of you, but I didn't! Did I? Fair do's! I didn't!'

Victor put our drinks into our hands. 'Thank you very much, Mr Briggs,' said Sigurd, his manners as automatic as blinking. I don't think I remembered to say thank you.

Unnerved now, Manfred peered out into the auditorium: why wasn't the audience booing? 'That fossil!' he giggled. 'Don't you know there's a whole industry out in China, turning out hoax fossils? Hundred quid, I paid!' He looked to Sigurd for a witness to back up his story. Sigurd averted his eyes. 'Found something advertised in Chinese script on eBay—God knows what it was—an alarm clock, antique chopsticks, for all I know! You weren't about to check what it really said, were you? Why would you check? This was your good friend Bruch telling you: it's a fossilized hand from Antarctica and it's yours for a snip at £10,000!' So expansive was Bruch that I wondered if he wanted us to clap him. The trouble he had gone to!

156

The ingenuity he had shown! This leech, this bloodsucker, this parasite.

But the hatred I felt for Bruch was nothing to what I felt for myself. All along I had had my doubts about miniature fossil hands for sale on eBay. And what had I done about it? Hadn't it crossed my mind that the photo could be an enlargement of anything—badger's burrow, a French toilet, a hole on a pitch-and-putt? But had I said so out loud? Too afraid of crossing Victor, of losing his good opinion, I stowed all my misgivings out of sight, like dirty magazines on top of a wardrobe. Every crime like this needs someone like me to look away and say nothing.

Sigurd was leaning up against me, uncomfortably heavy, like a dog seeking affection. I didn't want him anywhere near me, this accomplice, this conspirator. I tried to shift, but Sigurd had me pinned against the bulkhead. His drink was untouched. He was barely breathing for fear of what would happen next.

Uncle Victor gathered up the cups as if we had all finished, and emptied the dregs out of the door. 'Well?' he said eagerly.

'Well?' said Manfred lurching to his feet. The fire extinguisher slipped out of his grip and landed on his boot.

'Let's get on, then. No harm done,' said Victor equably. 'Never set much store by your data anyway, you being a foreigner. Always better to be self-reliant. Don't fret: I've got my facts straight.' His voice bounced along like a song in a pantomime—*join in, children, ladies, gentlemen!*

I thought it was just a saying, but Bruch's jaw really did drop. His mouth fell open in stark astonishment. Victor did not see it: he was already stumping back to the driver's van, jerking his elbows outwards from the shoulder to expand his lungs, rolling his head on his neck to ease muscle tension. At the base of the steps he flexed his knees once or twice, preparing for another stint at the wheel.

Manfred went after him. 'Don't you get it, Briggs? Those co-ordinates! I made them up! Invented them! Faked it! Listen, Briggs, there *are no co-ordinates*! I'm sorry. I'm sorry, Briggs, but face it! Give up! You've got your million back! Get us out of here before we all get killed!'

'Wasn't a bad guess. You were there or there about with your numbers,' said Victor generously. 'There or thereabouts. I'd pretty much narrowed it down already, of course. But you weren't far out.' And adjusting the slide rule of his reasoning to allow for a few minor glitches, my uncle went back to the job in hand. He was quite satisfied that Fate and Genius would steer him to the correct co-ordinates.

Manfred ran after him, fumbling at his Velcro-fastened breast pocket, pulling out the bank draft. 'Look! Here! Have it back! What is it? It's only money!'

'Oh, *that*,' said Victor, and something about the way he said it finally opened the Viking's eyes to the truth. The draft fluttering between his fingers, made out to Manfred Bruch for one million pounds, was worth nothing. There was no million pounds. The confidence trickster had met his match in one of his own victims.

Manfred started to laugh. It gave him a pain in his side, but he laughed anyway—a mewling, quacking laugh of sheer admiration. 'Shit, you're better than I am!' was what he said. And Victor laughed with him—smiled, anyway—and asked the Viking if he would be so kind as to rescue Sigurd's red face-mask before it blew away altogether.

The tissuey red circle of material was rolling gently over the ice, away from the van, and Manfred made a couple of grabs at it before it came to hand. He was talking to himself under his breath, cursing himself for being taken in by a rank amateur. By the time he turned round, the tank was moving, circling the spot where he stood, turning slowly around to retrace the track marks left in the snow by Manfred's mad dash towards the mirage.

By the time Manfred raised his first shout of protest, we were over the track marks and accelerating. By the time he realized what Victor was doing—by the time I realized—we were moving at ten miles an hour. The rear doors hung open. I remember one of the cups rolled along the floor and out of the door on to the snow. Manfred started to run, calling out: 'Briggs! No! Wait!' He ran and he gained ground. I watched him like someone in a film—unreal—the baddy getting his come-uppance. Sigurd meantime had struggled to his feet and was hanging from the hand straps, calling out to Bruch. *'Come on! Come on! Run! Run!'* crouching on hands and knees to reach out a hand. Manfred ran like a demon possessed.

Victor did not accelerate—not more than it took, anyway, to keep the sight of Bruch in his wing mirror, to keep ahead of him. The surface changed from smooth ice to fractured blocks and Bruch was leaping from step to step now, no longer shouting, his face contorted by agony, his eyes on us.

His eyes on my eyes.

*'Come on, Bruch! Come on!'*

Sigurd and I held on to whatever we could and tried to reach out our hands to him. The change of surface forced the tank to slow. But now it twisted its long, articulated back, rolling us from window to window, from seat leg to seat leg, set the doors banging open and shut. One moment I lost sight of Bruch, the next we almost had him, his outstretched hand nearly touching ours.

So when he turned his ankle on the treacherous blocks of ice, it was easy to read it in his face: how it felt to break a bone. I saw him pitch on his face; saw the

159

unnatural angle of his foot as he dragged himself upright again. *'ANYTHING!'* he screamed. *'ANYTHING!'* said his mouth, offering the world for a place aboard the bus. *'ANYTHING!'*

But Victor had worlds enough already. Victor had the prospect of worlds within worlds, with several worlds to spare. He maintained speed and switched on the cassette player. Victor never did suffer fools gladly.

For a long time, through the open rear doors, we watched the small figure crawling over the collage of deformed ice. For a long time we could hear him: sounds travel miles in the Antarctic. They last, too, those sounds. I don't imagine I will forget them if I live for a hundred years.

And what's the likelihood of that?

# Chapter Fifteen
## Looking Back

We never stopped looking back. Every time we came to a halt, I expected a figure, bare-headed, clad in a sky-blue snowsuit, to come toiling into sight. We both expected it. Sigurd said 'Good riddance', but he went on looking, waiting for the man with the broken ankle to catch up, to be taken back into the fold.

'I'll make Victor turn around. I'll make him go back for your dad,' I promised, holding his hand a little tighter. Once again we were walking ahead of the tank, lashed to it by safety ropes, prospecting for crevasses in our path.

'Italia Conti,' said Sigurd. It was like some foreign nobleman explaining his origins. But he was naming the drama school where he had studied acting. He was not Bruch's son at all. 'Apparently your uncle seemed to like the idea of Bruch being a family man—especially if he had a son. So, naturally, Bruch got himself a son! Advertised. Held auditions. I got the part. He's not my dad.'

After Bruch's confession, it should not have surprised me that Sigurd came from Great Yarmouth and not from Norway. Yet I had no end of trouble separating him from the tissue of lies he had come wrapped in.

'Maybe after your mother left, he just lost all sense of Right and Wrong!' I suggested, wanting to understand.

But there was no mother. Bruch was a bachelor. There

had been no massive debts, no personal sacrifices: Manfred had got Victor to pay for everything. He had been milking Victor for two years at least—research expenses, bribes to his fictional friend at NASA, bogus fossils, travel tickets, the cost of 'engaging a film crew'. There was no film crew—no film company of any kind. And yet man and boy had played their parts with such conviction that it was harder to credit the truth than the lies. It was harder to believe in the English Sigurd than the one with fractured English.

He had another name—of course he did—but it did not register in my head. There are only so many mental adjustments you can make when it's twenty degrees below.

'I told you he was a shot-peener!' I remonstrated with Sigurd. 'How could you *possibly* think he was a multi-millionaire?'

'How's anyone supposed to know what a shot-peener is?' Sigurd retorted. 'For all I knew, it was something in the Stock Exchange! He managed to convince Bruch he had money!'

Once again we looked back over our shoulders. Once more we told ourselves that Manfred Bruch would catch us up. But all that moved in the landscape behind us was the reeling, rolling Hagglund, its sun-bright windows obscuring the man behind the wheel. He could have been Tamburlaine the Great and we the conquered kings he forced to pull his chariot. Easier to believe than that it was my uncle Victor.

'He may have fallen down a crevasse,' I suggested 'At least then it would have been quick!'

'Good riddance,' said Sigurd, not for the first time. (I should say, in his defence, he was beside himself with fear.)

Hand-in-hand we walked towards the Transantarctic

Mountains now clearly visible. And if we had been walking through a minefield we could not have been more scared. Each footstep was against all reason. We were going further afield, when we should have been turning back. For all our feeble prodding about with ski sticks, we were effectively testing for crevasses with our own bodyweight.

'The snow's a different colour, apparently, and the surface dips, sort of,' I said, remembering my Ice books, as our pupils shut down against the brightness of an undulating landscape shaped by pressure ice, cloud shadow, and optical illusions.

Later I said, 'Why did you let it go so far? Why did you even agree to set out on this . . .'

'Briggs told Bruch he'd stop the bank draft. The idea was for us to fly out on the DC-6. *"What, no film crew? How terrible! Wherever can they be? Must go and find them!"* Out of it. Finish. Kaput. *Disparu.* You two would sit around waiting for us to come back. By the time you twigged, we'd have had seven clear days to cash the money and disappear. Bruch even spiked the camp radio, in case Victor felt the need to phone his bank or tried to cancel the draft. Everything was about the draft. Everything. Worthless piece of bloody paper. Then the plane went up in flames. Bloody ruined our whole game-plan. I wanted to duck out, but not *him.* Oh no. *Bruch* had a cheque for a million in his pocket, didn't he? And if the trip was off, Victor was going to cancel it, wasn't he? So he had to go on looking like a believer. When Victor said jump, Bruch jumped.'

'A million pounds!?'

'Well? He looked to be good for it! His cheques never bounced before! Manfred's stuffed him for thousands already! Know what it costs to do the Antarctic with that Pengwings outfit? Your uncle does: he paid for all four of us to come. Apparently Manfred always tries to swing it so that he gets a free holiday out of a sting. Reckons these kind of trips are perfect for lining up the next target; they attract just the right kind. Buenos Aires? Couldn't contain himself! Every direction he looked there was some rich old idiot begging to be ripped off, begging to put their money into a movie about themselves or their bloody passions. He was lining them up like skittles. Mimi and her romantic novels . . . Clough and his Performing Auks, Miss Adolphus and her Amazing Penguins . . .'

'He didn't have his gloves, you know,' I said.

'Who?'

'Manfred. Your dad.'

And suddenly the lack of gloves made Bruch real again—flesh and blood real, not a character in a play, not an object of disgust, but someone who had given Sigurd his first acting job, his big break, his first script. A huge sob burst out of him, and he came to a halt and he put his hands to his head and he swayed and keened and sobbed, *'Get him back, Sym! Get him back! Get him back! Get him back, Sym! Get Briggs to go back!'*

So I asked Victor to turn back: asked him for the sake of Sigurd, for my sake, for the sake of the Law, for the sake of his conscience, for the sake of not spoiling our nice outing—yes, I think I probably even said that . . . I don't know what I said. I only remember hugging him and hugging him and pressing my face against his, feeling the scales of peeling skin sharp as a dogfish, and the big pulse hopping in his neck, and me saying, 'I love you. I love you. I love you, Uncle Victor! Please don't leave Mr Bruch out there in the cold! I'm sure he's sorry! I'm sure he's really, really sorry!'

He heard what I said. He did. He didn't pretend not to have heard. He didn't tell me to buck up or to consider the facts of the case. He just wrapped both arms around

164

my head and kissed me on the eyes. 'There there! Soft article! You think I'd leave him to suffer? I hope I'm a tad more humanitarian than that, style of thing.'

And he was, I knew, because he had loved me when Dad didn't, and had taken care of us, and moved in and paid for the funeral and mowed the lawn and given me my Ice books and suggested a jaunt to Paris . . .

'That last drink would've finished him off in an hour or two,' Victor went on. 'Nothing to fret about on that score. I've been easing him out of the picture ever since we left Base Camp! A little something toxic in every hot drink he drank. I just made the last one plenty strong.'

No. There never was anything scones-and-cream about Uncle Victor's teabags.

'Flash monkey,' Victor puttered on. 'Thinking he could outwit me, style of thing. Still, he served the cause. That's no bad epitaph to put on a man's grave, is it? "He served the cause of Science".'


'Was the South Pole worth it, Titus?' I asked inside my head. 'One patch of snow just like all the rest. Was it worth anybody dying?'

Titus shrugged. *'Don't ask me if death's a tragedy, Sym. It's not the right question.'*


'So the reason all those people got ill back at Aurora . . . ?' I said to Uncle Victor, extricating myself from his arms. 'That was you, too.'

'Couldn't have a bunch of tourists tagging along, could I? Thinking they could do as they liked! Thinking they were on their hols! (Half of them soft in the head, as it is.) Just needed persuading to take the plane home, that's all. Give us elbow room. Leave us in peace.'

165

'So you poisoned them,' I said, trying to sound as if the logic of it was plain for all to see. 'Were they all dead, then, when we left . . . ?'

'Christmas, no, child! Drugged is all! Just put them out of my road for a mo!' He added, with military crispness, 'Had to free up the kit, didn't we? Had to free up the transport for the Big Push! Make certain of being first.'

I thought back to the sleeping Camp Aurora: the Pogsbaums, Clough, Tillie and Brenda and the rest. Not dead, then. Their nuisance value had not merited a fatal cup of Uncle Victor's lapsang souchong. Lucky them.

'Of course, when Bruch showed signs of pushing off back to Punta along with the others, I had to reassess the situation.' Uncle Victor used the most reasonable of tones. 'Had to nip that idea right in the bud. Happen he'd have tried to cash the bank draft, and me with nowt in the bank. He was planning on taking that Sigurd of yours with him, too, and that would never have done, eh? Eh?' He nudged me with his elbow over and over again. 'Eh? Eh? So the plane had to go.'

'Go? The plane? What, you mean you set f—'

I saw the DC-6 burn all over again, then: the fat orange tongue of fire unrolling through the fuselage, so bright that you could see the seats in silhouette even through solid metal; the wash of flame devouring the luggage on the ground.

Not just the luggage . . .

The plane had to go. And why? To stop Bruch trying to cash a dud cheque.


'Did you take morphine, Titus? Before you went outside. I always wondered. Did you?'

But Titus declined to say—declined, I think, to be in

166

the same room with people as worthless as us, let alone confide the intimate circumstances of his death.

I told Sigurd about the poisoning. Not about the plane, because that would have burned my mouth in the saying. But I told Sigurd that Bruch was certainly dead long since, of poisoning and cold. It was the only way to stop him looking over his shoulder, watching for Manfred to come limping into view.

'I thought I saw him,' said Sigurd. 'Just now. A man limping.' But he believed me, because he had learned better than to believe his eyes in Antarctica. We had them sussed now, those fictions of light—the mirages that promised palaces, the horizons scrawled with music, the undeserved haloes around the sun. We were getting used to the place, weren't we?

'I'll look after you,' said Sigurd staunchly. 'I'll be there for you.' His nose shone green where his nose-wiper had smeared sun block around. I didn't laugh out loud at the offer. You have to understand: he was beside himself with fear.

On foot, some of the surfaces were exhausting. The Hagglund made light work of sastrugi, but for us two, walking out ahead of the vehicle, testing for crevasses, it felt like pulling ourselves over a colony of giant tortoises, dead and deathly cold. The cold was stupefying. There is only one good thing about cold: it stops you thinking. It stops you thinking about the nice black journalist's wife and children in Maine. It stops you thinking about crevasses and empty fuel drums and a bank draft for a million pounds and fossil hands for sale on eBay . . .

The Hagglund, with robotic persistence, snapped at our

heels, sometimes almost over-running us. Uncle Victor, losing concentration, would let his foot rest heavy on the pedal and gain on us, and we were too tired to run, too cold to run. As we scrambled up one particular ice rumple higher than our heads, we reached a level with Victor in his driving cab. He was singing along to the tape deck and I could read his lips: karaoke Konitz.

> *Whenever the skies look grey to me*
> *And trouble begins to brew;*
> *Whenever the winter winds begin to blow,*
> *I concentrate on you!*
>
> *When fortune cries nay, nay to me*
> *And people declare 'You're through . . .'*

The snow on the other side of the rumple at least looked soft—no risk to our ankles. Sigurd and I jumped down together.

There was no time to fetch out the ice axes hanging from our belts—nowhere to sink their blades. We didn't go straight through, mind. Like snowy quicksand, the loose crystals swallowed first our boots then our legs. A slightly different colour, yes, I thought. Then, like sand through the neck of an hourglass, obeying gravity, the snow under our feet fell away, and we fell with it. A crust of snow had masked a crack in the ice: face-powder over a scar. Now, with a peculiar brittle sigh, the snow crust subsided into the fissure. We fell like hanged men through the scaffold trap, feet first, perfectly vertical, out of the blinding brightness and into a gloom as blue as deep water or Death.

168

# Chapter Sixteen
## Underground

The jerk was so sharp that I thought the rope had cut me in half. Sigurd's greater weight stopped my fall, began to draw me up and him down, but we collided in mid-air, a tangle of limbs and rope and screaming, and clung to each other, swinging sickeningly to and fro. Snow from the collapsing crust of the crevasse came down on our heads like Niagara—solid, smothering cataracts of snow-grit caking us with cold. I thought I'd suffocate. I thought the weight would snap the ropes. I thought the tank would plunge down after us, on top of us. I thought the Ross Shelf had cracked like a skating pond and that below me was nothing but the Ross Sea a mile down.

I thought that my hearing had been restored in the moment of my death, because my own screaming was so loud, but it was Sigurd, his chin on my shoulder, screeching into my ear. Then he made the mistake of looking upwards, and his mouth and nose filled up with falling snow and that silenced the banshee wail. His eye sockets, too, filled up with snow. His hat was gone, his head bare but for a crest of white, as if he had been cursed with instant old age. Skull-white and eyeless, this gargoyle clung to me, its mouth spewing snow.

Around us hung a blue world. Wherever sunlight penetrated the crevasse, the pure, ancient ice shone an iridescent blue—the colour of swimming pools or the Caribbean

Sea. From the lips of the opening hung countless sheets of wafer-thin ice, like the baleen gills of a whale, shavings of turquoise glowing with sunlight.

Sigurd struggled and thrashed about, setting us swinging again. I blew in his face until his eyes at least could open—*Calms the oil that greases the . . . something-or-other . . . can't remember what*—but he grew no calmer. His throat and nostrils were clogged with snow and he was suffocating. When he coughed, a mouthful of snow hit me in the face, but I doubt if he knew he was rid of it, because it had burned his gullet and tongue.

'Please hold still. Hold still, please!' My face was so cold that I couldn't shape the words. His ice axe was rammed against my stomach and I was afraid of it tearing the fabric or cutting through my rope. Sigurd went on struggling and grunting and trying to break free of me. Perhaps he thought I was holding him down underwater—that he could float to the surface of this blue fjord if he could just break free.

'Don't struggle! Keep still!' I said knowing he wouldn't understand me. Never could, never will be able to make myself understood. A goldfish speaking gibberish, that's me. 'The knots'll come undone if you don't keep still!'

Instantly Sigurd froze to catatonic stillness, his arms so tight around my body that I could not properly breathe. Above us, the roar of the tank grew and grew until it drowned out everything. I could picture Victor singing along to the music, thoughts flung far ahead into the realm of underground aliens. With the ridge of ice in his way, he wouldn't even see the crevasse on the other side— not until he came over the crest. Every metre he advanced, lowered us, on the ends of our rope, deeper and deeper into the blue ravine. *Look down, Victor! Please look down!* Into the slot of sky over our heads came the shadow of the Hagglund: an interruption to the sunlight, a noise big

170

enough to crumble the Transantarctic Mountains. Then, suddenly . . . silence. Not idling or the graunching of gears, but a juddering sigh and another cascade of snow.

In slamming on the brakes, Victor had stalled the engine. Now I could picture the twin vans straddling the ice rumple, steam rising off the bonnet, the smell of diesel rich in the air, the Nansen sled hanging back like a weary toddler. Our ropes threaded through the tie bars were the strings of twin puppets. Giant puppeteer, two puppets dangling. Uncle Victor's puppets. Pull us up, Uncle Victor!

'Have you out of there presently, don't you fret!'

'Presently,' I said to Sigurd.

'Pezenty,' he said back to me, mouth stiff with cold. And we hung there, faces as inexpressive as poker players. I brushed the snow out of his hair as best I could and blew it off his cheeks.

'*Reader's Digest*,' I said. 'When you get home, you can sell your story to *Reader's Digest*. Pay you a packet.'

'No kid?' he said, and a while later I saw his tongue moving behind his rigid lips in that way I had mistaken for prayer but which was actually Sigurd counting imaginary money.

'This happened to Captain Scott, you know? He and Taff Evans. On the first trip, the 1904 trip. They got out fine! Just took a while, that's all! They reckon that's why he made Taffy one of the five, you know?'

''ive?'

'One of the five who tried for the Pole. One of the five who . . .'

'*Don't finish that sentence, Sym,*' Titus advised.

'Well, anyway, they reckon that spending time like that—like this—made them . . .' But that was another sentence I couldn't finish. There was a terrible kind of intimacy in hanging face-to-face, clinging tightly to each other, but I didn't want Sigurd to get the wrong idea

171

about what was going through my head . . . If he was anything like Maxine, he'd just think I meant Scott was gay. There are only two kinds of love in Maxine's vocabulary: straight and gay. Friendship doesn't figure.

Another flurry of snow trickled in from the rim and Sigurd tilted his head at a sound I could not hear. 'What is it?' At first I thought it must be Victor singing, or Lee Konitz. But gradually I realized that the paper-thin stalactites—the rigid leaves of sea-blue ice above us—were resounding as the snow brushed over them. Wrapping my legs around Sigurd's body, I reached out with the ski pole and tapped the largest. It made a bell-clear note, like a clock chiming. The highest were far out of range of my lousy hearing—like the music only angels can hear. Or dogs.

Sigurd smiled, hearing far better (one of the angels, obviously). He took the ski pole out of my hand and tried it for himself. His arm muscles were jerked by spasms of cold; he could not open them fully away from his body at the armpits. But the vagueness cleared out of his eyes, and the effort of listening—even when I could not hear—fetched my own brain back from the dark.

'When I came home from South Africa . . .'

'Yes, Titus? What? I can't remember!' I could recall some of the things on the tray, on Uncle Victor's tray, underneath the embroidered tray-cloth, when he was training up my memory—a whistle, a fork, a pen, a peg, Pelmanism, 'time-wasting' . . . but I didn't want those. I wanted to remember what had happened at Gestingthorpe when Titus Oates came back home from the Boer War. Because it was high summer, then, and I needed to think warmth.

Sigurd tapped away at the tubular bells of ice, reaching out for a wider and wider range of notes. I noticed he had enough of a beard for the green sun block to stick

172

to each separate hair. He played the ice with all the ferocious delicacy of a conductor bullying an orchestra. 'At
home I play keyboards,' he confided, splitting his lips to
say it, and making them bleed.

'*When I came home from South Africa,*' said Titus, '*two
hundred and eighty people sat down to a village dinner of beef,
mutton, plum pudding and brown ale. Not to mention the children's tea: bread and butter and jam and tea. There was a
procession led by my sisters—and a steam roundabout—and
swings; coconut-shies and a brass band playing patriotic songs.
The local paper wrote a piece about me fit to curl one's hair
with embarrassment. Indeed I trust my sisters cut the paper up
to curl their ringlets with, since Ma obliged me to stand up and
talk some jingoistic tosh, and the paper quoted me.*'

And I passed all this information on to Sigurd—whole
sentences and everything—because Titus seemed to think
it would help to pass the time. 'His mother had the church
bells repaired, in thanksgiving for his safe return,' I
concluded.

But though I could picture it all, however hard I tried
I could not hear the church bells Mrs Oates had restored,
couldn't hear the summer sky choke up with the clamour
of them, and it filled me with completely irrational rage
to see Sigurd making music—to have the church bells
show me their open mouths but hear nothing, nothing,
nothing . . .

'Who is this Oates character?' said Sigurd.

In an effort to make me hear, he hit harder at the delicate leaves of ice hanging over our heads, and one of
them fractured and fell: a sword of Damocles. I felt it
brush my leg as it dropped—down and down and down—
into the colourless dark. The crevasse was so deep that
whole seconds passed before we heard it shatter. Suddenly
Sigurd was unable to raise the ski pole or play another
note. A moment later the pole slipped from his grip and

173

fell too. Hatless and wet-haired, he had begun to change colour below his green warpaint. The snow that had filled his mouth had burned his gullet, and his soft palate was starting to blister.

'Don't let him die, Titus,' I said. 'I like him.' And, like a plea in mitigation, 'He does play keyboard!'

'*Ripping,*' said Titus. '*Prefer the pianola myself. Flick of a switch.*'

'You always were a lazy sod. Make yourself useful. Go and show Victor how to put the Hagglund into reverse: he never got the knack. Flick of a switch.'

'*All right, but be so good as to remember what I said: motor sledges are a waste of time and money.*'

Once the stalled engine could be persuaded to restart, Uncle Victor did find reverse, no trouble. He did back away from the crevasse, and we were drawn up out of our blue gully towards a brilliant slit of pink sky. Two puppets dangling from either end of Uncle Victor's string. On the way past, we used our axes to smash the ice-leaves, so as not to cut ourselves on their razor-sharp edges. I don't remember what sound that made: the destruction of those exquisite glass organ pipes built from the teardrops of whole generations of angels.

And he was right, of course, Uncle Victor. If we had not been walking ahead of the tank, it would have driven straight into the crevasse and killed us all. If I had begun to doubt the truth of the things Victor said, the business of the crevasse made me think twice. Victor is a genius with an IQ of 184. And he has a Plan, which is more than anyone else does round here.


He bundled me round with sleeping bags and clothes, with the red silk skirt, with his tweed jacket and flan-nelette nightshirt and anything he could find in the big

174

suitcase. He rubbed my arms and spooned sips of warm Ribena between my lips. I tried to tell him that Sigurd was colder than I was, but he said 'First things first' and that he could not spare his right-hand girl, his apprentice, his journeyman, his Sym. The bifocal parts of his old spectacles looked like tear-drops rolling in the lenses.

'Uncle Victor,' I said, touching the ice pocking on his cheeks. 'Remember what Shackleton said to his wife?' My voice came out thin as the steam off tepid Ribena.

'Say again?'

'Shackleton. Wife. When he turned back. Gave up. South Pole.'

Uncle Victor began to sing something Konitz but without the tune. But I persisted anyway, hiding behind Ernest Shackleton for safety. No one thought ill of Shackleton for loving his wife. No one thought ill of Shackleton for giving up ninety-seven miles short of the Pole and turning for home. No one thought ill of Shackleton because he wanted to live more than he wanted the glory. '*"I thought you'd rather have a live donkey than a dead lion"*. That's what Shackleton—'

Before I had even finished speaking, Victor turned away. I thought he hadn't heard me, but he had.

'What about you, boy?' he asked, starting to chafe Sigurd's limbs, to rub warmth back into his body with a fistful of woollen jumper. 'Suppose you'd like to turn back, too. *Better a live donkey*, eh?' Sigurd blinked up at him, eyes bloodshot to the colour of port wine. 'You're not your father, lad! You have opinions, I'll be bound! Press on or turn back? The vote's split, manner of thing. You can cast the decider!'

For a long time, Sigurd's eyes fixed on the same things mine had—the four mugs of steaming Ribena on the table—(four?). Then he said:

'I very much want to go on, sir. If you think we can

175

reach Symmes's Hole, I truly want to see it! I told my father he'd got you all wrong. I told him he was scamming the wrong man. I told him: this Briggs man is really on to something!' Sigurd rolled his head from side to side on the leather seat and his golden hair fell across his face. I raised myself on one elbow and stared at him. Catching sight of me, his eyes filled up with tears. 'Oh, *I don't know!*' he burst out. *'I don't know if it's there or if it isn't!* I only know . . . I only know . . . that I *love Sym!* And wherever she goes I have to go with her! See her through! See her safe through!'

I don't know what my face showed—nothing, I suppose, since I assumed I was dreaming. I know Uncle Victor grew, then and there, in stature. His shoulders spread. His head lifted. His eyes closed as he savoured Sigurd's words. He was hearing something he had never heard before, not even from me—someone perfectly in tune with his Plan. 'Well, that's grand!' he breathed in a whisper. 'Eh, that's just grand, lad! Because it means I can tell you now.' He paused so that we would both know he was saying something truly momentous. 'It's *you* who's the crucial one, lad. Not t'other—whatsisname—that Bruch item. Means-to-an-end is all he ever was.' Victor was kneeling between the two bench seats. Now he laid a hand on each of us, in a kind of benediction. Giant puppeteer, a puppet on each hand. 'Made it part of the deal, I did, that Bruch brought his boy along. "A mate for my girl," I told him.' And Victor smiled, as if truer words had never been spoken. *'You're* the crucial one, lad. Not that spiv of a father. You and Sym! That was always the way I had it fixed up in my mind!' He pulled a red provision box towards him, up-ended it and tipped the contents out on to the floor—thrust at us boxes of raisins that our hands were too cold to open, flapjacks and cake bars in untearable foil. 'Eat! Eat!' he urged,

176

fetching us our mugs and his own, pausing only to pour the fourth away out of the door. 'Plenty more when we get there! Plenty more when we reach Home!'

---

## The East Essex & Halstead Times

*A stirring home-coming for local war hero*
*(contd from page 1)*

. . . the Lieutenant's conspicuous valour. We are indeed proud of him.

Lieut. Oates looks better than one might expect considering his experiences at the front, although a bullet wound in the thigh still causes him to limp.

---

It was annoying about the snowsuit. I don't know how you mend neoprene. Mum would know. Mum would mend it for me on the sewing machine. Maybe I can use gaffer tape. I suppose I shouldn't be surprised that it was sharp, that fragile wafer of ice, blue as sheet steel and still trembling with music as it fell. The edge on it was sharp as a razor. Shouldn't surprise me. It's just that I'd have thought to feel it at the time. Such a spectacularly deep cut.

Mum could have kissed it better. If she were only here.

# Chapter Seventeen
## Open Wounds

I notice Titus limps more than he did.

In Antarctica, in the cold, wounds don't heal, they re-open. It's Nature in reverse. After South Africa, the bullet wound in Titus's leg healed and left nothing but a long ragged scar in his upper thigh. But in the Antarctic it would have opened up again, flesh parting from flesh, laying bare the bone. Healing in reverse.

My father didn't like me, and now he's dead there's nothing I can do to make him like me. I thought I'd got over that. But wounds unheal here. It troubles me more and more, not less and less. You have to be pretty useless for even your own father not to like you. So how can I seriously expect anyone else . . .

'*Who says?*'

'Who says what, Titus?'

'*Who says that your father didn't like you? Wasn't me.*'

'Well, Uncle Victor . . .'

'*Oh,* him. *The man who says the Earth's hollow.*'

I thought about this. 'But it *feels* true that Dad didn't like me.'

'*Ah.*'

And he did not press the point, because friends aren't friends who tell you black is white just because you want it to be.

Anyway, I have someone else now who loves me.

*Dear Nikki,*

*Who would have thought it? The boy called Sigurd is in love with me! I would send you a photo if I had a camera. My hair is freeze-dried and there are sores around my mouth. If I stay here long enough, my body hair will start to grow till I look like a yak. But hey! They say love is blind, don't they? They say it's the person inside. Get thee to my lady's chamber and tell Maxine, let her paint an inch thick, it's the girl inside that counts. Yesterday Sigurd and I were wound in each other's arms for half an hour and if we hadn't been down a crevasse and dying by degrees, I might have sat on the teacher's desk when I got home and told you all how it was—my legs around his waist, making music. Uncle Victor says there are no rules here, no stupid social niceties. He says we should get to it, that thing that Maxine calls love.*

*Tell Mum I'm sorry*

*XSX*

'Well, what was I supposed to say?' said Sigurd once we were under way again and Victor was up front, driving. 'If I'd said any different, I'd have gone the same way as Bruch. Which of those drinks on the table do you think I'd have got if I'd said, *No, Mr Briggs: I want to go back, Mr Briggs. Let's go home, Mr Briggs. Your stupid John Symmes was an even bigger loser than you are.* The cup with the Vitamin C, d'you think? Or the one with the arsenic?'

I tore up my mental postcard to Nikki, then screwed up each of the pieces into tiny pellets, then flew in specially trained skuas to eat the pellets and fly out to sea in forty different directions. 'So you don't actually . . .' I said, 'you don't actually—you know—love me or anything. I mean, no worries! That's fine! I don't mind! Understood. I never really . . .'

'Well, of course I do! Of course I love you, Sym!' cried Sigurd, pitching his voice an octave lower, astonished that I should even ask. He threw his arms around me and pulled me close, so that our fat, bulgy suits were squashed flat between us and our various Velcro fastenings stuck to one another. He lifted my chin with one finger. The tip of his nose brushed mine. 'Why else would I say it? Believe me, there's no one I'd sooner be with than you! We're in this together. Didn't I say I'd always be there for you?'

'*There?*' said Titus tartly. '*Where?*'

'There. It's an expression,' I explained.

'*It's a geographical disposition.*'

'There. Here. Around. On hand. OK?'

'*Ah!*' said Titus, enlightened. '*Lurking, you mean.*'


'Uncle Victor . . . was I named after John Symmes?' I asked.

We had reached the mountains and—quite according to Plan—the Axel Heiberg Glacier, our route between the Horlick Mountains and the Queen Maud Mountains, through to the plateau. It flowed down from the sky—a vast river of ice; river rapids frozen in their course. After the confusion and chaos of the Shear Zone, it looked like a great open highroad to Heaven. The slope was shallow. The Hagglund coped, throwing its gruff voice into the mountains to be answered by growling, multiple echoes.

'You were indeed, lass. You were indeed. Your father had his head screwed on in those days. We might have been here long since if he'd not gone soft. That was the plan—for Larry to come along. We could have done this together, if it hadn't been for Larry's back-sliding.' Uncle Victor gave a snort of contempt, and his round and scaly head, red from snowburn, took on the shape of a boxing glove. 'The man lost his nerve. Think on, lass. Learn by

180

it. *He that sets his hand to the plough* . . .' (Sometimes you would think Uncle Victor was a Bible-reader, if he didn't have John Cleeves Symmes for his Messiah.) 'Don't know where the rot set in. Got soft, Larry did. Got flabby. Big disappointment to me, your father. Had the makings of a first-rate Second-in-Command.'

*Tell me about when I was little. Tell me about when I was small.* I had forgotten, until Victor started to talk, how I used to ask that all the time, toddling about with the photo albums, dumping them in my mother's lap. *Tell me about when I was little. Tell me about when I was small.* Little kids are such sentimentalists, always harking back to Happier Times.

'Right up until Iceland he was a trojan. One hundred per cent committed! Five-year plan we had. All sorted. Then the fire went out of him. Bit by bit. No backbone. No stamina for the spadework, the research.'

'He couldn't help getting ill, I suppose,' I said.

The boxing glove opened a little, showing a glimpse of pink dentures, a flicker of spittle. 'Ill? He didn't get ill! He got mediocre, is what! Settled for mediocrity and the second rate. Settled for shot-peening is what! Do-mes-ti-ci-ty.' Victor threw up his hands, the pain of betrayal vivid in his eyes. 'Started begrudging the money! Started fretting about bankruptcy, about paying the mortgage—the mortgage, I ask you! Tuh! Petty-mindedness. Every day he'd come up with some new, petty, ifsy-andsy-butsy piffling little . . . The man shrank, that's what! No word of a lie, Sym! The man shrank to *this*!' He held his finger and thumb together in my face, holding between them the smallness of my father's memory. Behind it came his face, pushing into mine; a face looming through the cot bars to say *Boo!* 'He *STOPPED BELIEVING*!' Victor confided, half angry, half apologizing that he had to be the one to break the bad news to me. And what bad news was that again?

My father was an alcoholic? My father experimented

181

on beagles in the basement? My father was partial to mouse-dropping sandwiches? My father was a cross-dresser? My father turned into a werewolf every full moon? No. Far, far worse. My father had *stopped believing* in John Cleeves Symmes.

*Tell me about when I was little. Tell me about when I was small.* Children are so sentimental.

It seems the rot set in in Iceland. At Snaefellsnes. Not finding the northerly Portal where Jules Verne said it would be, Larry Wates began to have doubts. He began to harbour heretical thoughts: that the shot-peening business was actually his livelihood, not just a way of affording the search for Symmes's Hole; that the need to keep the business afloat should come before the fun of exploring. Having re-mortgaged the house once, he wouldn't do it a second time—said his wife and daughter deserved a secure roof over their heads. Said an Antarctic trip was just too expensive.

In time, Larry Wates, back-slider of Croxley Green, grew resentful of the long hours he had to spend shot-peening while his business partner read Ice books and saved Larry's daughter from a shoddy education system.

'Jealousy, lass! Pure jealousy, that's what it was!'

In the end it was career planning that tipped the balance. As Victor said: 'I told Larry I was training you up for a trip into the Inner Spheres . . . and you know what? The shutters came down! Complete stone wall. Total breakdown in communications. There's none so deaf as them as don't want to hear!'

To think it! This father of mine so lacked vision, this Larry Wates, that he tried to cancel his daughter's appointment with Destiny. He said no to his only daughter becoming the first visitor to Symmes's hollow world; tried to stop her becoming an ambassador to the realm of Innerworld; tried to forbid a trip to Antarctica; said he refused to sacrifice her to Victor's Grand Plan.

182

*Tell me about when I was little. Tell me about when I was small.* Daughters are such sentimentalists. My father turned down the Eighth Wonder of the World in favour of keeping me safe! Dad said no: he refused to let Victor dump me down Symmes's Hole and feed me to the monsters in the basement.

*And the second band of iron broke, and the princess could both blink her eyes and move her hands.*

'Did Mum know?'

'Lillian? Nay. Women lack the imagination for truly Great Projects. No steel in them. Shopping and knitting, that's about their weight. Shopping and cooking and breeding and knitting. Leaky too: not to be trusted with a secret. She has her strengths, Lillian, but don't bother to go looking to your mother for scientific rigour. I never did. But Larry! You'd've thought my own chum, my own business partner—my own Second-in-Command—could be counted on to show a bit of backbone! Wouldn't you? Eh?' His eyes, magnified behind his glasses, appealed to me to see the tragedy of the situation: his best friend had let him down.

'So it wasn't that he didn't . . . you know . . . *love me*, sort of thing,' I said tentatively.

'Call it *Love*, do you, to mollycoddle a child? Call it Love to rob her of her chances, eh?' Victor roared. 'Larry wasn't stupid! He could have played his part! As it was, he just . . . he just . . . just . . . made himself a *nuisance*, pure and simple. Obstacle in't road!'

A barrier to enlightenment, in fact. How extraordinarily lucky then, wasn't it, that this Larry Wates should have died so young.

'So he had to go, didn't he, Uncle Victor? Like the aeroplane. Have I got it right?'

'Exactly. His dying, that freed up the funds a good bit,' said Victor, nodding in agreement with himself, and recovering his good temper as he remembered. 'There was his life insurance, for a start. Took out a big business loan on the strength of that—sold off the heavy machinery, stopped paying the bills . . . Cut down on the rent I was paying on my place! Moving in with your mother meant I could sell up, style of thing. Channel it all into the Project!'

I felt wiser now. Though sometimes a dose of enlightenment tastes a lot like swallowing bleach.


'Dad loved me, Titus.' (I would have told my proper boyfriend, Sigurd, because that's what people do, isn't it? But Sigurd never knew the people involved. He didn't know about the skull-rats or the jackals at the window or the wine vinegar or the punches or the golden syrup dripping off the mantelpiece. Titus has known me a long time. He's my 125-year-old-and-valued friend.) 'Dad loved me, Titus! Uncle Victor poisoned him for it—emptied the bank, wrecked the business, murdered him for it—but Dad loved me!'

Titus had turned his blanket-cloth hat inside-out and was studiously picking out clumps of curly black hair from its stained and grubby lining. It's a casualty of cold weather and not enough food and having to wear your hat all the time, even in bed: your hair starts to fall out. Mine is.

'Dad loved me all along, Titus!' I said again.

He looked up and gave a gentle little smile. *'Naturally,'* he said. *'Who wouldn't?'*

Dear Titus. Sweet thing to say. What an excellent friend to have in a crisis. What a mate. Warmed by his words, I pocketed him, like a slab of wholesome Kendal mint-cake, for later.

# Chapter Eighteen

*'If you want to please me very much, you will fall down when I shoot you.'—Oates*

'I'll help you kill him, if you like,' said Sigurd when I told him about Victor murdering my father.

It took me aback to begin with, but the more I thought about it, the more it appealed: the idea of killing Uncle Victor.

'Just do me a favour and pretend to go along with him, for now,' Sigurd added, 'or he may turn on us, like he did on Manfred.'

By rights, we ought to strand him, I decided, as he had stranded Manfred Bruch. But then he would always be there, creeping into the corner of my eye, into the landscape of my dreams, like Manfred was always limping into view.

No, we should poison him, I decided, as he had poisoned Manfred, as he had poisoned my dad and anyone who stood in his way. There are no soft social niceties out here, Uncle Victor—like courts or the Law. Just natural justice.

'Sym and I would like to go in the back van now,' said Sigurd, with a brazen and suggestive smirk. 'For a bit of . . . you know.'

I half expected Victor to roar and bluster, to deplore the decline in moral standards, the laxity of youth, to lament bygone days when young people showed self control and joined Duke of Edinburgh Award Schemes sooner than fornicate like rutting stags . . . But of course he didn't. When I am old, I shall take a soapbox at Hyde Park Corner and harangue passers-by about the moral decline in uncles.

It was all right for Sigurd: he knew why he had made the suggestion to go in the back van 'for a bit of . . . you know'. Me, I wished someone would show me what script we were working from. Was this just an excuse to search the van for Victor's teabags? Or was it for 'a bit of you know', because he was in love with me?

Either way, I never thought it would be like this. I never thought (as Sigurd's mouth closed over mine) that I would be left thinking anything at all, let alone about the snowburn inside his mouth or that the CCTV camera was still on and that Victor was watching us, checking on us, spying on us. After a minute or two, the red light went out. But Sigurd said we had to keep up the pretence, just in case it was a test and Uncle Victor turned the camera on again to check we truly were misbehaving ourselves. That's what Sigurd said, anyway, as he wrestled with my clothing and his own.

How you do it in the Antarctic is this: first you have to take off your overmitts, then your big jacket, then your quilted shell-jacket, then your fleece jacket and glove-liners, your neck-gaiter and body-bib and salopettes . . . I recalled how Scott's men used to play a game called Furl Topgallant Sails that consisted of trying to rip the shirts off each other's backs. But there, you see: why was I letting my thoughts wander at all at a time like this?

Next you have to find the top of your tracksuit bottoms, and the tight waistband of your long thermal pants. By

186

that time, even in the shelter of the van, your hands are getting cold so you can't feel details or fastenings . . .

When Sigurd's chilly hands found the crumpled red silk of my Paris skirt packed down the leg of my thermals, he rather lost momentum. I explained about the slit made by the falling icicle, and how I was hoping the silk would keep the cold from getting in, and when he found the silk had stuck to all the blood, he peeled it off ever so gently and fetched the first aid kit. 'Can you do it?' he said glumly. 'I don't really do blood.'

And there, inside the first aid box, were the home-made tea bags! All that were left of them, anyway. They were colour coded: red label and mint green; blue for murder and yellow for cowards? I didn't know. Neither of us knew. That was the trouble. Which ones would kill? Which would bring on nothing worse than a stomach-ache? Which would send Victor to sleep and which would perk him up with a mild dose of tannin? I don't know what I had expected: instructions for use? A skull and crossbones? Government health warnings?

We had to abandon the idea of being poisoners, because how can you poison a man with camomile, or finish him with what might turn out to be Earl Grey?

In torrid whispers, heads close, reminding one another of what he had done to us, we settled on killing Uncle Victor by brute force. With an ice axe. (I should say, in our defence, that we were very, very scared.)

An ice axe has four blades: a standard cutting-edge, a banana blade, a semi-tubular one for boring holes in the ice for tent pegs and suchlike—and a hammer adze. If you fall over on a glacier or if a gust of wind threatens to throw you to your death, you're supposed to grab the axe-head with one hand and the shaft with the other and ram the banana blade into the ice. Jon taught us that a hundred years ago, when we were innocent tourists and children and not paying close attention. If his ice axe lesson explained how to brain a man, I can't have been listening. But as we watched and waited for Victor to sleep, we twisted the complex weapons in our hands and wondered how it should be done.

'Why didn't you say? About your leg?' Sigurd asked accusingly. But what answer could I give? At school, if you're ill, there's the sick bay to go to, lessons to miss, an advantage to be gained. Where would it get me now, here? Also, since belief is optional in these parts, I'm choosing *not to believe* in the cut in my leg. This is not a good place for getting injured.

'Sleep, Uncle Victor.'

Now that Manfred was gone, there was no one to share the driving. Sigurd insisted he didn't know how, and I couldn't reach the pedals. At long last, Victor was obliged to stop and rest.

The no-noise of the Ice Shelf was left behind, and the mountains were not quiet at all. Thuds and rumbles emanated from the steep, black fangs of rock, as somewhere, out-of-sight, avalanches slipped down, seracs crumbled, wind blundered off the Polar Plateau into the first solid object in its path.

We two lay quite still—stationary—knowing we had reached the spot where we would kill Uncle Victor, where he would die, where we would dispose of him in a shallow grave hacked out with the correct blade of a regulation ice axe. (When people find us—when the search parties pick up our trail—we don't want to get into trouble, do we?)

In the end, we settled on using the hammer adze, what with Sigurd not doing blood.

We waited for Victor to fall asleep: his seat swung back and away from the steering column, his body sprawled in the tub seat (so much less therapeutic than the Vibro-Chair®). When we were sure he was asleep, we would

188

creep up either side of the van, wrench open the doors and . . .

I imagined his eyes flickering beneath his lids as he dreamed of his underground El Dorado. I hoped his dreams would be in black-and-white, though, so they'd make less mess when they spilled.

And then, as we waited, my memory gave a violent, reflex twitch of its muscles. I didn't ask to remember. I didn't want to. But suddenly I realized that, of course, I already knew of an assassin whose advice we could ask, someone who had already killed with an ice axe. I had read his confession in one of those many, many Ice books Victor gave me as he trained me up to be his underworld Ice Maiden.

'Tell me again how it's done, Titus,' I said.

'*On the way back from the depot-laying trip, Bowers and Crean and Cherry got into big trouble between Safety Camp and Hut Point. The sea ice had thawed and it was breaking up under them. They camped overnight on an ice floe—woke up to find the floe had split in half. Nothing but a streak of water where Guts had been. Poor Guts. That's why the killer whales turned up. And the skuas. Horseflesh on the menu. Anyway, Bowers and Co. managed to jump the other ponies from floe to floe and get them pretty close to the shore. The rest of us were there by then, trying everything we could to get them off. They tried to jump Punch over the gap, but he didn't make it. He went in.*'

Titus paused, swallowing, turning his ice pick over and over in his hand, testing the sharpness of the tip with the ball of his thumb. (It wasn't much of a tool in comparison with our fancy four-bladed jobs.) '*Poor old thing,*' said Titus, blinking over-fast. '*Struggling in the water. Terrified. Freezing. He'd go under, then come up again, coughing, shrieking . . . I could see his eyes coming up through the water towards me . . . The killers were closing in for a feast. Couldn't have that.*

189

'Difficult to put in a clean blow, though, what with him thrashing about and me wet through and starting to freeze up. It took a few . . . We were nose to nose, pretty much. And I kept remembering feeding him on the trek we'd just done, building ice walls for him—and for what? This? All for it to end like this.

'There was a terrific storm on the voyage from England— waves pounding over the ship, flooding the pony quarters all night long, knocking them over. Spent all night propping the little beggars back on their feet. Seeing Punch there in the water, I could remember myself, arms round his neck, dragging him to his feet over and over—Come on, old boy. Come on . . .

'Made my gorge heave, but I couldn't leave him alive in the water, not with the whales there. So I hit him. And hit him again. And again. Until he went quiet and sank.

'After that Birdie Bowers's horse went down, too, and I could see the beast was done for. I should have done Birdie a favour and killed that one, too—he didn't ask me to—said it was his horse and he'd do it himself, but what does a Navy man know about animals? Nothing . . . Thing is, I knew I'd be sick if I had to kill another horse the way I had Punch. So I showed him where to put the ice pick in—here or here . . .' And Titus spread a hand shaking with cold, wet with blood, across his own face (streaming with saltwater and melting ice) to show where the skull is most vulnerable to a sharp blow . . . 'The ponies weren't of my choosing, poor little duffers, and I'd've chosen better, but you get fond of a beast—even the demons who want to break your shins or bite the ears off your head . . . I've done better work than that day on the sea ice, I have to say.'

Then he took hold of the pick by its head, and turned the handle towards me.

'Of course to get the right degree of force, you have to take a back swing, and the movement scares the beast and it jerks aside, and the point goes through the cheek or bounces off the mane *and then you're in trouble, because the pony's trying to get away from you, whereas up to then you had its trust . . .'*

I reached out for the handle . . .

*'Be sure and bury the creature's head. You may be glad of it on the way back. You know, we dug up Christopher's head, but it was rotten.'*

I took hold of the handle but it was soft to the touch and recoiled from my fingers, and I woke and found I had, in my sleep, pushed my hand into Sigurd's face as he slept on the bench seat opposite.

So I told Sigurd I didn't think I would be killing Uncle Victor with an ice axe, and he said that he had come to much the same conclusion himself, though he did not describe his dream and I didn't describe mine. There's a fearful intimacy about sharing dreams.


I don't know who Axel Heiberg was. A hole in my knowledge. A paragraph I skipped. A page Dad burned, I don't know. I do know that the glacier named after him used to be called something else: this torrent of ice pouring down out of the sky. This Amundsen's Glacier. There are wave terraces built into it of contorted bands of blue and white ice. There are chasms, icefalls, and splaying crevasses in this stairway to the Plateau. Seracs—ice pinnacles—stand here and there, in the shape of chimneys and sometimes, when the sun is in one particular quadrant of the sky, you could mistake them for figures or statues. Like Lot's wife in the Bible, who looked back and was turned to salt.

The angle of ascent was getting steeper. Our boots were good, but not good enough. As Sigurd and I walked ahead of the Hagglund, prodding ominous dips in the snow, we struggled to keep our feet. Terrifying. Once, where there was no snow for the tracks to grip, the tank slid backwards, dragging us off our feet. Terrifying. Twice, three times we saw (or imagined) a dip in the snow with a yellowish tinge to it, and edged sideways and made detours. The noise of every manoeuvre was duplicated—multiplied by countless echoes bouncing back off walls of rock. We trudged on, sealed up inside our own thoughts, like vacuum-packed mackerel and no scissors to prise us open.

But then suddenly Sigurd pointed up at a serac on the slopes above us and began grinning and waving. 'I didn't know you had a sister! Look, she's the spitting image of you! It *is* you!' And to prove it he cupped his hands round his mouth and called out. 'Hellooo!'

The figure on the mountainside duly returned his call. *'Hellooo!'* To my eyes it looked like a child on Hallowe'en, draped in a sheet. But in comparison with how I knew I was looking, it seemed quite a compliment. Sigurd called again: *'DO YOU LOVE ME, SYM? I LOVE YOU!'* and out of the jumble of echoes came the distinct reply: *'I LOVE YOU!'* The mountain growled its disapproval, like a pair of elderly oppressive parents, and then the serac laughed out loud— a girl's voice that could only have been mine. Sigurd looked at me shyly out of the corner of his eye and nodded towards the mountain, wanting me to join in, wanting me to send him a message via this snow-haired go-between. *'I'LL LOVE YOU FOR EVER, SIGURD!'* he called, falsetto, so that the girl on the mountainside declared her undying love and I covered my face in delicious embarrassment. The echoes streamed past my head like banners. It was fun! It was lovely! The sun shone with real warmth on the back of my head, and something trickled through me that was just as pleasant. He wanted me to call out myself—looked at me intently, all smiles and bright blue eyes, and nodded again towards the mountain, egging me on. Well and why not? We were practically lovers . . .

192

'*I LOVE*—'

Then the first shot rang out, and we threw ourselves on our stomachs and slid helplessly downhill on slippery neoprene, tangling in our own safety ropes. It was Manfred Bruch! It had to be him! Dogging our footsteps, he had lain in ambush, knowing the route we would take, and now he had us in his sights! I pictured him, foot turned under, bare hands drawn up his sleeves, panning and zooming, fading and cutting through the lens of a telescopic rifle. Orange, like Sunny Delight, stained the snow where Sigurd crouched on hands and knees, shuddering.

Then the glacier cracked its knuckles again, ice moving with jerky but imperceptible slowness, giving off cracks as loud as pistol shots. Not Manfred Bruch after all, but a far more dangerous enemy: unthinking, implacable Nature. Our nerves were stretched like piano wires and this place was systematically breaking them, note by note. The glacier's thunderous rumblings weren't funny any more: they tied my guts in knots. Its snapping fibres broke our hearts with every deafening crack.


After lunch, as we were refuelling and I was holding the funnel for Uncle Victor, Sigurd held his belly and said he had to go. A bolt of fear went through me, in case his stomach ache meant he had somehow earned Victor's annoyance and he was poisoned, too. But Sigurd himself did not seem worried, and I was proud of him for walking off out of sight, to relieve himself in privacy.

We waited and waited, I to congratulate him on his bravery, Victor to get under way.

'I'll have to come and go, of course,' Victor said, tipping the heavy can. From inside it came half-thawed diesel— a sort of diesel Slush-Puppy. 'I'll have to keep the Outside World informed about my observations. But you and whatsisname—the boy—you can establish yourselves. Permanent like. Job for the young that. Pioneering. By! What I'd give to be your age again!'

'Establish ourselves?'

'Blaze the way, manner of thing.'

One pair of humans. For delivery to the inner spheres of the Earth.

'To my way of thinking, their Science will be more advanced. Politics, too. Meritocracy, wouldn't be surprised. If my projections are right, it won't be a bad place to raise nippers.'

A breeding pair, even.

'Look at those first settlers in America! Virginia! Look where that led!' said Victor triumphantly.

Wrong. The first ones died. I know I had a shoddy education, Victor, but the Virginians weren't the first colonists in America. The first settlers died. To a man. To a girl. I don't say so, though, because I promised Sigurd not to cross Victor, not to do anything to make him mad. Wait till Sigurd hears that ours was a one-way journey—only ever a one-way journey; no return ticket; no going back. Victor means us to set up home together in the Underworld.

'How will *you* get back, uncle?' I asked. 'After you leave us there. There's not enough diesel for anything. Fifty kilometres. Anything.' Was he envisaging an industrialized Underworld, then, complete with transport for the use of visitors? Scott's motor sleds recycled, perhaps. Alien jetpacks. RentaSled. A bus terminus. A Mercedes concession. Would they have diesel as well as five-star unleaded in their subterranean pumps? Uncle Victor didn't answer my question about how he was going to get home. Oh, I'm sure he *has* an answer. I think the question may have offended him by calling his planning into doubt.

\*     \*     \*

194

Ten minutes passed but we thought nothing of that. Victor in particular thought nothing of it; after all, he was hard put even to remember Sigurd's name. Then a voice came down the mountain:

'*I've found it! It's here! Come quick!*' It was a high, hallooing voice—echoes muddling the words into one another—but the urgency still plain, the wild joy unmistakable. '*I've found it! They're down there! I've seen them! Come quick. Come now! Come quick. Come see! I'M UP HERE!*'

My leg was stiff from sitting. The glacier ice was slick. Along the rim of the white highway a crevasse of prodigious width bared its sapphire teeth. But we did not stop to think.

'*Come quick! There's someone down there! It was true what you said! My God! It's vast! And look at that!*'

Victor was running and skidding, crawling and slipping, sinking his axe into the ice to get purchase, sobbing with the exertion. I hoped he wouldn't slip. I hoped Sigurd wouldn't do anything foolish until we got there. I hoped the faces he was seeing were friendly. Then I didn't think anything any more, except where to put my feet, how to walk and not to fall, how to suck in the cold air without paying for it in pain, how to keep the strain off my left leg . . . When Sigurd stopped calling, I was terrified.

We must have climbed a hundred metres, cursing the lack of crampons, scared by the crevasse but all the time drawn to it, for where else would Sigurd *be* on this great white down-escalator to the sky! How far could he possibly have got in so short a time and why would a call of nature have brought him so far from the tank? He can't have been looking for a bush! After the flatness of the Shelf the gradient of the glacier was enough to make us sweat. 'Wait, uncle!'

Victor was in no mood to wait. The cracks of the moving ice had no power to make him even flinch, so intent was he on reaching Sigurd's side—seeing whatever Sigurd was seeing.

'Uncle, wait!'

'*Cry out, lad! Let's hear you!*' Victor bawled through cupped hands, his goggles on top of his head, his jacket pulled loose at the throat.

'We'd be quicker in the tank!' I called, and turned round and looked back.

From lower down the mountain, you might even have mistaken me for a figure carved in ice. Or Lot's wife, turned to salt.

At first the sun was so bright in the glass of the windows that I could not see which way the Hagglund was facing—only the exhaust fumes hovering in the air above it. Then I saw the flash of the wing mirrors as it completed its turn and started out along the railway lines of its own tracks. Sigurd. He had cut loose the Nansen and thrown things out of the van on to the ice—dark mounds of cloth and equipment. A big suitcase. Tea bags. They made it look as if the vehicle had answered a call of Nature. Now he sped away, stealing the Hagglund, seizing the slimmest of chances not to die. Shedding surplus baggage in the process.

You have to admire his cleverness: to use the echo-effect to suggest he was above us on the mountain. You have to admire his forethought, in testing out, ahead of time, whether it would work or not: throwing his voice to the ice-girl on the mountain, hearing her return it.

Perhaps I should just say, in his defence, that he was very, very scared.

Behind me, somewhere in the mountains, a corniche of snow subsided. Or perhaps it was an icefall breaking from its crag, or a serac crumbling.

Polish the windows of Glasstown, Deighton, and tell the Captain I'm coming home tonight.

# Chapter Nineteen

*'Between you and me, things aren't quite as rosy as they might be.'—Oates*

We have come a long way. The air up here is thinner. Fear falls like acid rain; Victor must surely feel it. He is shedding skin like a bird moulting. He's shedding weight, too. He eats as he would at home, holding true to the articles of his dietary religion. And yet we are burning calories like it's Bonfire Night. I can see their ash floating past my eyes as they burn.

Gaffer tape doesn't last, I notice. There's red silk spilling out through the slit in my salopettes, but the cold is so intense that often I can't feel it, only the stiffening of tendons, the beating of my heart, the clinging of my lungs to my backbone like two sick pigeons in a tree. We are hauling the sled towards the summit of the Axel Heiberg—Amundsen's glacier. A few icefalls, then we'll be on the Polar Plateau. A white hole. Life in negative. Not just a lack of anything, but a space ready to devour existence itself. Off it comes the wind, incessant, everlasting, inexhaustible wind. It never stops to draw breath. It licks the heat off you like a great animal toying with its food. They say the Ice tries to break a man open and reduce him to the essence. Won't find anything inside me, eh, Titus?

*'Time to find out, dearie.'*

'Sigurd knew. He got the measure of me. I really thought Sigurd liked me. But he was just a con-merchant, like the other one.'

*'Far too young for you, anyway,'* says Titus, straight-backed and bristling slightly. *'125 is altogether a better age.'*

'I thought Uncle Victor loved me. But he only wants to drop me in a hole in the ground—sacrifice me to the great god Symmes. It's Symmes he loves. The whole idea of Symmes. Even the books he gave me—even all my lovely books—the books where I read about you! They were just Victor *educating me up* for all this stuff. Even my name . . . Even my name was a part of it—part of his great Obsession.'

*'People do the oddest things,'* says Titus, whirling one fur mitten on the end of its tape. *'My mother was so grief-stricken when I died that she slept in my bedroom for the rest of her life—to feel close to me, I suppose, surrounded by my things. But she burned my Polar diaries.'*

Burned them? His diaries? The words he had formed in his head; the words he had shaped by the movement of his hand? The pages he had brushed with the side of his wrist as he wrote? She burned them. Unimaginable.

*'Don't struggle too hard to understand people, Sym. They're hideously complicated. Unhappy people do the oddest, most terrible things, just trying to keep despair at bay. All you have to do is accept them . . . go round them . . . take avoiding action.'*


When we put up the tent, it wrestles and buffets around our heads like the ravings of the mad, and although Sigurd probably off-loaded it with the best of intentions, he forgot to off-load the pegs. We lash it down to the sled, but it is really only our weight that holds it to the ground. And we are lightweights now, both of us. So the wind still picks up the tent at the corners. We are nothing but swag in a giant's sack, the cloth lashing around our ears, making as much din as a dozen snare drums. It is impossible to talk.

For all kinds of reasons.

We have to get the sled down the icefalls; it's our life-support capsule. I've come to hate it, like a convict must hate his ball-and-chain. But in a place where everything else is ten million years old, it represents civilization, I suppose: salvage from a previous life.

Somewhere along the way, we must have passed the Butcher's Shop: the place where Amundsen culled his dogs from thirty to eighteen. Too many to feed, and their meat was needed. It's a dog-eat-dog world up here. Their ghosts have taken a liking to us because I can feel their jaws around my thigh and I can hear their howling all the time, all the time.

Except from Glasstown, of course.

There the windows are tight shut and the fires are lit. There, Florence Chambers and Titus Oates tell each other stories, play bagatelle, and wax nostalgic to the sound of the pianola. I am . . . she is . . . teaching Titus the words of Cole Porter:

*Whenever the skies look grey to me*
*And trouble begins to brew . . .*

. . . which is quite a feat for an Edwardian, I can tell you. Titus reciprocates with 'The Turnip and the Fly'—a cleaner version, I suspect, than the one he sang at Hut Point. He sings baritone, but his range is . . . well, limitless. A free-range baritone, you might say. For his voice goes as deep as regret and as high as . . . as high as here: this airless place. He is anywhere I am. He is inside me and my brain closes round him like hands round a warm drink. In fact

199

he's more a part of me than my own limbs, because even though Amundsen's dog-ghosts sink their teeth into my cut thigh, they can't reach deep enough to rip out Titus. And, oh, I am so glad of him.

Even though no one else in the world can find me now, he is never out of reach. Even though Time is a one-way street and it's not taking me anywhere I want to go, with Titus I can travel to and fro through Time—to the Boer War, the Indian raj, the Curragh Races, Gestingthorpe in high summer, Hut Point . . . There was an Otes at the Battle of Hastings in 1066, you know? (I wonder if he was scared, too.) From the windows of Glasstown I can see into the future, as well—as far forward as my fifteenth birthday, when Titus has promised to take me to the top of the Eiffel Tower! I can't express how glad I am of him.

Uncle Victor also has plans for my fifteenth birthday. He pictures it happening in one of the inner spheres of the hollow Earth. He described it to me in the tent yesterday but what with the noise from the loose fabric rattling and thrashing at our heads all I could picture was a piñata with us inside and a thousand maniacal kids thwacking it with sticks. I don't any longer listen, I'm afraid, to his theories of cold fusion and hydroponic food production or how sunlight is deflected underground. I have to concentrate very hard, you see, to get deep enough inside my head, and it doesn't allow for listening and nodding and watching his lips so as to fill in the gaps in my hearing, and agreeing and asking sensible questions. And minding.


Sometimes, when I help Mum change the beds at home and a snow of dust flies up, it does terrible things to her airways. She starts wheezing and coughing and forgetting how to breathe. The effect is the same up here— Polar asthma. The air is thin, the air pressure is low, and each breath has only half the oxygen in it. Your pulses race and your heart thumps like someone live trying to get out of a sealed coffin. Whose sloughed skin and blanket-fluff and dust-mite droppings are these, flurrying and whirling about our heads as we disturb this white bed of a landscape? This is the kind of place where Nature recommends you don't exert yourself, ha ha! This is the kind of place where Nature doesn't recommend strapping a harness across your chest and leaning into it till your head throbs like a Belisha beacon and your chest cavity feels like a portion of Chinese spare ribs.

That's why it's so good to go instead to the Turf Club in Ghezira, and watch Titus playing polo, his long legs tucked tight around his latest protégé of a pony. The only things Titus has ever 'trained up' for his personal use are horses and beagle pups. Never apprentice girls as breeding stock for the Underworld.

*'Meet my friend Roly Barnard. He can run faster backwards than most people can run forwards. You can win money betting on him! Go on. He won't mind.'*

I miss my own friends, though. If I were back in England now, at school, I reckon I'd have a bit more to say for myself than I did—though I'd have to be careful: no one likes it, do they, when someone swanks about expensive foreign holidays? Here's a questionnaire for you, Nikki, about holiday romances.

---

**WHAT COULD *YOU* PICK UP ON HOLIDAY?!!!**

*What's your idea of a hot destination!?!*
    *A Croxley Green*
    *B the Polar Plateau*
    *C the Underworld*

---

*What would you pack (apart from a six-pack)!!!?*
  A *Snow goggles*
  B *a copy of* The Peninsular War
  C *morphine*

*Who would you choose to go long-haul with??!!!*
  A *Pengwings Expeditions*
  B *your uncle*
  C *Italia Conti*

*What is your perfect holiday date?*
  *2006*
  *1912*
  *1066*

*What dish would you and your holiday dish share!???!!!*
  A *Beach b-b-q*
  B *city restaurant*
  C *herring in formaldehyde*

*What would you wear to score!?!?!*
  A *Snow goggles*
  B *10 layers of neoprene*
  C *an Edwardian riding habit*

*Which of these foreign languages could you get your tongue round???!!??!*
  A *Norwegian*
  B *Swearing*
  C *Lying*

*Oh, those memories! What's your idea of a great souvenir??!!*
  A *My hair*
  B *a husky*
  C *a Hagglund all-terrain vehicle*

*PS: Sorry if snow goggles crop up rather a lot, Nikki; it's because my eyes are giving me trouble.*
*PPS: I'd've sent a picture postcard, but there'd be nothing on it. Only way you could paint the Polar Plateau is to leave the paper blank.*

At the sight of Sigurd driving the Hagglund away, Uncle Victor tore off his glasses and threw them on the ground in anger. The metal bridge had frozen to his face, though, and he ripped off a large piece of skin from the space between his eyes. I don't believe he even noticed. Luckily, I picked up the glasses, because when he realized that he had left his snow goggles in the driver's van, he needed to use mine. At least I *thought* it was lucky to have pocketed Victor's glasses, except that when I got them out of my pocket I found that both lenses were missing. They must have dropped out when they hit the ground.

The ultra-violet light reflects off the snow and burns the cornea. At first it feels like when you peel onions, then like when you open the oven door and something's burning and the smoke is acrid in your face.

Then it gets really bad.

Now there's the added joy of ice crystals. They form a haze in the air—like tiny fragments of razor blade that slice into the eye. A sandstorm, but of ice.

At school, Nats obsessively doodles eyes during lessons. Always eyes. The longer the lesson, the fuller the lashes, the more biro-black the iris and eyebrow. I can picture them now, like Egyptian hieroglyphs looking at me, looking at me, and I'd like a page of them here now: Nats's weird talismanic eyes like the ones the Greeks painted on the prows of their boats so as not to lose their way.

'What do you miss most?' I asked the man with the most beautiful eyes on the planet.

203

'*The smell of damp earth,*' he said. '*It's so dry here in India, don't you find?*'

Actually the whole business of eBay fossils and Thoughtisfree.com and Manfred and Sigurd (and similar sharp pieces of razor blade), sets me brooding about Maxine. I hope Waldron is not just another Manfred. I hope he is the genuine article and not a Chinese replica. I hope Maxine is not one in a long line of internet conquests. I hope that Waldron is his real name (insofar as I'd wish that on anyone) and that he won't take her money or anything else she doesn't want to give. I hope he's nice. After all, who am I to criticize her for liking the older man?

There again, everyone's capable of deception; that's another thing I've learned. So maybe it's not just Waldron whose honesty I should be doubting. Maybe the great internet romance didn't all happen *quite* as Maxine said— the parties, the flowers, the glamour, the passion—or maybe she gave us the edited highlights. Maybe it never happened at all, in fact. Any of it. A happy thought. 'Bet it only ever happened in her head,' I whisper gloatingly to Titus.

'*Only?*' says Titus sharply, and tramps off for a cigarette.


Though we have skis in the Nansen, it has become impossible to ski. The sastrugi here have surfaces like millions of fishhooks. When you fall, they try to keep hold of you. I didn't notice when it began: so unobservant. I don't remember much between here and the icefalls. Strange that I can remember the names of all Titus's horses, but not how we got down the icefalls. There must have been icefalls, because this is Amundsen's glacier and I've read a dozen times his account of reaching the Pole. 'It all went like a dream.' (Must have had very different dreams from me, is all I can say.)

204

The tent, when we camp, wrestles with us. Through the groundsheet, I can still feel the fishhook sastrugi, except when the wind lifts us clear off the ground before dropping us back down again. You could probably tenderize octopuses like this. Never mind hitting them on a rock: just put them in a waterproof bag and slam it up and down on hooked ice. Our sleeping bags writhe and heave as we lie in them. It doesn't help ease the nausea that comes with altitude and a diet of sild and dried dates and Oxo broth. But sleep solves all that.

Sleep is there the moment we get out of the wind. Despite the noise and the hunger and the raging thirst, the need to light the emergency primus and thaw snow, the need to make the broth . . . sleep slows movement as if we were under water. No need for Victor's narcotic teabags here; I have to fight my way through long folds of sleep like heavy velvet curtains before I can shove food into my mouth. Romeo and Juliet never made more eagerly for bed than I do for my sleeping bag—my sanctuary from Victor's endless talking, my wormhole to another solar system, my portal into my interior world. There's a masculine smell in my stolen Pengwings sleeping bag. The top part comes right over your head and zips completely closed: the perfect hiding-place when the Devil has his hooves over his eyes and is counting to twenty. Nudged by the wall of the unsecured tent, I feel as if someone restless is lying against my back, their body against the curve of my spine.

'I'm sorry I brought you here again, Titus.'

*'Don't mention it, Sym. I wasn't doing anything else in particular.'*

I would like to turn over and see his eyes, but then I am asleep—as quickly as that—like the Wolf falling down the Three Pigs' chimney into a cauldron of boiling dreams.

I dream I'm riding pillion on Titus's motorcycle, down

205

a stony road. The suspension of these old bikes is terrible, but with my arms around his waist, I can feel the curve of his ribcage through his linen shirt, the big, syncopated beat of his heart and the swell of his diaphragm as he takes quick gulps of the sweet, flowery air. The Boers are shooting at us and I can see the holes their bullets make in the cloth of my school coat, but they don't seem to have hit me yet. From time to time, Boer outriders on motorbikes and side-car, or on horseback, draw level and enquire politely if he would care to surrender. But Titus declines, equally polite but insistent. The bike is almost out of petrol, but he has arranged with his friend Roly Barnard for an alternative means of transport to be waiting: a hot-air balloon.

It billows in the distance, a funnel of blood-red silk; I can hear the roar of the burners, big as aeroplane jet engines—pouring their heat into its envelope. We have to drive through the blast of flame, and I expect it to incinerate us, but it scorches nothing but my eyes. Already the basket beneath it is bumping along the ground. Guy ropes trailing, the balloon swells and bellies and strains, fuller and fuller, eager to be airborne. Titus dismounts before the bike has even stopped moving—and I must have done, too, because now we are in the basket of the balloon.

But Titus has left something behind—his honour?—his pet deer? He swings his great long legs back over the basket-side and, without the smallest difficulty, drops to the ground. For some reason, though, I can't persuade my own legs to move, to bend, to lift over the towering sides of the basket, now crenellated and garrisoned like a castle wall. Looking up, I realize that it is not a silk balloon envelope hovering over me at all, but the solid sphere of a planet, open at the base and full of fire.

'*Get out! Get out!*' yells Titus, and I want to, but my leg

206

is so painful and my eyelids are stuck together with gum
Arabic, and the basket is tipping so violently . . .

'Get out! Get out, lass!'

Uncle Victor, waking and instantly determined to get
going, crawled out of his bag, and shouldered his way
out of the round tent door. The tent, relieved of his weight,
had no reason to hold its shape. It rolled over. The ground-
sheet became the side wall, and like a windsock the whole
thing strained away from the Nansen, moulded by the
wind into a flaccid sack. Victor was on the outside; I was
left inside.

Even when I am out of my bag I can't at first find the
door hole, because I am lying on top of it. Empty food
jars ricochet about like giant bluebottles. A torch hits me
in the face. Also my boots. My boots! Mustn't lose my
boots, no matter what! Both sleeping bags wind themselves around me. Briefly I can see Victor's silhouette
through the wall as he tries to get hold of the tent. Then
I am through the hole, dragging the sleeping bags with
me willy-nilly, holding a boot in each hand, plunging like
a diver out of a diving bell into freezing water.

The sled is hopping—actually hopping—over the ice,
dragged by the guy ropes and the blowing tent. Free to
rise even further into the air, the tent instantly fills with
wind, emptying out bits of equipment—the torch, my
axe. We daren't grab the ropes to haul it in; the sled
runners would smash our feet or legs. So there's nothing
to do but watch as the tent drags the sled along—a
great kite rattling in the sky. The sled begins to pick up
speed. In socked feet, I can't run on these fishhook
sastrugi.

Uncle Victor stands lifting his hands and letting them
drop back to his sides, swearing vilely. I push my feet
into my boots but it's hard—it's hard, Titus!—it's hard,
Mum! You use so many muscles in your leg to get into

207

a pair of boots! As I run, laces flying, laces catching in the ghastly frozen Astroturf, the bandage round my thigh slips down. Getting skinny. Smoke from the burning calories is stinging my eyes.

As the sled baulks at a seam in the ice, I catch up and swing my axe at it—at the half hitches fastening the ropes to the sled. But they've swollen into Gordian knots of compacted ice and at once the sled is off again, beetling along faster than huskies or a skidoo could pull it.

In the end, the ropes snap off the tent. It rises and rises and rises, tumbling and diminishing in size, until an opaque roof of white haze swallows it from sight. A kilometre away our sled lies on its side: lacings frayed, pulling-harnesses spilled out on to the ice.

'Now look what you've done,' says Uncle Victor ambling up behind me.


We are ugly, Neanderthal people, big pawed, knock-kneed, drunken, reeling people, no better than the apes—can't join fingertip to thumb-tip—wiping our noses on pads of sheep's wool, eyes fixed on the ground in front of our feet. Mindless, Ice Age people with nothing in mind but food and shelter and sleeping out the pain. Stupid, bovine people shoved from side to side by wind and weariness. Yeti people, round-shouldered and slow, looking for somewhere to become extinct.

But yes. All right, yes! Buck up! Maybe Victor's right! Never say die! If Victor's right, there's a chance we won't. Die, I mean. By tonight or tomorrow night, he says, we'll find Symmes's Hole and climb down into its cavernous gloomy warmth. Be greeted by pallid albino faces. Smiling, maybe! He knows so much. The number of rivets in the Forth Bridge—the melting point of glass—everything! Perhaps he has been right all along! Yes! By tonight we'll

208

find Symmes's Hole! We will! We must! This is an adventure! That's what happens in adventures!

*'What happened to me, Sym?'* snaps Titus, and for some reason he's really angry. I didn't ask him to come to mind, but suddenly he's there anyway, and he's shouting. *'What happened to me, Sym?'*

And he's so real that I can see the way the hairs spring from his hairline, the length of his lashes, and the rim of white around the hazel of his eyes. And he's ragingly angry. *'What became of Lawrence Oates? Was he snatched up to heaven like Elijah in a chariot of fire? What happened? Answer me!'*

But I can't answer him. I can see the water-vapour on his breath, the darkness of tomorrow's beard beneath his skin, the asymmetry of his lips. That's why I can't afford to answer him.

*'What became of me when I went outside into the blizzard? Did I put on wings of snow?'*

'No, Titus.'

*'Or get trampled by the stampeding ghosts of all those poor ponies I slaughtered?'*

'No.'

*'Was I suckled like Romulus and Remus, maybe, by a colony of cheerful dinosaurs?'*

'No, Titus.'

*'No! Use your common sense, girl. Use your head!'*

I don't want to use my head. My head aches.

*'Do you think I'm held prisoner in the palace of the Ice Queen, with a sliver of ice in my heart?'*

'Don't, Titus, don't.'

*'What happened to me? Did I scurry underground like the White Rabbit, into Symmes's Wonderland?'*

'No. Stop.'

*'Use your common sense, Sym!'*

He is so real that I can feel the warmth emanating from his body and see the pulse beat in his throat and the dark hair move above his wristwatch at the brush of his cuff. And in all my life I have never wanted anything, anyone so much; never so much wanted Time to stop. Here. Now. No more thinking. No more deciding. Because if I speak the words in my mouth, he will be gone—will blow out like a flame and leave me in the dark, with nothing but the Fear and the Cold. I pull my hands up inside my sleeves, so that I won't make a grab for him. I shut my eyes so as not to see how his lips shape and release each word and how the pupils of his eyes dilate and contract with the force of emotion:

*'Answer me, Sym! Because I'm perpetually thirty-two, maybe you think I'm Christ Almighty? Maybe you think I went for a three-day warm in Hell, then rose again on the third day?'*

But I refuse to say. Because I love him, and you'd give anything, wouldn't you? You'd give anything for someone you love not to die alone and in scalding agony?

He is everything, everything, everything I ever admired and wanted and couldn't have. He is everything I needed and couldn't find in real life.

Of course he is.

That's why I invented him.


'All right! You died! Lawrence Oates died! He crawled on and on until the pain paralysed him—until the walls of his lungs froze and he couldn't breathe, and the vitreous in his eyeballs froze and blinded him, and his arms wouldn't lift his face off the ground any more and his damaged thighbone snapped. Then he froze to death and the snow buried him!'

There is no Hole. There is no cosy subterranean world inside a hollow Earth. Victor believes in it because he wants it so much to be there. He's mad. He has probably been mad for years.

I do not pass on this stunning insight to Titus. Because of course he cannot hear it. He isn't there either—doesn't exist, hasn't existed for ninety years. In fact my Titus never existed. Just a pretend friend. Just someone I invented, out of loneliness. *Like little kids do-hoo-hoo. Like the little kids do.* Once you understand about madness, you're not allowed to go on being mad, are you? You have to grow up, buck up, shape up, wise up, get real, marshal your facts, think on.

I must open my eyes now, because otherwise the tears will make my lashes freeze together. You have to be careful crying in this kind of cold. I ease one hand out of its big glove and quickly wipe the sockets of my eyes.

And there, ten metres ahead, back turned on the perpetual wind—from under that blanket-cloth cap, from above the collar of that strangely homely, Navy-issue cardigan, Captain 'Titus' Oates flashes me the most dazzling of smiles.

It is all the smiles I have craved from every face I ever met.

*'Thank God for sanity!'* he says, speaking through the frozen clouds of his own breath. *'Stick with me, girl. We know this place, you and I. That's what's going to get you out of here.'*

# Chapter Twenty
### *'It was not a very big hole.'—Oates*

But it's not true, Titus. I don't know spit! It's right what they say: you can read everything written, but nothing prepares you . . . What do I know that's going to be any use at all?

*'Cherry used to use wads of old tea leaves to . . .'*

'All right, I know. I'll give that a try, but that's nothing . . .'

*'Not poisoned ones, of course.'*

'Obviously.'

So I make compresses for my eyes, using Twinings English Breakfast Blend teabags, doing as Apsley Cherry-Garard did ninety years ago, and it does give a bit of relief from the pain of the snowblindness. But it's not exactly Air-Sea Rescue, is it?

*'Birdie found that taping over his specs . . .'*

'All right, all right, Titus. But it's like throwing bread rolls at a charging rhino is all I'm saying.' So I tape over Victor's glasses, doing as Birdie Bowers did ninety years ago to protect his eyes from scorching, leaving nothing but a pinprick-sized hole to see through. Victor goes on using my snow goggles and I use the taped glasses. From any distance I must look as if I was born without eyes. Snowblind leading the snowblind. Ah well, I always preferred looking inwards to looking out.

Unfortunately the sun-block is back on board the Hagglund, so my own skin is starting to blister and scab. What a joyous sight we would make for my mother now: two public monuments pocked by air pollution. Victims of Polar shot-peening. That's what it is, you know, shot-peening. It's blasting things clean by bombarding them with . . . with what? My concentration is terrible up here. Whole sentences—whole thoughts go astray and wander off into the haze to be lost for ever. No wonder grey and white are the colours of old age.

'What about Mum?' I asked, wondering if he had even given her a thought in all this, wondering if she would ever find out the circumstances of our death. I am perfectly sure he never phoned her that night long ago in Paris, never gained her blessing for this infernal trip. Just lied to me, as to everybody else.

'Don't you fret on her account, Sym. Lillian and I have an understanding on that front.' And he crossed his middle finger over his index finger and gave a wink. Plainly he could see himself back in Croxley Green, after his triumphant return, feet up on the coffee table, my mother cooking his supper. 'She'll be right proud, lass. Don't you fret. I'll look after her. We go way back. We've always had an understanding, Lillian and I.'

No.

I am almost grateful to you, Victor. Tell me there are worlds-within-worlds. By all means. Who am I to argue? Tell me there are dragons in the sky. Tell me that space dust is the sperm of cosmic whales, that Man was made to walk on his hands, that money grows on trees. But the Fount of All Knowledge ran dry the moment you said my mother and you 'have an understanding'. I'd laugh if I thought I could ever stop. Muster your data, Sym. Keep your eye on the ball. Verify your facts. Revise your subject. Pursue your argument. Answer the question. Open your

213

eyes. Use your loaf. Check your answers. Remember your manners. Do as you're told. Tell the truth. The truth is, Victor, there are some things that are, and there are things that just ain't so. Even if Mum never finds out that you stole her passport and emptied the bank, bankrupted the family business, kidnapped her daughter, and murdered her husband, she still thinks you are a pompous boor—a humourless, hectoring know-all and a bit of a bully. She is just too polite to say so, knowing how reliant we have been on you since Dad died. There are some things that don't need learning; they just are, Victor. And there are some things that just ain't so.

It wasn't much of a blizzard: we should be grateful. It could have lasted days, but it was no more than a squall. We had to take shelter: the tent was gone and there wasn't time to build a snow-hole. Although I do know how, in theory. You pile up your belongings and pack snow around them, then pull the belongings out and crawl inside the hollow.

*'I didn't know that. That's ripping. In our day it was just cutting ice blocks to build ice walls—or not letting your tent blow away in the first place, of course.'*

'Thank you, Titus. All this useful knowledge, eh? If we keep this up I may even find a use for the Atomic Table or the Golden Numbers.'

*'Or the Four Horsemen of the Apocalypse. They're my favourite.'*

Maybe that's how God made the Earth, do you think? He piled his ski-suit and rucksack and giant Parisian suit-case together into a mound and packed snow round them, then plucked out the insides. Perhaps God's curled up, even now, inside His giant hollow planet, sleeping out the blizzard that blew up on the Eighth Day.

214

Anyway, there wasn't time—when the squall came, I mean—to build a snow-hole. So Victor and I climbed into either end of the Nansen, and wrapped ourselves in everything that came to hand, re-laced the covers over us and waited. The wind was shoving and shouldering the sled, moving it over the ice. I could imagine it picking up momentum, slipping faster and faster downhill towards crevasses, portals, sinkholes, plate-glass windows of ice that would shatter and spill out smiling albino aliens and stuffed dinosaurs. The wind howled and bayed on every side. I asked Titus to wrap me in his arms and keep me warm, but if he did, his body was even colder than mine.

And when the squall passed, the laces were frozen solid. My fingers were icy, without feeling. Claustrophobia and half a metre of snow were pressing down on me like soil. I was buried alive. *Help, somebody!*

But there is no one within a thousand miles.

So what was there to do but tug at the canvas and lacings until the edges parted and let the snow cascade in on me?

I thought, as I emerged, that the blizzard had eaten us. There was nothing left above the surface but snow, and for a moment I thought we'd died and stopped existing, there was so little to show for us: just a white wilderness smoothed to the consistency of fluffy cappuccino by the new fall of snow.

'Where are you, Uncle Victor?!'

Frantically, I went looking for the other end of the sled, using mittened hands and my ice axe, digging and digging down through the snow until I hit the metal frame and the lacings showed through like surgical sutures in a belly, or a sailor's shroud. It was just like opening a grave and Uncle Victor the corpse in it: his face blue with cold, rotten with snow-burn; square, dark holes where his eyes should have been.

Teabags.

I tossed them away into the snow. 'Victor? *Uncle Victor!*'

'Any time now, lass. Any time now,' said the corpse, opening its eyes, rising from its resting place among the waterproofs and corned beef, the foil blankets and the methylated spirit. 'Just over the horizon, by my reckoning.'

But before we could reach his Shangri-La over the horizon (not that there was a horizon) we had to unearth the sled from its drift, and when it came to pulling, we sank to our knees, barely able to shift it through the deep, soft, wet porridge of new snow.

Actually, the snow's not new. Nothing in this place is new. The wind grinds the surface off centuries of compacted snow and blows it about a bit, that's all. Just the same old snow, recycled over and over. Just the same old snow going round and round. Like an astronaut drinking his own piss.

I said something to Uncle Victor just now about shot-peening: how someone could use all this razor-ice to peen dirt off stone and rust off metal. It was a mistake. His shot-peening partner's treachery must have been playing on his mind. Frostbite swells up in a hand or a foot like a great black bubo; Dad's desertion had swollen in the same way, into an obscene canker on Victor's brain.

'Petty minded, provincial little Luddite!' he spat, over-spilling with venom. 'I could have put up with him leaving all the spadework to me, idle lummock! I could've tolerated his *losing interest*! But when he started trying to interfere with my work . . .'

\*     \*     \*

216

It seems it was the antibiotics that caused the final rift between Uncle Victor and my father: an experiment of crucial importance. Germs, bacteria, infections of the Overworld must on no account be allowed to pollute the Worlds Within: one look at the fate of the Amerindians proved that. Terrestrial infections must not be passed on to the Insiders. And so naturally Uncle Victor experimented with ways of ridding the human organism of every contagion. A course of antibiotics—strong enough to exterminate the sludge in a drain let alone streptococci and scarlet fever. And who did he use for this experiment? Well, his apprentice, of course. His right-hand girl. His trainee ambassador. He needed to see if, like a toilet or a scalpel, she could be made germ-free.

'Had to cut it short,' said Victor resentfully. 'Your hearing started to go. But the science was valid enough! Anyone can see that! Even you can see that, can't you, and you're not the brightest match in the box! Not him, though. Not that petty-minded Luddite, your father. He tried to stop the whole project!'

I could remember it, of course: swallowing huge numbers of Smartie-like sweets suspended in spoonfuls of honey, hiding the treat from my father, because (Victor said) Dad begrudged the honey. It was to be our little secret: Victor's and mine.

'So really . . . you took away my hearing, too,' I said.

'Say again?' said Victor.


When the White Darkness sets in, it's such a kindness. All shadows disappear—the sky, the ground—leaving nothing but a milky, trembling nothingness. It's a sweet light, a pleasant light, like lying under a sheet on a summer morning: the presence of light without any of the usual complications—like being able to see. Perfect ignorance

217

was like this, I remember: a feeling of enlightenment without ever quite grasping what was really going on. They call it The White Darkness. A window opaque with condensation. A cataract over the eyeball. The White Darkness. With the tip of my ski I draw an eye in the snow—not as good as Nats could do, but an eye—just to prove to myself that I can see what I've drawn; that I'm not blind. When Odysseus entered the Underworld, the Dead pressed in on all sides, jostling for a glimpse of a living man. Maybe The White Darkness is woven out of reject, leftover ghosts.

Diamond ice twinkling in the white haze stirs memories of those gilt-mirrored changing rooms back in chic Paris. Get out your credit card, Uncle Victor: we've reached the ultimate Changing Room. In the smoke-filled mirrors stands my true reflection: what I'll look like when I'm gone. Nothing! Zippo! Nobody!

*'I believe your pemmican must have disagreed with you at breakfast this morning.'*

'Oh. Am I whingeing?'

*'Just a little, perhaps. This place does lower the spirits.'*

'I'm sorry. How's your leg?'

*'Which one?'*

'The one with the bullet hole.'

*'Oh, pff, that. It was never a very big hole in the first place. Watch out.'*

The weight of the sled brings me to a dead stop. Uncle Victor has stopped pulling. The looming whiteness has elongated into a corridor and standing at its far end, veiled by the drifting mist, are four—five—figures shapeless in their voluminous robes. It is a sight so unnerving that I drop my ice axe, and the thud, as it hits the ground, reverberates like thunder. The ground is hollow.

I would run towards the motionless strangers, but for that hollow wowing under my feet. We are standing on a drum-skin of ice. How thick? A metre? A hand-span? 'Uncle Victor. Keep perfectly still!' I say.

I don't believe Victor could move his feet if he wanted. He is standing staring at the shapes in the mist. One hand creeps tentatively into the air and he waves like a little child, mittens folding over at the knuckles, a big grin cracking open his face, water vapour sobbing from his mouth. 'Hello?'

I retrace my steps towards the sled, trying to place my feet exactly where I placed them before. Two steps. Three steps . . . *Boom. Boom. Boom.* I tug the skis out from under the covers. 'Put these on, Uncle Victor. They'll spread your weight.' Rather than add to my own body-weight by carrying Victor's skis, I kick them ahead of my own, over the ice. 'Put those on, Uncle Victor.' He ignores me, eyes fixed on the deputation of aliens standing stock still in the white haze. Like a dog, I want to hunker down, stretch myself out along the ice, make myself weightless and invisible. Every noise is magnified by the huge sounding-box beneath our feet. But this is no place to stand still and stare. We ought to go back, get off this bone-china plate of ice. Instead, we scuff forward—I on my skis, Victor on legs that buckle and totter—until we ought to be face-to-face with the strangers.

As usual, size and distance have deluded us. The figures aren't human. They aren't even human in scale. They're bigger and further off. They're three metres, four, five metres tall. And they're not robed guards or placid ambassadors from another world; they're bulgy outcrops of craggy ice rising like termite hills out of the ice-sheet. They are twisted blisters of deformed ice pushed up by the same massive forces that suspended this glass roof magically over a cavernous Nothing.

'I know where we are,' I say, though I say it very quietly in case the weight of decibels is enough to shatter

219

the glass. 'This is the Devil's Ballroom.' Such an unscientific name; Victor will think I'm being melodramatic—'This place is Hell on Earth; this place is the Devil's Ballroom.' I wish I knew what else to call it, but I don't. The name is in my head—*The Devil's Ballroom, The Devil's Ballroom*—and it doesn't leave room for anything else. 'Amundsen came here, uncle. This is not a good place to be. There's nothing underneath us.' In a desperate effort to make him understand, I stamp my ski twice. *Boom, boom.* 'Listen, uncle. Hollow!'

Victor turns on me a face so agitated that I think the figures in the fog, the tantalizing illusion of life, must have finally broken his heart. But then he crouches down and begins hacking at the ground with his axe. *Boom. Boom.* I wait for the floor to shatter under me like a car windscreen. 'Help me, lass! Look sharp! Got to see!'

Nothing I say or do stops him except snatching the axe out of his hands and starting to hack at one of the anthills instead. If he has to see what's underneath us, let him at least do it this way! I have to take off my skis to get close enough, smashing my way into a monstrous knobbly egg of vuggy ice, filling my face with needles of flying sharpness. The impact runs back up my arms and sets off explosions of pain in my elbows and shoulders, in my neck and spine. If this *were* a person I would be hacking off its head. If it were Victor, I'd be glad!

I chant inside my head: *You took my dad! You took my hearing! You brought me here!* The blows of the axe no longer hurt. In fact I have the strength of ten and the rhythm of a pile driver: *You stole, and you killed, and you lied, and you bullied, and you did for us . . .* The hollow head and shoulders of the frigid alien crumble, cave in, and drop down through its ugly hollow body, falling and falling into the space beneath. If the fragments touch bottom at all, I can't hear it. The antibiotics Victor fed me made me deaf. And besides, the noise is drowned out by the thunderous, quaking, bass percussion of echoes booming around the Devil's Ballroom. I can feel the very ice trembling under my boots. My last blow nearly decapitates Victor who is struggling to *climb up* the trunk of the ice-chimney. 'What the hell are you doing, you fool?' I scream at him.

He has hauled himself up, the heels of his hands resting, as it were, on the coping of the ice-chimney, so as to peer down. And I can see that the look on his face isn't pain at all, but manic delight. He rips off my snow-goggles, the better to see, and throws them away. 'We're here, lass! We're here! We've made it! Didn't I tell you? Didn't I tell them all along no one believed me but I showed 'em I bloody showed 'em nobody else me I did it I found it I got here it's mine!' Then he drops down with a crunch of boots that crazes the ice where he lands, and he drags the sled towards him by the ropes, so that the iron crossbar slams into his own legs. He needs to stand on the sled to gain height—'You first, lass! You first!' Crouching down to embrace my knees, he lifts me bodily towards the opening.

The pain in my cut thigh is momentarily bigger and blacker than the darkness below; I can't lift a hand to help myself. A smell ten thousand years old comes up the chimney of ice—and a draught that blows stray hair into my mouth, as Victor attempts to feed me into the Underworld like a worm into some gross, petrified cuckoo. I kick him in the head and spread-eagle myself across the opening, so that he cannot force me down it.

His open-mouthed smile is one of total bewilderment: a genius faced with the task of explaining quantum theory to a rather stupid dog. 'Don't you understand, lassie?' he says slowly and deliberately. 'It's Symmes's Hole! There's not one . . . there's whole clusters!'

Then his generosity and patience are all spent, and he

clambers up again, flings me aside, jealous of anyone reaching the Truth before him. Lifting first one leg, then the other, he slides his feet into the chimney—'Uncle, NO!'—and lifts his hands from the rim.

Inside his snowsuit he is a thing of skin and bone. But his chubby, puffy, out-sized layers of thermal quilting wedge in the opening at the hip. He sticks up, like a Victorian chimney sweep, writhing and swearing, his hood down, eyelids blown open and shut independently by the force of the wind, begging me to hand him the axe so that he can make the opening wider and climb down to the Inner Worlds.

I lie where he threw me, the axe within reach of my hand. And why not? Why shouldn't I? Good riddance, I should say. Good riddance and damn you to hell.

'Get down, uncle! Please get down! You're scaring me! Be careful! You'll fall! There's nothing there! Just a big nothing!'

He wriggles and strains, his clothing bunching up around his neck and face; a fat Santa stuck in the chimney-top.

'Give me the bloody axe, you stupid child. God give me patience! I'm surrounded by fools and idiots!'

I grub up one of the dirty canvas hauling-harnesses and thrust it up at him. 'At least put this on. Look! Put this on, uncle. You don't want to fall, do you? You can lower yourself down! But it could be hundreds of—!'

His hands flail over his head, with frustration and exertion, like a toddler in a tantrum. I try and suit my voice to the age of this demented child in front of me, wanting, wanting, wanting his own way, thwarted by a world that won't do as it's told:

'Whatever's there is an awfully long way down, Victor. You don't want to find out the hard way, do you? Why don't *you lower yourself down*, at least? Put the harness on?

222

You can lower yourself down then, can't you? I'll get the torch, look. You can have a . . .'

'Yes, yes,' he snaps, tormented by impatience, and struggles his arms into the harness without bothering to untwist it or distinguish front from back, all the while telling me to join him, giving me strict instructions to put on my own harness and follow him. The idea of harnesses is his now, of course. 'Well? Look sharp! Get yours on! Think on!' And I have to go through the motions of putting on my pulling harness and stepping up on to the sled as if I will follow him—two trapeze artists in a death-defying act above an audience of watching aliens. 'Jump to it, Sym! Pass me the axe. Jump to it!'

'No! Uncle! Please! Don't leave me here alone! Stay here with me! We should stay together! We shouldn't get separated! Everyone says . . .'

But genius has taken over—as genius always has done, tyrannizing Victor's life, shouting in his ear that he is a man of destiny and dazzling merit. He has suddenly realized that without his big, down-filled overjacket he might fit through the ragged throat of the ice-chimney. So he tugs and rends at the poppers, throws aside his bear-paw mittens to find the tag of the zip, shrugs his shoulders out of their quilting, his arms out of the sleeves, his wrists out of the cuffs—forgetting the small fact that, along with the jacket, he has taken off the harness as well.

The slick whistle of neoprene rubbing against ice, and he is gone, hands over his head. I am standing on the sled. I reach out—try to grab something, anything—but pitch up against an empty funnel.

Even so, his face, in falling, is turned up towards mine, so I see the look that crosses it. Realization. True enlightenment.

Dark takes him in the blink of an eye.

# Chapter Twenty-One
*'Oh! he was a gentleman, quite a*
*gentleman, and always a gentleman!'*
*—Tom Crean, of Oates*

Bulging-obese with Uncle Victor's jacket crammed on
over my own, I sit for a long time at the foot of the ice-
chimney, sheltering in its lee, my back against its pocked
and goitred surface. The appalling wind slices across its
opening, as over the neck of an empty bottle, howling.

'Good riddance,' I say, trying the phrase for size, zipping
the jacket as high as the zip will go.

'*Oh?*'

'He destroyed me, Titus. He murdered my dad. He's
murdered me.'

Titus also sits with his back to the funnel, eyes screwed
up so hard that his white teeth are bared. The hollow
between his cheekbone and jaw is deeper now, the skin
stretched almost transparent. With a penknife, he is cutting
through the laces of his boot, from the top of the shin,
all the way down, *click, click, click.*

'The bastard destroyed me!'

He doesn't contradict me, because a friend isn't a friend
who tells you black is white. He simply says: '*As Scott
destroyed me. But do you think he meant to? Do you think it
was done with malice?*'

224

Why can he not be angry? Now's the time to be angry. Not before, with me. Now. 'Well? You hated Scott! Now I hate Victor, just the same!'

'*Me, hate Scott?*' He seems surprised.

'Yes, the Owner! You did, you hated Scott!'

'*Hate him? I loved the man.*'

'After what he did to you? After the way . . .'

'*Oh, early on I couldn't abide him. Skipped Sunday service because Scott led the prayers. Couldn't stick his vain, sanctimonious, two-faced . . . Let's just say, I harboured unChristian thoughts about him sometimes. Whenever we were in the same room. Sometimes when we weren't. But in the end? Out on the Barrier? In the end, I loved the man. We all did. Loved every hair of his head. Because his heart was good and his intentions were sound. And because . . .*' He looks around him at the Plateau's white maze of hazy alleyways, as if the right leafy words might blow past. His voice is as soft and dizzying as smoke around the brain. '*God save us, girl, who else* was *there to love? It would have been a precious foolish thing, to waste time hating each other.*' And he stops what he is doing and lifts his arm, so that I can lean in against his chest and press my forehead against the damp wool of his cardigan. I can smell his sweat. Long time now since he and the others stripped to their drawers to wash with handfuls of snow. Ninety-one years.

'Everyone loved you, Titus. Always. The magnificent Captain Oates? Everyone who met you. Everyone loved you.'

'*Ah! That's Death for you,*' he says with a twitch of the nose, dipping his eyes in embarrassment. '*Does wonders for a man's reputation, don't you know. There's simply nothing like it for making people speak well of you. Come on. Time to go.*' But we continue to sit and watch the covers of the sled flapping in the wind, the two empty harnesses rolling over and over on the ends of their ropes. Hatred erodes in the wind. I dare say I shall shed it all in time, along with my hair.

'I could always say—when I get home, I mean—I could always say Victor *did* find Symmes's Hole,' I suggest. 'Died bravely making the Greatest Scientific Discovery of All Time. Who'd be any the wiser? Or worse off? Who'd care?'

Titus fixes me with that penetrating stare of his; the one that would make a charging bull elephant stop, think twice, apologize and saunter off.

'Well, all right, I won't say it. But I hope he found something. Paradise. At the bottom of the hole. Some kind. Paradise. We were very fond of him once. The family. I think. If I can remember.' My skin is so cold that my tears feel like molten lead running down, running down. Sobbing hurts the vertebrae of my spine, too, but it can't be helped. It would be a precious foolish thing, to go on hating Uncle Victor for the rest of my life; and the rest of my life doesn't really allow time for postponing the tears.

*'Tell you what, dearie. Given the whole Universe to choose from, I doubt God would site Paradise down here, in the U-bend under His sink. Eh? God, this is an awful place, Sym. Can't we be cutting along now?'*

But I haven't the heart to bend my leg, put weight on it, raise myself to my feet. I roll on to hands and knees, but go nowhere—abject, submissive under the whip-cracking wind, fawning on the jostling snow-ghosts in the hope they will spare me for another day, another hour. At any moment the fragile glass rink of the Devil's Ballroom may crack and open under me. What the hell. How could the blackness down there be any blacker than the hole inside me?

*'Hey, Sym! I trust you are not forgetting: you are with the fortunate Captain Oates? You may shelter under my good luck.'*

'Oh, goody.'

*'What? I told you before: I'm the luckiest of men! Think! Two years more and it could all have been ours: the Great War! Lice and rats. Drowning in mud. Shrapnel wounds. Phosgene gas.*

226

*One among millions known only unto God. Would that have
been somehow preferable? Is that what you wish on me?'*

'You might not have died in the Great War.'

*'Well, then what would you call lucky? If the dogs had come?'*

'Yes!'

*'Rescued in the nick of time—on my thirty-second birthday?'*

'Yes!'

*'And just how much would this horse-riding, boxing, camel-
racing, sailing, cricketing, skiing, motorcycling, soldiering man
of yours have enjoyed life with amputated hands and feet? No
one could ever accuse me of that kind of bravery.'*

And Titus beams: his sunniest of smiles. *'Instead, what
were we, the five of us? Household names! Celebrities! Scott and
Birdie and Doctor Bill and Taffy and I!'*

'The Famous Five.'

*'I should decline to know of Enid Blyton, but yes, The Famous
Five.'*

'Without the cakes and buns.'

*'Or Timmy the Dog.'*

'Oh! Timmy the Dog! If you'd had Intrepid Timmy, you
could have sent him off with a note in his collar to fetch
help!'

*'Eaten him, anyway.'*

That's how it's done, you see. It's the same way people
get horses out of burning buildings. When the whole
world's on fire around you, you use a blindfold. Everyone
needs someone like Titus for a blindfold.

That reminds me: I must find my snow-goggles. I crawl
across the ice to find them, then turn towards the sled.
The wind slides me along on my fleecy knuckles and
neoprene knees. I'm a curling stone skidding towards my
target. There is no possible way that I can haul the sled
on my own. So I pull all the dregs of food out of it—
biscuits, raisins, curry powder, cocoa powder, glucose
tablets—pour them into a plastic bag, all in together—

227

and push it into my sleeping bag. I push that inside Victor's sleeping bag, along with the foil blankets. The wind has stolen all but one of the skis.

*'Those Norskies had their heads screwed on right, you know. They could even sail better than I could,'* says Titus.

'Everyone could sail better than you, Titus. You were a liability in a boat.' But I take his hint to use the remaining ski as a mast, and the covers of the sled as a sail, as Amundsen did, scudding home from the Pole. At least then I can sleep inside it. Or be easier spotted from the air.

But stupid, stupid, stupid, ignorant, mindless, useless idiot fool that I am—victim of a shoddy education—I unlace the sled covers without turning the sled side-on to the wind.

With a crack like a galleon losing its mainmast, the wind swoops under the covers and fills them. Faster than a life-jacket inflating, the sled swallows the full force of the Plateau wind, rears up, leaps into the air. It has absurd ambitions to fly, this slab of steel and fibreglass, this thing that has wrenched my guts into piles of spaghetti with its massive, immovable weight. Its runners slice through the air a hair's breadth above my head, then it crashes down on its prow and somersaults away across the Devil's Ballroom—end over end, spinning and waltzing to the music of the wind.

I run. I run and run and run—not after it, but in the opposite direction—into the haze, cold ripping at my throat, feeling the ice juddering under my feet: *BOOM BOOM BOOM!* It's the noise of a hurtling sled prancing and cartwheeling, over and over, slamming down repeatedly on to a drumskin of delicate frozen snow. It is a noise loud enough to walk on.

When, finally, the ballroom floor is holed—when the Nansen crashes nose-first through the fragile platform of ice—when the glass shatters—the fractures spread out with the speed of shockwaves, crazing the entire land-

228

scape. From the edge of the Devil's Ballroom, not knowing if my feet are on plate glass or solid ground, whether I have run far enough or whether I too will fall, I stand and watch the Devil roll up a section of his ballroom floor and reveal the basement beneath.

I shut my eyes sooner than see the drop.

On and on, the noise of catastrophe. Then a silence like the end of the world.

*'What, not dancing?'* whispers Titus into the nape of my neck.

'No. You and I were always wallflowers.'

*'In that case, perhaps we should be leaving. I'll rustle up a coach and four.'*


When there's enough sun to cast a shadow, I'll use my body shadow and wristwatch to keep my bearing. I'll be a sundial. Of course I'm not sure which bearing I want to keep; I've only a memory of the GPS in the tank telling me it's north-east or north-north-east. At home in the summer, when Victor taught me how to do it, using the sundial in the garden, we had to adjust for British Summer Time. Just a hunch, but I reckon you don't have to adjust for British Summer Time down here.

I suppose vampires must get lost everywhere they go. Is it vampires? Who have no shadows? I'm a vampire, then. In the White Darkness I have no shadow.

Doesn't surprise me any more that the wind could pick up the Nansen and chuck it through the air. Seen chunks of ice as big as cars burst volcanically out of the ground in a pumice cloud of snow and ice—just kicked there by the wind. Twice, gusts picked me up and threw me thirty metres. Victor's extra jacket cushioned me. Like blubber on a sealion. I'd like to say I picked myself up after I landed and exclaimed, *Oh, Toto! I don't think we're in Kansas any more!*

but that wasn't what I said. An ancient language, Anglo-Saxon, and very useful when all that's holding you to the ground is a pack of ghost-dogs with their teeth in your thigh.


The sun gives more back than my shadow. I am clambering over the monstrous carcass of some dead, fanged dragon—a morass of rocks and peaks and glacial slides that take the feet from under me and spill me down long chutes of white pain, when suddenly—a flash of light on glass. For the longest time, I assume it's ice. But because it holds my attention, my face turns towards it, and whichever way my face turns, I can't help walking, so I walk towards it. It reminds me of the sun flashing in the windows of the Hagglund as it drove away. Eventually the flicker and flash turn into twin circles of light.

Glasses?

Extraordinary. Impossible. A hallucination. An illusion. Except that it happens.

*'I found my little white pipe on the way back from the Pole,'* says Titus. *'Dropped it on the way going, found it coming back. Raised my spirits no end.'*

Victor's glasses. The lenses from his glasses, I mean. I have to take off one glove to pick them up. Raises a laugh, if not my spirits. What a fluke! What a fantastically futile fluke! It makes me laugh out loud—bark like a dog, dislodging the ice crusted round my nose and mouth and hanging from my eyebrows and fur-trimmed hood. Good for Uncle Victor! Keeping me on the straight and narrow. Keeping me on course. Keeping my eye on the . . .

The lenses lie in the palm of my hand, the teardrop bifocals looking dolefully up at me. Then I can see through them into his eyes, into his face, into the time before we got here. My uncle Victor. When Dad died, the one sight that made me cry was a pair of his shoes in the hall, moulded into the shape of his feet. Things. It's things that get to you. Silky blouses slithering on to a railway platform; a budgie in a bank; a mobile phone spinning on a glass-top table.

'Sorry. So sorry,' I say to Titus, sinking to my knees. 'I've tried, but I can't do it. My eyes hurt too much. My leg. Too tired. Need to lie down. Need to stop.'

*'Canty up, Sym! See it out! Just keep in my lee!'*

Like good King Wenceslas . . . 'in her master's steps she trod, where the snow lay dinted . . .'. But Titus is making no footprints, or else the blizzard is filling them in the instant. In any case, I haven't the strength to take one more step. Sorry.

*'Give it to me, Sym!'* says Titus. *'Give it to me to carry.'*

'What?'

*'The pain, Sym. Give it to me.'*

'Oh. No. No, thank you all the same.'

*'Give it to me, Sym! Give it to me to carry!'*

'Not to worry. Don't trouble. Why should you?'

*'Because I'm the one who loves you enough. I'm the one who cares if you live or die.'*

It's true: everyone needs a reason to stay alive—someone who justifies your existence. Someone who loves you. Not beyond all reason. Just loves you. Even just shows an interest. Even someone who doesn't exist, or isn't yours. No, no! They don't even have to love you! They just have to be there to love! Target for your arrows. Magnetic Pole to drag on your compass needle and stop it spinning and spinning and tell you where you're heading and . . . Someone to soak up all the yearning. That's what I think. That's what I deduce. I've mustered my facts. And that's what I—

*'Give me the pain, Sym! I'll pull it for you. Are you tired? I'm not! I'll carry the weariness, Sym!'* And he leans over me, his face close to mine, his cheek rubbing mine. Sharp with beard, it scratches my cheek like frostburn. When he takes his face away, it is ice-pocked, the blue lips split and

231

bleeding, the cornea of his eyes scraped red by the iron-filing flecks of ice in the wind. I ought to protest harder, but it is pleasant to be loved. Everyone knows that.

'You've done enough,' I say.

People are always putting on him. Wanting him to have been perfect. Wanting him to have been braver than they ever could be. I won't impose. I wouldn't have let him go outside in the first place.

*'Listen to me, Sym. I got it wrong. I should have walked out earlier. Then my dying might have made a difference. Five days earlier, and it might have made a difference. Five days when the others could have eaten my rations! Five days less of marching at the pace of a man crippled in both legs. Each morning it took me three hours to put on my boots—three hours when the others could have been pressing on! Five days earlier and the last blizzard might not have pinned them down. Five days earlier and they might have made it to One Ton! But I funked it. I didn't want to die on my own. God knows, I wanted to be dead, but I didn't know how to commit suicide without a gun. They refused to leave me behind in my sleeping bag, though I begged them . . . My hands were gone. I couldn't even take the coward's way out. My hands were gone, girl, so I couldn't get the morphia out of my pocket. So I waited and I hoped to die, but I didn't and I didn't, because . . . because—who knows why? Because I was made so deep-down, ingrained bloody-minded—or because I was so dashed fit to begin with—or because the pain hadn't finished with me.'*

Poor Titus. He doesn't understand. It's not dying or bravery or The Ice that makes him wonderful—indispensable. It's not the dagger of ice in his heart but the sliver of Indian sunshine. It's being lousy at spelling, and crying for joy when his horse won a race, and thinking he could sail a yacht because his grandfather was an admiral, and chasing his own motorbike down a mud-baked road, and keeping a deer in the coalhole . . . It's the colour of his eyes and the silken rope of his voice.

It's being thirty-two and beautiful as a dog moon . . . He shouldn't have gone outside. Young men ought to be left to grow old. Friends ought to stay together. I would have made him stay out of pure selfishness—because I couldn't have brought myself to part with him. I would have let him stay and be afraid, like ordinary people are. Like me.

*'I hoped I'd die in my sleep, but I didn't! So—God love them for it—my good, my dear, my beloved friends unlaced the tent flap—do you really think I could have undone frozen knots on my own, with my fingers gone?—and I crawled out of the tent and let the blizzard do me the last kindness. But I'd waited too long! So in the end my death didn't change anything—didn't save anyone! Let me make a difference this time, Sym! Give me the pain.'*

The pain in my eyes is less, it's true. While I keep them shut, it's less. So I don't open my eyes, even though I can still sense his face a breath away from mine. It is enough; knowing it's there.

I understand the game now, Nikki, Maxine. I could answer the questionnaires in the magazines now. What is passion for? It's for when the words run out. That's when to come down out of the nursery: when you can't see the stairs for the white, glaring darkness, but you don't care any more if you fall. When there's nothing left between sky and earth or as far as the eye can see, except Need. It's like a blizzard unpicking flesh and bone and what's real and what's not . . .

Interesting. People talk about it being hot—boys being hot, love being hot. But it's more like a blizzard, really. Whiteout. Or a kind of madness. Like the imagination: it's a different place.

Obliteration. I know that's how it would be now, if Titus and I were to make love. I know. I have the knowledge. Of course I do. I'm an animal, aren't I, full of ancient instincts? Instincts old as the Human Race. Instincts as old as the dinosaurs, almost. It's good to know.

233

A bit late. A bit irrelevant, since no one takes their clothes off here and anyway I'll be dead shortly. But it's good to know how it would have been.

So, like Snow White in her coffin of glass, I think I'll just wait here to be kissed and raised back to life. About ninety years from now. That will be soon enough. I'll just lie down here, and Titus can lie down beside me and I can get a few things clear—a last few outstanding questions. Like they say at the end of whodunits: just a few things I don't understand, Titus.

'Is there life after death, Titus?'

*'Well, I'm alive, aren't I?'*

Don't understand. Always so contrary and argumentative, this man in my head. Always wanting it both ways.

*'I was alive in the thoughts of my mother when she slept in my old bedroom; now I'm alive in your head, for the duration. I continue to exist in the fevered jungles of your unusual brain. That's why you have to go on.'*

'But no Heaven?'

*'Don't know. It's not Judgement Day yet. We should both find that out simultaneously.'*

'And ghosts?'

The wind teems with mile-high ghosts of blown snow, bending and flexing across the white landscape. But none of them are Titus. He is at peace—buried somewhere here—intact like that Jurassic dinosaur, preserved in the very instant of death. Somewhere near here, Captain Lawrence Edward Grace Oates lies preserved by the cold that cradled him in its arms before any woman could.

I could sleep here. Like him. I could do that. Look. Even without meaning to, I've lain down full-length. Falling snow has obscured my ski-suit already. I look as if I'm dissolving into the ground. 'I'll just stay here, Titus. Your body's here somewhere. It's a good place to be.'

*'No it's not.'*

234

'Durr. Course it's a good place. You're here, aren't you.'

'*No. I'm not,*' says Titus and none too gently. I wish he would just lie down and be quiet. Of course he's here. His body is preserved in the ice somewhere, even if it is lonely and separated from the tent with his friends in it. '*I'M NOT HERE!*' He's shouting it now. Perhaps he thinks that without my hearing aid I can't hear the hero who lives inside my head. Silly man. Why deny it? He went to such pains to make me admit the truth—that he crawled out and died in the snow. Forget Symmes. Forget nesting planets-within-a-planet . . . No. A shallow grave. An eiderdown of snow. Right here, maybe! Just a few centimetres below me now! His body just a few centimetres below mine . . .

'*THE ICE SHELF IS MOVING, YOU FOOL!*' shouts Titus. '*The surface is moving! All the time! New stuff welling up in the centre, pushing the old ice outwards! Only a few miles a year but never stopping—on and on and on! Carrying everything with it: Bill and Birdie and the Owner wrapped in their tent. Taffy Evans under his cairn: all carried along inside a river of ice—all the time sinking lower, like dead fish. Sinking through the ice, the saltwater gnawing the ice from under them!*' He is shrieking now—so loudly that it pains my eardrums and makes me screw up my face, splitting my lips, leaking warm blood into my mouth. '*In the end, the Shelf ships everything into the sea! To wash about in the sea! Lawrence Oates hasn't been in Antarctica for years, Sym! Twenty years ago his body dropped out of the bottom of the ice shelf and into the sea! OATES IS GONE! His body was food for the leopard seals and the crabs!*'

'NO!' Sheer horror makes me pull myself up on to my knees and arch my back to shake it off. Wet drowning dark. Squirming, teeming, grotesque life down in the savage, restless cold. I hold my breath, because I'm already there in my imagination—in the ocean—delivered there on a bier of ice. Snow White's coffin of glass fractures round me into shards of pain and I have to arch my back repeatedly to shake off a stiff shell of snow. In the small of my back it creaks like old age.

No white, eternal rest, then? Nothing but a bulldozer of ice pushing me down and out to sea? This place doesn't want anything or anybody! It's so intent on being pure that it spits out everything living, everything that's ever been alive! The carcasses of Scott's useless ponies, the carcasses of Scott and Evans and Birdie and . . . What kind of graveyard spews out its dead? I hate it! It's like a patch of leprosy on the planet—can't feel cold, can't feel pain . . . All the time it's sloughing its dead, white skin—purging itself: those bloodstains from Amundsen's chopped-up dogs, all the droppings from those sled-ponies and explorers and eco-tourists and penguins and seabirds and dinosaurs and . . .

I don't want to be in this frigid bitch of a place! I don't want to be in a dead place that doesn't even want my dead body! I don't want to be shouted down by this bastard never-ending wind! I don't want to be shipped into the sea out of the bottom of a glacier! I don't want to be food for the leopard seals and the crabs! I want to be somewhere that wants me!

And I rise to my knees and then my feet, gloves dragging across the snow—put them on, Sym, put them on. Can't feel my hands. Wind shoving at me, bullying me, so that I reel from side to side, lumbering along—a dinosaur—gasping and groaning and swearing and staggering, my feet sliding off to right and left, my oozing eyes shut. Beside me, Titus is carrying the pain—I can see it behind him in the shape of a sled; he leaning into the harness, the runners baulking and biting into the granite hard ripples of ice. So chivalric. Always the perfect gentleman . . . His shape is blurred by swirling snow, but now and then—when he turns to urge me on—I can see his face quite clearly, even through my closed lids. His beauty has been blackened and pitted and eroded away like old stone. Hardly recognizable. His cap is gone. He is wearing no boots, and only one of the reindeer-skin *finneskoes* that ought to cover his socks. His hands are bare.

The sun dies. Wind-driven snow rages at us, infuriated to see two interlopers still on their feet, intent on beating us down. But Titus is to one side of me, shielding me from the worst gusts—the ones that would lift me clear off the ground. He is shielding me from the fear, too, carrying it for me. Always the perfect . . .

Every moment my body-heat is being peeled off me, like gold leaf off the Happy Prince. No pain now—only a blizzard of sleep and a very, very slow and distant drumming which is my heart or maybe my soul not liking to be penned up any more in such a little space. There is a calculation I could do to work out my life expectancy. If I could just be fagged. But Titus is alongside me, so Time has no reality anyway. It might be the twenty-first century. It might be 1912. Minutes or whole years might be passing, but he is carrying Time, too, inside his useless, frost-bitten fists. Always the perfect . . .

Always.

Can't get one hand back into its glove. Get it into a pocket, Sym, into one of the pockets. Can't feel the opening. Can't see round the great bulk of my quilted body to guide my hand home into the side pocket of Victor's big jacket. So put it *inside* the jacket, Sym.

Victor's jacket never fully zipped up over mine. I push my hand inside, into the no-warmth of my armpit, into the interior map-pocket that doesn't have a zip. Hand almost too swollen to fit. Doesn't feel any warmer— doesn't feel anything. Must be warmer. Fingers start to hurt as though they're dipped in acid. Blood trying to flow through. Fingertips start to scald and throb—even to feel. Can feel, for instance, that the pocket is not empty.

# Chapter Twenty-Two
## Fire and Ice

Fancy kit. Really nifty. Worth a fortune. The girls at school would really covet this. Chances are, though, it doesn't exist. Just an illusion. Delusion. Hallucination. Hypothermia does that to you. The mind starts to play tricks.

Tricks? The mind's a three-ring circus! Music. Lights. Happiness. Wonder. Colour. All my life I've gone there when Life got too drab or unkind or lonely or miserable, and it's hardly ever let me down. Why should I wonder at the stunts it's pulling now?

Red, for instance. Red like the silk skirt twirling in the changing-room mirror. Red like the blood on my snowsuit. Red, like a London pillar box agape for all those postcards of penguins. That's what I'm seeing. I don't blink in astonishment at it. Normally the body does things like blinking without being asked. At the end—in the cold—it stops volunteering: to blink, swallow, shiver, think, breathe . . . The non-existent red island, in its sea of white, blurs in and out of focus; the liquid in the membrane of my eyes is trying to freeze. With my good left hand, I pinch my eyelids together until the liquid thaws and I can momentarily see again. How funny. How very twenty-first century. In Ancient Days, the prophet Elijah saw a chariot of fire swinging down out of the sky to carry him off to Heaven.

Me, I see a Hagglund all-terrain amphibious vehicle.

238

It's just standing there, like a doner kebab van waiting for trade on a Saturday night. Perhaps it's a *Flying Dutchman* of a van, a ghostly vessel doomed to cruise the kerbs of Antarctica until Captain Sigurd finds a woman who loves him for himself.

Have a long wait, the little shit.

Or maybe I'm the ghost. And this is the job allocated to me for all eternity—to haunt the frozen sea lanes of the frozen Ross Sea for ever, driving a ghostly Hagglund. Are ghosts prey to weariness? Do ghosts sleep? I want nothing now but to sleep. Had a ten-storey building collapsed on me, it couldn't weigh heavier than the sleep bearing down on me right now. To pull myself up the metal steps at the rear is to climb a slippery pole up out of black molasses wearing concrete pyjamas.

Certainly Sigurd's face says I'm a ghost, when he sees me through the window. 'You can't come in!' he says. (I do lip-reading, me.) But there is nothing he can do to stop me, sitting as he is, piled round with upholstery and empty food containers, two blankets and two sleeping bags. He has wrenched every cushion out of its seat to pile around him. A guy, buried up to his neck in a bonfire of foam pallets, only his head sticks up out of the top. I doubt he has moved for a day.

'You ran out,' I say.

'Go to hell!'

'Of diesel. You ran out.'

'Can't come in. Is he with you?'

And I nod, because I think he must mean Titus.

'Can't come in. Can't come in. Can't come in!'

'First-aid'ox,' I tell him. 'Ad'enalin. I'n dead.'

And then the sleep enfolds me, in black, billowing clouds, forbidding breathing, preventing me from ever crossing the immensity of frozen wilderness between me and the first-aid box on the shelf beside my hand. I topple forward on top of Sigurd, my skull hitting him in the face with a gristly crack.


And I am burning on a grid-iron. Sparks prick every nerve ending. My skin is scalding. My tendons shrink and shrivel up short till the bones crack. There are skewers buried hilt-deep in my elbows, knees, shoulders, hips. Flames of pain in every colour of the spectrum wash over me, flaying my flesh and crazing my skull into a dozen unmendable shards of pain. The circulation coming back hurts like rats chewing on my tendons. Cramp, but in seventeen places at once. Didn't they used to tear traitors apart with hooks buried in their flesh and tied off to galloping horses? My ribcage subsides over the hot coals and my skeleton falls apart. And still the fire is powerless to melt the core of cold inside me. Coming back to life isn't something I'd wish on my worst enemy.

'I fried the engine,' says my worst enemy violently rubbing my back and arms and legs. 'Turned off too quick. Bang. Melted something. Shut up, can't you?'

No, I don't think I can. I wasn't aware I was screaming. The headache is so bad that I can't form words or move my hands, only scream. I'm conscious that it's a fearful waste of energy to scream, but it takes me a long time to stop.

The van looks like a flop house—cushions and limbs everywhere, empty adrenalin syringes on the floor. Disgrace. Offends my tidy nature. Sigurd and I lie in each other's arms, conserving body heat, as the books tell you to do. It is the most unromantic clinch since Germany embraced Poland.

Even in melting the ice, heating the ice water over the primus to make a warm drink, the last of the methylated spirit runs out and the blue flame dies on its wick, like hope extinguished. The Ribena comes at room tempera-

240

ture. Unfortunately the 'room' is a stalled vehicle in the Antarctic wilderness. At some stage Sigurd has tried to suck ice to quench his thirst. It just about destroyed the surface of his tongue and the inside of his cheeks. His face has the look of an anorexic gerbil. His nose, where my forehead struck him, hasn't even the energy to bleed.

But who am I to talk? There's an owl pellet where my brain used to be. I can barely remember my name. There is nothing in my head for a long, long time, except surviving, and I'm not even sure I want to do that. Then Sigurd asks, 'What happened to him? Is he dead?'

And the thought is more powerful than adrenalin. I pull myself to my feet and throw open the door and shout and shout, loud as a mewling kitten: 'TITUS! TITUS! WHERE ARE YOU? WHERE ARE YOU? WHERE ARE YOU?' Curtains of light, intricately embroidered with sprigs of snow, billow out from an open sky. I shout over my shoulder, 'Didn't you see him when I got here? He was right beside me! Which way did he go?' but there's no reply from Sigurd either. The icefields shift under their restless tilth of snow-blow. Dizzying movement is everywhere. But none of it is Titus. There is no lame, hunched figure hauling a shadowy sled; no nonchalant, shirt-sleeved soldier smoking a pipe; no sulky explorer leaning his chin on the grip of a single long ski-pole; no Inniskillen Dragoon steering his horse with knees and crop; no leather-jacketed scruff chasing his runaway motorbike across the sastrugi. I look and I look, but there is nothing and no one for a thousand miles. I call and call, but he won't come when I call. He always used to say: *Women are a great nuisance.*

Sigurd is petrified. 'He's out there? Your uncle's out there?'

'Of course not. Victor's dead.'

Relief caves him in at the chest. 'Did you kill him?'

'No. You did.' It's not true and it's not fair, but he

deserves it. I don't terribly like Sigurd whatever-his-name-is.

'So who are you talking to?' he asks, high-pitched, crouching up on hands and knees, tongue poking the burned lining of his cheeks.

'Someone who helped me. Someone I need inside my head.'

'You're mad! You're just as mad as he was!' And there's a kind of awe in Sigurd's voice, as if I've finally managed to rise above the unremarkable into the realms of scary. 'Shut the door, will you?'

I will. But first I face out towards the glaring expanse of the Barrier, where sometimes palaces float and suns multiply and miracles occur. 'God bless and keep you, Titus, until you come home.'

'Shut the door, you mad—'

And I do.

I can't bear to be the one who finds out the bad news—that it's unusable. So I get Sigurd to reach inside Victor's jacket—into the map pocket—and fetch out Mimi's stolen satellite telephone stashed there.

Up until now, it quite slipped my mind.


Victor was not totally mad, then. Not as mad as I accused him of being. He did have a plan for getting home from Symmes's Hole, after we got there. He was going to phone for a lift. Not entirely mad, then. Just mad nor'-nor'-east.

Mimi's swish Iridium 9505 still has the price ticket stuck to it: $2,800. And it is still switched on. If it weren't, it would be about as useful as a house-brick, since we don't know the PIN numbers. I suggest calling 999; Sigurd says it's American so we should use 911. I say maybe only the price ticket is American. He says it's the nationality of the satellite that matters, not the telephone. But neither number sets phones ringing in New York or Punta Arenas or Christchurch or the Falklands. We neither of us know the dialling code for the UK. So in the end we ring last-number-dialled, and get some raucous friend of Mimi's.

*'Hi there! Fern isn't here right now. Well, I guess you worked that one out for yourself, he-hee-heee! But I want you to know I'm really and truly S-A-D to miss your call, so if you'd like to . . .'*

The telephone chirrups once, its battery staggering with cold and weariness. *'Speak real slow, now, and don't forget to say what time and day you called, cos naughty me, I don't always check out my messages and sometimes I'm gone overnight—though don't you go getting the wrong idea, know what I mean, m'sweetheart?'*

The telephone cheeps again, its heartbeat failing as surely as ours will within the day.

Finally the signal to speak. I give the geographic co-ordinates of our position (guesswork) while Sigurd clam-ours *'Mayday Mayday Mayday Emergency! Emergency!'* in the background. My speech is as slurred as any drunk's. After the battery gives out, we sit with the thing between us, looking at it, as if it might come spontaneously back to life. Strange to think of our voices escaping this frigid wilderness and lying coiled in the corner of some stranger's living room in Maine or Florida or Los Angeles.

How long before Mimi's friend checks her answer-phone? What chance of her hearing the garbled message or taking it seriously? What chance of our words reaching the right ears, or of rescuers caring enough to search? What price good weather? What chance of clear skies? What likelihood of being spotted from the air?

And yet we sleep, because at least we've *done* some-thing, re-aroused the possibility of surviving, whereas, before, both of us had quite stopped believing in rescue. We eat every last scrap of food there is—curry paste, cling peaches, fish roe, raisins, cocoa, indigestion tablets, milk powder, and three fruit gums—then bury ourselves in the upholstery and sleep.

'We could always . . . you know,' says Sigurd. 'I don't mind.'

'Not if you were the last schmuck in the universe,' I say and he doesn't seem to mind that either.

There is a hollow inside me big enough for twelve nesting planets and as cold as Outer Space.


Within a few paces of the bonnet gapes a curved crevasse, like an idiot grin gouged in the face of a snowman. Seeing it in the nick of time, Sigurd slammed on the brakes and immediately switched off the engine instead of letting it idle for ten minutes like it says in big letters on the dashboard. The oil pressure essential to the turbo-charged air-cooling system suddenly slumped, and the engine overheated so much that bits of it melted. I only mention this because I think it's funny. The Hagglund didn't die of cold: it overheated. That strikes me as funny, for some reason.

It does mean one *slightly* important thing. There is still fuel in the tanks.

There might be only one litre. It might be only a slush of freezing diesel. Whatever there is, it won't power a wrecked engine. But it does mean we can go out in a blaze of glory.

'You're mad!' says Sigurd. (I've noticed he says that a lot.)

I make the fuse out of the piping on the cushions, coiling it up inside the methylated spirit bottle for an hour or two in case there's a vestige of meths for it to soak up.

'You're out of your mind!' says Sigurd watching me pull it out again.

244

I plait my hair and cut off twenty centimetres of it to put on the end of the fuse—just to get an extra burst of heat where it's needed.

'If you think I'm going to let you . . . !' says Sigurd following me out of the van.

I push my wick of hair in at the filler cap, weighted with a few Argentinian coins to get it to the bottom of the fuel tank. I think cassette tape burns as well, so Lee Konitz may come in useful. Best keep him dry for now, though.

'They should've locked you both up—you and the psychopath!' says Sigurd, watching me grind out a trench for the fuse to lie in, so the wind won't blow it out.

'We can shelter behind that,' I say, pointing out a pressure ridge a metre or so high.

'And I say we don't. How about that, then?' says Sigurd, following me back inside the van, snatching up a thermal blanket for fear I should gain some unfair advantage over him in the competition to keep warm. We huddle down again among the cushions, two pit bull terriers too weary to do anything but snarl at one another. 'You hear voices. You see things. You're cracked,' says Sigurd.

Am I? When the bombs are falling, what's so clever about staying outdoors? Inside my head I've built this air-raid shelter . . . At least there was one there earlier . . .

I didn't say that out loud, but almost in answer to the mention of air raids, comes the sound. I don't hear it myself, of course. I've told Sigurd he is the one who has to listen; has to be our ears. Now he doesn't want to tell me what he's heard, for fear of what I'll do, but I see the noise fly into his head, the hope flare up in his eyes, the struggle to keep the news to himself: he has heard an aircraft engine!

It might be a holiday flight or a search plane; an airliner at 50,000 feet en route for Australia, or a military plane delivering personnel to the Scott-Amundsen Base. It might be the Law in pursuit of those who stole a half-million dollar vehicle, or a mercy dash financed by Mimi Dormiere-St-Pierre. Doesn't matter. It's the end.

I get up and go outside, Lee Konitz in one hand, the storm-lighter in the other, and Sigurd at my heels, bear-paw gloves swinging round his ankles. Festooned in blankets and coats and cushions, I'm a shambling bag-woman under the arches on the coldest night of the year, trying to justify herself to the Salvation Army. 'A hundred miles more, that's why! They'll see us at least a hundred miles further off!' I have no idea what I'm talking about.

It's a great tool, the storm-lighter—a cross between a blowtorch and the thing you use to light a gas oven. Even the strongest wind can't blow it out—or so Jon told us a million years ago. In the hope he is right, I set about stripping the music tape out of its cassette and bunching it into kindling. Somewhere in the sky above is an aeroplane, and if it isn't hundreds of miles away, if it's flying at low altitude, if it's looking, if we're incredibly lucky, the pilot might just see an explosion or a column of black smoke.

'*I Love Paris*' frizzles into black vermicelli. We take shelter behind the pressure ridge. Whatever happens, at least we'll be warm for half an hour. I can't remember warm. I have allowed for kindling, for wind, for flying debris, for sitting out the wait. I just didn't allow for Sigurd's loveable nature.

Suddenly he hits me and jumps to his feet. 'What are we, sodding Vikings?' he shouts. 'I'm not doing this!' And he rushes back towards the tank, to pull the fuse out of the fuel cap. His gloves swing and bound, like terriers trying to bite him. His boots slide on the ice and he skids up against the metal body of the van. Steadying himself with one hand, he reaches to pull out the fuse. Then he

246

screams and screams and screams, because his bare hand is welded by cold to the freezing metal, stuck fast, as with superglue, except that through his palm and spread fingers it feels more like a scalding kettle.

Flame trickles along the fuse, closer and closer. Put it out, Sym.

It's a really excellent fuse, considering I've never made one before. If I put it out, the plane won't see us, and if the plane doesn't see us, we're dead anyway.

But Sigurd is trying to tear his hand free, to rip the skin off his palm and fingers, screaming and screaming and stretching and straining but still unable to reach the fuse with his other hand. The fire bubbles happily along the fuse, closer and closer to his feet, and even though he kicks at the ground, trying to scuff ice over the fuse, it persists in burning. There's no stopping it. Unless I stop it.

I won't put it out.

I'll go back inside the van instead.

With all the upholstery pulled out of the seat frames, the wall of the Hagglund is bare. It is massively insulated, but there's Sigurd's ice axe and there's a wheel-jack and a handful of seconds. And there's desperation. And there's terror, stronger and sharper than any crowbar. In the end, I just direct the storm-lighter at the hole I've gouged in the insulation, blistering paint, filling the air with noxious smoke, coughing and gasping, tears leaking from my grazed eyes. I light a cushion and push it into the hole. Any moment now, the fuse will ignite my wick of hair in the bottom of the fuel tank, or the dregs of diesel, or the fumes swirling above it. I'm too tired to be this afraid, Titus. Mum. Nikki. I'm too tired to decide whether to freeze or burn.

The explosion is of swearwords, as the van's metal rises a few degrees—enough degrees—and the ice sealing

247

Sigurd's hand melts and sets him free. And I'm out and running and hoping the tank won't blow and hoping it will and hearing the plane, and we're calling out to it . . . As if two children's voices could possibly carry as far as the sky.

Far too long has passed. Even before we take cover behind the pressure ice, it's plain my seamless planning has gone for nothing. The Hagglund doesn't explode. There's no gigantic orange mushroom cloud. No track rods or luggage racks come spinning past our ears. This is no stunt from a disaster-and-destruction movie.

Victim of a shoddy education, you see. Diesel's not like petrol. Not when it's cold. Not when there's so little. It doesn't even catch fire. *Only one step from the sublime to the ridiculous.* And all I can manage to think of is my plait of hair lying in the bottom of the tank. I begrudge my hair.

Even I can hear the aeroplane now. The noise flexes the sky, to see if its dull white melamine can be broken. Sigurd hugs his hurt hand to his stomach and rocks to and fro.

Then, suddenly, flames are looking out at us through the windows, jigging, jumpy, jazzy-coloured passengers gawping out at the scenery, all set for the journey of a lifetime on their big red bus. The cushion I lit has ignited another—also, instruction manual and maps, food wrappers and cotton wool. Sigurd runs to the back door and throws inside the cushions we brought out with us— feeds the fire, like someone hurling meat into a lion's den. The windows crack. The sludge-cold diesel ignites with a grudging thump. Within two minutes, the cater-pillar tracks have begun to flex and burn, the smoke to billow blackly. Our eyes follow it up into the sky, watch the wind twist and strand and wash it away.

'What now?' says Sigurd aghast. 'What if they don't come?'

Be quiet, Sigurd. Enjoy the warmth. Don't think about it. Just enjoy the warmth.

'But what if we wait and they haven't seen and they don't come?'

I shrug. 'Take off our clothes, I s'pose.'

His face is a treat. I'd laugh, but my mouth isn't up to laughing any more; I have to do that on the inside too.

'Get it over fast, I mean. Take off our clothes and get it over quick.'

As Napoleon said, *Come what may, there's always Death.*

# Chapter Twenty-Three
*'I do not regret this journey'—Scott*

What kind of word is 'big' to describe Antarctica? To begin to capture anything here, 'big' would need twenty-seven syllables.

Words can't cope. The space between the letters ought to make them elastic enough, but they aren't. The tails under the g's and y's and q's and j's ought to help them grip, but they slide about helplessly. Cliffs are the length of counties. Icebergs are the size of cities. Prospects run as far as the sky. Parallel lines never meet because there's no disappearing point. Adjectives die on the wing the moment they see Antarctica, and plummet on to the Plateau. Words are no good.

Mimi's friend Fern deleted the phone message, thinking it was kids messing about. We never stood a snowball's chance in Hell.

The co-ordinates that I guessed were entirely wrong, anyway.

A hail squall obliterated the tracks of the Hagglund showing which route it had taken out of Camp Aurora. No Hansel and Gretel trail.

Not a snowball's chance in Hell.

\*     \*     \*

*Buum boom boom.* It is all around me, making the air vibrate, making the air in my lungs vibrate. When I first woke, I thought it was the noise of the Devil's Ballroom. Or my heart beating with terror. *Boom boom boom.* There's a music to it, starting with strong, loud bangs about my head, thumping downwards through my body and on by, pattering away towards silence. A hollow symphony of timpani.

Arriving after the destruction of the plane, the Americans at McMurdo Base suspected terrorism, and took over the search, concentrating all their efforts on looking for submarines out at sea. The only reason terrorists would go to Antarctica is to find out the meaning of terror, that's what I think. No one was searching the Barrier or the Queen Maud Mountains. I knew all along: Sigurd and I never had more than a snowball's chance in Hell.

Fortunately Hell happens to be tucked away here at the bottom of the planet, in the last place on Earth. And sometimes even snowballs get a lucky break.

*Boom. Boom. Boom.* The icebreaker's hull is smashing its way through pack ice, splitting it with the bow, forcing a path between the fracture, crumbling the pieces smaller and smaller as it pushes them aside. The brash ice whispers past, caressing the ship's sides like a lover.

Apparently, a tourist aircraft flying at 2,000 metres was suddenly confronted by a tent tumbling through the sky, ropes trailing, the Pengwings logo perfectly legible on its billowing sides. Calculating that it could not have been aloft for many minutes, the pilot noted his position and reported it. On the same day, Mimi Dormiere-St-Pierre found my

251

postcard home, in her snowsuit's back pocket, telling Mum what Victor was planning. The search switched south-wards—to the Barrier itself—rather than out at sea. In the end, one of the search planes did spot the burning Hagglund.

Every snowball deserves a lucky break.


'You'll come back,' says Bob. 'You don't think so now, but you'll see. It gets to you, this place.' Mike agrees. He says less, but his face is equally sure I won't be able to resist the lure of The Ice.

I shake my head. We're sitting on deck and, on either side of us, towers of ice soar to the height of skyscrapers, fissured and etched by wind and water, colonized by birds and sunlight. The colour is blinding—a bombardment of vivid greens and blue and red that pound away at the brain. The glitter on the water is a firing squad shooting from point-blank range. It is beautiful past all descrip-tion. There's not a chance I'm coming back. I never want to see the place again. Like Cherry-Garard said ninety years ago, the good memories are swallowed up by the bad.

*Boom. Boom. Boom.* The noise of the ice-breaker drives the memories through my skull, like it or not:

A sled somersaulting over a crust of ice like a paper cup blowing in the wind;

A face with teabags for eyes;

Turquoise xylophones of wafer-thin ice;

A man running on a broken ankle;

Sun dogs and ghost dogs.

*Boom. Boom. Boom.* The noise is like the piston rods driving some huge mechanism inside a hollow planet.

'You did good. For a first-timer, you did all right! You did some bright stuff!' Bob enthuses. 'You could do like us! Get a job with one of the travel companies. Give talks—

the whole tour thing, you know!' And Mike agrees and nods. It's a triumph of optimism on their part, since I don't even speak right now, let alone give talks. It is hard to focus on their faces, because I am still suffering from Long Eye. 'The four-metre look into a three-metre room', they call it. It comes of peering into an endless whiteness. It is a kind of battle-fatigue.

I can't face Sigurd. We keep to opposite ends of the ship, and Mike, (sensing that events haven't forged undying friendship between us) seems to have mounted guard over me, so that Sigurd can't come near. I sit on a steamer chair, all tucked up in blankets and quilts and borrowed clothing, and the *Battleship Potemkin* (or whatever it's called) bullies its way out through the ice towards the open sea. I'm a celebrity being escorted through a jostling crowd of gawping paparazzi penguins and skuas. No photographs, please; I am not exactly looking my best.

Mimi and Clough; the Colonel, the Pogsbaums, Ms Adolphus and the rest were all flown out long since. But for some reason it was decided to send me home aboard a ship bound for New Zealand, rather than by the South American route. I don't know who decided, only that it wasn't me. I haven't been doing decisions lately. Perhaps Pengwings are anxious to avoid adverse publicity. The state of me wouldn't exactly sell Antarctica as a health cure or a life-affirming experience.

Trouble is, Sigurd is nervous of what I'll say about him when I finally open my mouth—scared that my account of events will land him in jail. I suppose I could tar-and-feather him with criminal wrongdoings if I wanted: conspiracy to defraud, travelling under a false identity, impersonating a good guy, reckless endangerment of life. Taking and driving away.

I can't be fagged. Sigurd doesn't know that yet, so he's still in fear of me, but I can't see what I'd gain by shopping him. As Titus said, the thing is to go round such people; to take avoiding action. One day, if Manfred's body is found out on the Barrier, the bank draft in his pocket may set whiskers twitching. But for myself I am content not to speak ill of the dead. Let people go on thinking Manfred Bruch was a gullible innocent, obsessed by the same cocka-mamie theories as my uncle. I wonder which label the Viking would hate most: Fraudster or Anorak?

At first I thought I could not speak. About Sigurd. About the dead. About anything. Too hollow inside. No happiness, no unhappiness, no words, no anything. Like the Plateau. It seemed as if The Ice had frozen shut my mouth, finally perfected the cocoon that I've been weaving around myself since Dad died. When they all came at me with their questions and their compassion and their first aid and their curiosity and their reassurance and their incomprehension, it was much easier just to turn my face to the wall.

I wanted to go to Glasstown. It would be like running inside a church and claiming sanctuary in the old days, when they were after you. In the end, they'd get me when I came out, but not for a while. Not yet. When I went looking, though, the windows of Glasstown were all smashed, the streets deserted, its buildings condemned as unsafe.

And I couldn't find Titus anywhere. I shut my eyes, like closing the blinds in a house, and vowed not to open them again.

But the sky is radiant with buttery yellow iceblink, and beneath it heaves a sea that's a gaudy swill of cobalt blue, inky navy, sage, emerald, and holly green cluttered with snowy bergy bits. Pancake ice, delicate as pierced stone tracery, rises and falls on the swell. Mountains and sculpted icebergs leap up on all sides: killer whales frozen in the very act of breaching. It is fabulously lovely. It demands to be seen.

And curiosity, like warmth, is creeping back into my bloodstream.

Bob says we could have been nowhere near the Devil's Ballroom—that we could never have crossed the Axel Heiberg on foot and been found where we were. He sits with a map on his knee, trying to work out where we really were, which geographical features I must have mistaken for which others. Mike nods his agreement, but keeps trying to take the map and fold it away. 'I don't think Sym wants to . . .' It's true that my curiosity doesn't extend to where I have or haven't been.

The solid world turns on its axis and, in some place that isn't the Antarctic Ocean, people wake up. Bob goes to make an international telephone call using a satellite phone that has been to the Devil's Ballroom and back in the pocket of a madman. Mike never says anything at all when Bob's not there, but that's all right; silence doesn't strike me as awkward these days. It is the natural order of things.

Presently Mike leans forward and folds back the blankets from over my three layers of socks. He does it without comment, but I must have looked puzzled, because he ducks his head and says: 'There's this animal called a dassie. It can only get going in the morning when the sun shines on its feet.'

In the sky overhead a snowy albatross flies in a figure-of-eight directly over the ship, its shadow crossing and re-crossing me. And suddenly I have to tell him.

I have to say about Titus—how he was there! How he helped! How he carried the pain! How he fetched me out of there! How he pulled me through as surely as he hauled a sled over the Beardmore Glacier ninety years ago! Sucking in breath enough to speak has the strangest effect, for although it's as cold as hoarfrost, it seems to *thaw* the clod of ice behind my eyes. Tears stream down my face and drip on to the penguins on my borrowed sweatshirt. And the words pour out of me, about Titus. Oh, he was a gentleman, quite a gentleman, and always a gentleman!

'You see? She's out of her tree! Just like her uncle! Round the twist! Cracked!' It's Sigurd, his big-bandaged hand held up in front of his chest like a boxing glove, in his mouth a gumshield of sores and blistering. 'You can't believe a word she says! Talks to herself. Hears voices. She's mad!'

Mike stands up, placing himself between me and Sigurd who is brandishing Fright like a weapon. He doesn't say anything, just stands and deters Sigurd from coming any closer; stands and waits until Sigurd, like a wolf faced-down by firelight, turns and skulks away.

'Poor chap,' says Mike. Everyone aboard the *Battleship Potemkin* pities Sigurd for the loss of his father, the ordeal he has been through, his troubled state of mind. They just don't know what to do about him. Whereas me . . .

'It was the same with Shackleton!' exclaims Mike, sitting down again as if nothing has happened, thrusting hand-kerchiefs at me from almost all his pockets. His face is bright with delight. I was expecting a soothing pat on the head; a 'Yes, yes, dear, now get some sleep.' But he is eager to hear more about my mysterious companion, eager to agree that such things can and do happen. 'I read it about Shackleton! When Shackleton poled up on the wrong side of South Georgia and had to walk all the way across it—two of them! Exhausted! Lost! Half dead from rowing a thousand miles. They both said afterwards they could sense a third person was with them! Incredible! When I read that I thought "Oh yeah!" but with you saying that . . . Incredible!'

At least he doesn't think I'm mad. He doesn't understand how it is—was—between Titus and me, but at least he doesn't think I'm mad. He doesn't know quite *how* incredible, nor shall I tell him, but I've just realized something, and it's roaring around my head like a swarm of bees.

'Mike,' I say. 'Is it true Scott's tent isn't on the Barrier any more?'

256

'His huts are. You went there . . . No! We never got there, did we? Next time. I'll have to take you next—'

'Not the huts. The tent where he died. His body. Wilson. Bowers. The death tent.'

'The search party burned them where they were, if that's what you mean,' says Mike. 'Didn't take the bodies home. Just built an ice-cairn over them.'

'Yes, I know that! But the cairn—the death tent—Is it true the Ice Shelf emptied it into the sea years ago? Tell me. It's really important. Tell me!'

It must seem an odd question coming from someone who has only just rediscovered the power of speech; an odd piece of knowledge to need in a hurry.

'Don't think anyone knows, for sure,' says Mike cautiously. 'Some people say twenty-five years ago. Some say ten years from now. Some people think it's getting there about now. No way of knowing for sure.'

Exactly! There is—there was—no way of knowing. And I *didn't know*! I didn't! Everything else I knew—deep down—must have. Titus was of my making! Everything Titus ever said to me, could only have come from inside me. Things I've read. Things I imagined.

But I *didn't know* about the Ice Shelf moving! I never knew that the bodies of Scott and Wilson and Birdie and Oates were being shoved along by a great tide of ice! I thought the Ross Shelf would always be holding them!

Communion bread between its flat white palms of ice.

So how could Titus ever have said that to me? That figure beside me. The one who leaned across me? The one whose face brushed mine? How could he possibly have told me something I truly didn't know? Oh, Titus! Tell me what it means! Tell me what to make of it! Tell me what to think?

'When we get home—after you're better, I mean,' says Mike, cutting across this extraordinary, bewildering

thought, 'I suppose you wouldn't like to . . . you know—
I mean, say if you wouldn't, but just if you might like to
. . . meet up. Do something. Go out. Somewhere.
Something. Make a trip?'

*Boom. Boom. Boom.* I stretch up in my chair, to see what
isthmus of ice we are forcing a sea-path through. But we
are in open water, so the noise can't be coming from the
ship's bows. It must be coming from somewhere inside.

'I'm fourteen,' I say.

Mike is mortified. 'Oh, God! I'm sorry! Fourteen? I
thought you must be much older. The way you handled
yourself, I mean. And looked . . . not now, I don't mean,
but before . . . Wow! God, I'm sorry! Fourteen! God! All
the men at Aurora were trying to pluck up the nerve to
ask you out. Fourteen! Sorry. Sorry, sorry. Forget I spoke.
Fourteen! You look older.'

The tiny kernel of an iceberg—once the size of Essex but
melted now to the size of a book—bobs in the ocean, making
the green ice inside it wink and blink like semaphore. A
school of fish breaks surface like a fusillade of shots fired in
salute over a grave. Then, inside my head, a familiar voice:

*'And the third band of iron broke, and the princess could blink
her eyes and move her hands and was entirely free to speak.'*

Oh, Titus! It's so good to see you. So unbelievably good.
Thank you.

*'Don't mention it, Sym.'*

Blushing, embarrassed by his mistake, Mike is gathering up his belongings, offering to leave me in peace.
He hastily re-covers my feet. But that's all right, because
the dassie is well and truly awake now. Mike trips over
a leg of the chair and heads off in full retreat.

'Oh, Mike!' I call after him, so that he turns in the
companionway and bangs his head on a lifeboat. 'Keep
in touch, won't you?' I say. 'I'm planning on being older
in a year or two.'

# Scott of the Antarctic

When Captain Robert Falcon Scott set out for the South Pole in 1911, it was not his first attempt to reach it. He had tried unsuccessfully in 1904. This was to be primarily a scientific expedition, commissioned by the Royal Geographical Society, but the surprise arrival in Antarctica of Roald Amundsen, intent on claiming the honour for Norway of being first to the Pole, enraged Scott who believed that England had a moral right to it. Though no one said as much, a race had begun.

Scott's expedition plan involved dogs, ponies, motor sledges, and manpower. The man he chose to take charge of the ponies was not Royal Navy, like the rest, but an Army officer, Captain Lawrence Oates. Unfortunately, Oates was not allowed to choose the ponies and was horrified by the shabby animals put in his care. He took a strong and immediate dislike to Scott, though won the affectionate respect of everyone (including Scott), with his quiet, laconic, anarchic nature. They called him 'The Soldier', or 'Napoleon' (whose picture he pinned to his bunk), or 'Farmer Hayseed' (because he so delighted in looking scruffy). Or Titus (after the Jacobean rabble-rouser, Titus Oates). Despite an old leg wound, which had left him with a limp (and a commendation for the Victoria Cross), he was immensely fit and relished hard work.

The plan involved two expeditions. During the first summer they would set up a series of food dumps at intervals all the way across the Ross Ice Shelf to the Transantarctic Mountains, then hurry back to base at Hut Point and sit out the Polar winter. As soon as spring arrived they would set off across the Shelf, via their supply dumps, and climb the Beardmore Glacier to the Polar Plateau and the South Pole.

On the first expedition the motor sleds broke down almost at once, and the ponies were a liability. In trying to relieve their suffering, Scott took the fatal decision to off-load provisions early and turn back. Oates strongly objected, saying that 'One Ton' food dump needed to be further out on the Shelf. He was overruled.

Amundsen's journey went, in his own words, 'like a dream'. This was no lucky accident: he had immense experience, skill, and wisdom. He used dog teams to pull the sleds, and when the loads grew lighter and fewer dogs were needed, he killed the weakest and fed their meat to the strong. That is simply how such journeys are made in the Arctic Circle. He also got lucky—found a glacier just where he needed one in order to get up to the Plateau, and enjoyed 'good' weather (a relative term in Antarctica, of course). Amundsen reached the geographic South Pole on 14 December 1911. It did not delight him: he had really wanted to conquer the North Pole, but someone had beaten him to it.

Meanwhile Scott, too, was marching. A big company set out, but stage by stage, as planned, the support party peeled off and turned back, leaving just a chosen core of the fit and fortunate few to attempt the last leg. But the British met with filthy weather, fell behind schedule, used up supplies too fast. Oates's ponies died one by one . . . but got them to the Mountains, which had been their purpose. An attempt on the Pole was still possible.

The worst that could happen, to Scott's way of thinking, was that they would find the Norwegian had got there first.

It was not the worst thing that could happen.

Five men made up the final 'Pole Party'. No dogs: Scott disliked them and saw more grandeur in the idea of men hauling the sleds themselves across the Plateau. Captain Oates was already more exhausted than he cared to admit, but rejoiced in being chosen as one of the five, because he thought his regiment might be pleased. Scott, Dr Bill, Taff Evans, 'Birdie' Bowers, and 'Soldier' dragged two sleds over 200 miles of Polar Plateau—only to find Amundsen had impaled all their dreams on a Norwegian flag. There was nothing to do but turn round and head back, knowing their supplies were dangerously low.

It should have been possible. A close-run thing, but possible. But the temperature dropped, the weather worsened: winter came early that year. On reduced rations, Taff Evans—a great bear of a man—was literally starving. He had terrible frostbite, too. Nearing the Ross Ice Shelf he probably fell and banged his head. Within days he collapsed and died. Four men struggled onwards, outwardly confident, inwardly racked with anxiety, grimly hoping for the best. Gradually everyone realized that The Soldier, too, was done for.

The last entry in Oates's diary records digging up the remains of a dead pony in the hope of something to eat. *'Dug up Christopher's head for food, but it was rotten.'* After that, his hands were too frostbitten to write. His feet had long since been destroyed by the cold. It cost him agonies to walk, even to exist. He knew he was holding up his comrades, wasting precious time, lessening their chances. But he failed to die.

On 16 March, his thirty-second birthday, he woke and struggled out of his sleeping bag. 'I am just going outside

261

and I may be some time,' he told his companions, and crawled out into a blizzard to die.

Dr Wilson, writing a note to Oates's mother, tucking it inside his diary, said, *'I have never seen or heard of such courage as he showed from first to last . . . never a word or a sign of complaint or of the pain.'*

Three stumbled on towards One Ton Depot. If Scott had listened to Oates about where it needed to be, they would have reached it. As it was, a blizzard pinned them down eleven miles short. They sat in their tent and waited—waited, starved, and froze to death, racked with scurvy and frostbite. Their bodies were found the following spring and entombed then and there under a cairn of ice.

Captain Oates's body was never found.

# Many Thanks

*'A book must be an ice-axe to break the sea frozen inside us'—Kafka*

It was this quotation that led to this book. So I suppose I must be indebted, firstly, to Franz Kafka. He was actually talking about reading—saying we should only read books that hammer into us some swingeing truth. But it is a perfect word picture, too, of why authors *write* books. My thanks go also to:

**The Antarctic Centre, Christchurch, New Zealand**, especially Roger Harris;
**Ranulph Fiennes** for his graphic descriptions, bravery, and decided opinions;
**The Kelly Tarlton Centre, Auckland**;
**Sue Limb** for turning her own childhood obsession into a brilliant biography, *Captain Oates, Soldier and Explorer*;
**The Oates Museum at Selborne, Hampshire**;
everyone at **Oxford University Press**;
**Francis Spufford**, whose beautiful book *I May Be Some Time* includes my favourite account of Scott's last Antarctic journey;
the girls of **St Gabriel's School** for confiding how and when they use imaginings;

263

**Craig Vear**, composer of 'Antarctica', who shared his first-hand experience of a place where I have never actually been, and who really did play music on the ice-leaves;

all those involved in the making of *The Last Place on Earth*[*] (based on the book by Roland Huntford)—contentious but enthralling television; in particular the actor who played Oates and was my template for Titus—**Richard Morant**—an entirely sweet-natured man—unlike the Captain, I suspect, for all he was so loved and admired by those who knew him.

Speaking of whom: I just hope that by some fluke of Time, Space, or Divine Grace, **Lawrence Edward Grace Oates** is aware that the nose of his memorial in Eton College has been rubbed shiny by generations of boys touching it for good luck—and of how many people, writers included, have carried his story among life's crevasses and frozen reaches, like an ice axe.

[*] © Central Independent Television 1994 Carlton DVD